THE PROMISE OF
TOMORROW

SAMANTHA TONGE

B

First published in Great Britain in 2024 by Boldwood Books Ltd.

Cover Design by Lizzie Gardiner

Cover Illustration: Shutterstock and Adobe Stock

A CIP catalogue record for this book is available from the British Library.

Paperback ISBN 978-1-83518-999-3

Large Print ISBN 978-1-83533-000-5

Hardback ISBN 978-1-83518-998-6

Ebook ISBN 978-1-83533-001-2

Kindle ISBN 978-1-83533-002-9

Audio CD ISBN 978-1-83518-993-1

MP3 CD ISBN 978-1-83518-994-8

Digital audio download ISBN 978-1-83518-995-5

Boldwood Books Ltd
23 Bowerdean Street
London SW6 3TN
www.boldwoodbooks.com

Still standing. Still falling. Still succeeding. Still failing.
Still picking myself up.
Still never giving up.
Still smiling.
Still standing.
This one's for me.

PROLOGUE
21 DECEMBER 2004

Elena held Teddy tightly. He always understood and gave the best hugs.

'Mummy's had an accident,' she whispered to her bear, as if saying the words more loudly might cause a bad outcome. 'The police came to the door. Daddy's gone with them to the hospital. Auntie Gayle is downstairs making me something to eat but I'm not hungry. Not even for a slice of my birthday cake that we never got to cut. Mummy iced a big number ten on top.'

She pushed back the covers and shivered, despite burning up with the hot tears that made her feel sick, along with the temperature Gayle said she was running. Tonight the roads were icy and the police thought that was one reason the other car hit Mummy's. Elena was about to look out of the window. She was tempted to sneak outside, to cool off – to desperately look for her driving down the street as if nothing had happened. However, the phone rang and Auntie Gayle's voice carried upstairs. Elena went onto the landing.

'Elena is okay, Don, upstairs in bed. No... don't worry, I'll stay here for as long as it takes.' Auntie Gayle listened for several minutes. 'Are the doctors sure?' she asked eventually, voice wavering. 'There's really no hope she'll recover?'

The landing spun for a moment before Elena dropped Teddy on the floor and rushed downstairs. Auntie Gayle's eyes filled and she passed her the phone. When the call ended, after Daddy said goodbye, Elena threw up on the floor. She'd never heard him cry before.

* * *

The next morning, Elena woke up and beside her, on the pillow, lay a playing card with a fancy back. The king of hearts? She had no idea where it came from. She yawned and sat up. Teddy lay, nestled in her arms, undisturbed by the jolt that ripped through Elena's body as it all came back. The police, the call with Daddy and then... Elena *had* sneaked out; she'd gone to the woods and... She gulped at the memory of the stranger in the purple shawl, of the terrible promise Elena had made to help her mum... Shaking, she covered her face with her hands. They dropped away when the door creaked. It opened slowly and Auntie Gayle came in.

'I've let you sleep in, sweetheart, but you should know that... You see... this morning the hospital rang and...'

Holding her breath, Elena stared at Auntie Gayle, willing her words to be happy ones.

1

ELENA

Twenty years later

Rory came back into the house carrying a large glass tank. Mouth open, Elena moved out of the way, unaware that this eyesore would be the least of her problems by the end of the evening.

Her colleague had already dumped two suitcases and a bag of outdoor gear in her hallway, whistling as if he'd lived here all his life. The crisp air tried to reach in, but Elena swiftly closed the door on the inky November night. At a recent work party, a few gins had loosened his tongue about the hell of living in an apartment that was being renovated. He hoped it would be finished by Christmas. Elena had a spare room in her detached house, and in a rare show of impulsive behaviour, she had suggested he crash at hers. After all, how weird could it be living with someone from the office?

Perhaps *very*, now she thought. Elena jerked her head towards the glass tank. 'You've got a lot of explaining to do.' She tried to look annoyed, but a sheepish look had crossed Rory's face, so unlike the assured one she was used to.

'We need to get going, I'll tell you everything later. The fireworks venue opens soon,' he said swiftly and shivered. 'Unless we stay in, fire on, a cosy movie playing, and get takeout, my shout. Amazing as it was, I can still feel the breeze going right through me from this morning's skydive. It's a while since I did the last one. I'd forgotten what it was like in winter.'

Inwardly she rolled her eyes. Why did he have to jump out of an aeroplane to have a good time? 'Rory Bunker, it's Bonfire Night. It's actual law to stand out in the cold and wish you were anywhere else.'

Rory gazed around and shook his head. 'How have I never visited your place before? Wow. Who were the previous owners? The Kardashians?' With his floppy curly hair, Rory gave that cute, boyish smile that might have been irritating on a grown man, but somehow he got away with it. He leant against the wall. Average height, slim, with the casual confidence of a cowboy movie star, blowing on his gun after a shootout in a corral. 'Talk about palatial, and what with being in a private cul-de-sac with fake sentry boxes at the entrance to it...'

'Palatial, my arse,' she muttered and blushed. However, his words reminded Elena of when she'd first moved in, unable to quite believe the property was hers. To the left was the lounge, airy in mint and cream, with the welcoming wide arms of a comfortable oat-coloured sofa, and an unassuming television in the corner – reading was more her thing. A dining room ahead had French patio doors that looked out onto a large, sensible square of lawn. To the right was a kitchen with a breakfast bar in the middle, surrounded by marble work units. On one stood a coffee machine and rows of biscuit packets. A mini fire extinguisher hung from the wall in a prominent position – safety first, with Elena. The hallway was spacious, with the nut-white decor and ceiling high above the second floor. Dark wooden banisters curved upstairs, passing bedroom doors as they reached the top. As for the sentry boxes, the property developers had insisted they added class to the street. The residents took themselves a little less seriously and had put scarecrows in them for Halloween last week.

Not that she'd tell anyone, least of all Rory, but those sentry boxes gave Elena's home a much appreciated, added sense of security.

'It's not like you couldn't afford a place like this,' she said.

'It's not like I'll give up my exhilaratingly expensive hobbies for mere bricks and mortar.'

Their relationship was an honest one that suited the cut and thrust of them both being marketing executives for a large, dynamic manufacturer, Bingley Biscuits. However, the common ground between them was sparse, apart from their choice of career. Sensible Elena led a life that was adventurous only vicariously, through book characters. Whereas Rory mountaineered and whitewater rafted for real – he found any spectator sport, like League football, boring. And at work Rory focussed on facts and statistics, packet format and colour, consumer trends, footfall areas in supermarkets. Whereas Elena was more inspired by the story a product could tell its customers, in order to become an impulse buy or their regular favourite.

She took the heavy glass tank from him, trusting that Rory knew better, by now, than to ask if she could manage. Elena disappeared into the kitchen. After washing her hands, she returned to put on her belted plum trench coat, matching scarf and wool-felt beanie. The Wheatsheaf pub was the site for the fireworks display and it backed onto a field. It was thirty minutes away on foot, the other side of the Cariswell, a south Manchester village that thought it was better than everywhere else. By walking, both of them could enjoy a drink. Once at the end of the drive, Elena nipped back to check she'd locked up properly and then the two of them set off. Her elderly next door neighbour tapped the inside of his front window and waved.

'Fantastic.' Elena groaned and waved back. 'By the end of your stay, Tahoor will have us engaged and the wedding breakfast menu chosen. He's horrified that I'm thirty next month and *not even courting.*'

'Don't worry, I won't do a single thing to encourage him.' Rory waved at Tahoor and linked his arm through hers, leaning in. He increased their pace as she went to glare, but couldn't help smiling instead, even though he was more annoying than fog on Bonfire Night. The humour between them, despite their differences, had more than once saved the day when they'd clashed over a project. They were halfway to the pub, in the village, when the aroma of garlic and seafood wafted out of a bistro with subtle lighting and no prices on the menu. Cariswell prided itself on not having a single branded high street store. A real shame, in Elena's opinion, she'd have loved a Superdrug or The Works. The shops were upmarket, such as the designer boutique, herbal emporium, and organic cheese and meat deli. Even the charity shop shouted high-end, with its antique books, vintage garments and collectible porcelain pieces.

A group of young women passed by, Rory oblivious to their appreciative glances, with his pink scarf, the jaunty baker boy hat and bell bottom jeans. The refined way he moved underplayed his sporty strength. Rory dressed as he liked, from the beaded necklace he'd worn to the staff Christmas party, to the denim trucker jacket when the heating failed and the office became chilly. A fluid style, a fluid mind, a carefree attitude – everything Elena lacked. Looking at him sometimes felt like seeing the Elena she should be. He'd worked freelance for Bingley Biscuits during the last year, and formally given up contract work and joined the company officially at the end of the summer. Their professional clashes shouldn't have been unsurprising. Her leisure time involved reading cliffhangers, unlike his, which saw him scaling cliff edges. And her nightlife involved dinner with friends or cinema trips, whereas he'd recently dated a trapeze artist.

Elena didn't do dates. Not often. Certainly not serious ones.

A coldness wrapped around her bones, as if the November chill had found a way through her coat.

Falling in love wasn't an option, not for Elena, not until after her thirtieth birthday, in six weeks' time. The hairs stood up on the back of her neck because of the reckless promise she'd made, twenty years ago, that foreboding night, on the common near her parents' house; the promise that guaranteed terrible repercussions for her big three-o.

A shiver ran down her spine.

When they arrived, the pub was packed. Rory ordered two hot chocolates, Elena declining a shot of rum in hers. Whilst fact-lover Rory chatted to the server, passing on the essential information of how drinking chocolate had been traced way back to 1700 BC in Mexico, she sipped her drink, enjoying the cosy atmosphere. They headed outside and found a space right at the front, directly behind a thin line of rope at the edge of the field. Elena breathed in the sweet cocoa steam. Most people avoided the wintry air until the giant bonfire was lit. It stood a car length away, with gnarled branches sticking out next to straight, manmade furniture scraps.

'That glass tank...' Elena stared Rory straight in the face and raised one eyebrow.

'Brandy and Snap live inside.'

'Who? All I saw was a bundle of twigs.'

'Two Indian stick insects. Female. You should be impressed – they don't need men to reproduce. How's that for women's empowerment?'

Slowly Elena looked him up and down. 'More like wishful thinking.'

He laughed, softly.

'No one told me *three* of you would be moving in, and that's aside from the prospect of dozens of babies. What if they get out?' Her brow furrowed.

'Julian, my neighbour, who you met when I had those drinks at mine to celebrate joining the company permanently...'

'The vet? Hasn't he been ill? How's he doing now?'

'Yeah, much better. Well, someone abandoned over a hundred of them on his surgery's doorstep... Imagine having to re-home that many? He showed me the tanks. I put my hand in one to straighten a twig and these two crawled onto my fingers. They swayed from side to side and clung on tight, as if their lives depended on me. I swear they gave me puppy eyes.'

'Emotional manipulation of the highest degree? Brandy and Snap have gone up in my estimation. But wouldn't it have been kinder to release them into the wild?'

'Nope. Indian stick insects are non-native to the UK.'

'Do they bite? Release poison?'

'Elena! Thousands of children across the country look after them. They are more likely to sing nursery rhymes or knit booties. In any case, Julian's illness was stress-related, so if I could help in any way...'

She lifted up her mug, took another sip, and the smooth

chocolate froth stroked her taste buds. 'How did you arrive at those names? Talk about having the biscuit business on the brain.'

'Because they kind of look like brandy snaps,' he said.

'Rory, stick insects *so* don't.'

He shrugged and smiled like he did, at work, when they disagreed over something small. 'In all my twenty-seven years, I've never done pets, although I've always thought an insect would be cool. These can even grow back broken legs. Snap is missing one at the moment. At least they won't be scared by all the noise tonight, like a dog would.'

A bang went off in the distance and Elena jumped.

'Elena Swan, my gutsy colleague, full of drive, known for never giving up on a pitch...'

Too right. Neither did Rory. Derek, their boss, said it was great to have two team members coming at projects from different angles, as it meant they covered all the bases.

'The office's appointed first aider who doesn't faint at the sight of blood,' he continued, 'the organiser of many a staff trip out to a noisy nightclub – don't go pretending that *you're* scared of fireworks?'

Deep breaths. He was right, even though those booming dance nights out were more for her hardworking colleagues' sake – she preferred the quiet. Elena stood taller. Her thirtieth birthday was looming, but a woman like her surely had nothing to fear? She swallowed. That promise would never be called in. It wouldn't. She'd made it as a child. Adult Elena wouldn't have to keep her side of the deal. She was being stupid still worrying about it, all these years later. She took a large gulp of reassuring hot chocolate as Rory swayed to music pumped out by a local DJ. He transitioned smoothly from one move to the other, not spilling so much as a sip of his drink, in a world of his own for a moment, or so it seemed. Rory lived his life as if no one was watching.

Whereas the nearer her big birthday came, Elena lived hers under the close gaze of the past.

It was tough working alongside someone who reflected back at you the type of life you might have led if it hadn't been for one chance meeting, when you were ten, with a stranger in a purple shawl.

The bonfire blazed, releasing soot, as if sending a smoke signal to ticket holders to gather around. Rory tapped into his phone, reeling off event-appropriate statistics to the family standing next to him, their faces glazed, such as the average sparkler burns at one thousand degrees centigrade and fireworks are able to travel up to one hundred and fifty miles per hour. Didn't he realise how much he sounded like a mansplainer? His commentary was halted by a loud cheer as the organisers announced the display was about to begin. Elena drained her mug and gave hers and Rory's to one of the bar servers trudging past with a tray.

Bouquets of colour, bursting stars, falling fireflies... Elena was rapt, as if she was little again and lost in a Disney movie – unlike numbers man Rory, who was googling how light travels faster than sound and that's why the sky lights up before you hear the pop. As the show came to an end, she went to suggest they dart off early, to avoid queues at the bar and then...

Her eyes narrowed.

Oh no! A sparkling object flew, out of nowhere, across the field.

Past the bonfire. Thank goodness it missed that man in the hi vis jacket and...

What? Now it... No... no, no, no! It was heading towards her.

A voice shouted, 'Watch out!'

Too late. A thud. Pain. She went numb. The object had whacked her in the chest.

Elena gasped as a sense of panic sucked the breath from her lungs. Rory stared at her in horror. A firework had lodged itself in a gap at the front of her coat. As sparks continued to travel along the fuse to the firework's main head, people screamed and backed away, dragging children by hands and dogs by leads.

2

ELENA

Elena's mouth dried as spectators screamed. Her knees weakened, and she couldn't blink. Holding his breath, jaw set in a determined line, Rory leant forwards. His fingers curled around the firework and he jiggled it, perspiration glistening on his forehead, despite the frosty air. For Elena it was as if time passed in slow motion.

Is Rory mad? He could die as well.

But please, please let him succeed. Hurry, hurry, hurry.

What if it goes off?

Oh Mum. Dad. I'm sorry. I'll miss you both so much.

Have I lived my life to the full?

Or played it safe?

Since making that promise, years ago, have I squeezed the most out of every day?

Rory winced as the fuse touched his hand before... He did it! Rory dislodged the firework. Lifting it high, he turned around and lobbed it to the far left of the bonfire, an area cordoned off and free from bystanders. The crowd crouched down and waited. Nothing. No bang. No light. The loudest noise came from the right of the bonfire, from a group of shouting teenagers circled by adults.

Gulping now, spasms of raw emotion running through her chest, Elena looked down. The firework really was gone.

'Let's get inside. You're shaking,' said Rory.

'Like your voice,' she stuttered. They stared at each other and he leant forwards and... Oh. Rory embraced her firmly. But it felt... right. 'I'll... I'll be fine, it's just... shock,' she said, and a tear rolled down her cheek as she pulled away. 'You're the one who's injured. We need to get that burn seen to.'

Followed by pairs of sympathetic eyes, he put an arm around her shoulders and steered Elena into the pub. Rory was about to explain to the landlord what had happened, but Elena took over. Flustered, the landlord led them through the building filled with banter and the clink of beer glasses. It smelt of fried food, after-shave and hops, and Elena escaped gratefully into a private room out the back. In a hurry, he left them sitting on a small sofa, him muttering something about the cops. On the way out, he instructed one of his servers to make coffee.

'It might have gone off in your face, Rory,' she said in an unsteady tone.

'But it didn't.'

'I can't thank you enough. I owe you. Big time.'

'Looks like Brandy and Snap can stay, then.' He attempted a grin that didn't arrive. 'Only joking.'

'You've earned them a home for the next few weeks. Seriously. You're a hero.'

A lump rose in her throat and he didn't know where to look. Some heroes wore capes, others dressed like bats, but her hero loved necklaces and jaunty baker boy hats. An uncomfortable sensation rose within her. She'd always been quietly scornful of his mad weekend adventures, his dramatic tales of base jumping or navigating fast-moving rapids. But if it hadn't been for his bold nature today, the freak accident could have ended in a much worse way.

Unable to push away the image in her head of the firework caught in her coat, Elena closed her eyes, as if hoping to bring the curtain down on a dire theatre show, but only managing to provoke an encore. In those seconds, the firework pressed against her chest, her life had played before her, like a documentary on fast-forward – not the things she'd done, but the things she'd hadn't. Oh, she was always up for a night dancing or Bongo Bingo – even if, often, that was to avoid disappointing the rest of the crowd – and Elena happily took on the role of organising the staff's social calendar. She wasn't a hermit. However, she had never gone on an aeroplane to some tropical location. She'd told herself it was because she enjoyed holidaying in England so much. Was that really true? Because she loved hot weather and lying in the garden when the sun was out, but surely that was what the tropics were like too. She'd never smoked pot or got blind drunk as a youngster, like her friends, afraid of losing her senses and dropping her guard against... against the past coming back and seeking retribution. The wildest thing Elena had done in recent times was to have her long mouse-brown hair bobbed and dyed blonde. As her big birthday approached, it had become harder to push the thoughts away that she'd controlled for almost two decades and now threatened to burst out, like a Jack in the Box with an evil clown face. Those thoughts had filled her with a sense of dread and sent her to the hairdresser's, on a whim, on a mission, to grab life by the hand and let it lead her where it wanted, and—

Her eyes snapped open.

But no! Elena was *not* that fearful person. She was successful, go-getting, a high achiever. Everyone said so – a resilient woman who'd never taken a single day off sick in her whole career, not even when she'd had food poisoning or sprained her typing wrist; the optimist who lifted others up. She put herself out there, socially and professionally.

'Come on. Let's go. I need takeout and a large gin,' she muttered.

The landlord came back, a paramedic and a police officer trailing behind him. 'A group of young lads were messing about,' he said and ran a hand over his bald head, cheeks an angry red. 'They wanted to throw a firework into the bonfire to see what would happen, with no consideration for the explosion and flying debris it might cause. Damn idiots! One of them plays cricket, is apparently an ace fielder, so was chosen to do the dirty deed, but threw it too hard.' He cleared his throat. 'Look. I can't apologise enough. We had that far side supervised but his mates pushed through the cordon further up the field, to cause a diversion. Obviously, along with the police' – he shot the police officer an embarrassed glance – 'we'll be investigating what happened and will take extra measures, next year, to make sure nothing like this ever happens again.' He pushed a couple of ten-pound notes into Elena's hands. 'A full refund, of course.'

'Luckily for everyone it looks like the firework was a dud. It's been put in a bucket of water,' said the officer.

'Those fools soon shut up when I told them they could have been up on a manslaughter charge,' said the landlord, looking momentarily pleased with himself.

The officer took out his notebook and turned the pages, as a server brought in two coffees. 'We've already had several callouts tonight, with unsafe displays in back gardens and fireworks thrown at motorists. We've taken these lads down the station. Throwing fireworks is illegal, as is underage selling. You have to be eighteen to purchase. We'll be looking into where they bought it.' He asked Rory and Elena questions, gave her his number and then left the paramedic to examine them both. Elena insisted she was fine, even though her heart still pulsated, like a clock tick-tocking down to another potential tragedy. The paramedic dressed Rory's hand, carefully avoiding his silver chain bracelet with a tiny compass hanging from it. She told him to get it checked out by the nurse at his GP surgery in a couple of days. She wanted Elena to go to hospital for a once-over, but Elena refused. Didn't want a fuss.

The landlord came back. 'Two free dinners is the least I can offer you. Let me find a quiet corner.'

'I appreciate that but I just want to get home,' said Elena, and Rory glanced at her.

'But—'

Rory stood up. 'Thanks for the offer, mate, perhaps another time.' He ordered a taxi as they left the pub.

Elena didn't say a word to him on the way back, pretending to scroll on her phone. When they walked into her house, Rory went to take her coat but she stepped back.

'I'm all right. Thanks, though,' she said, not used to leaning on someone else, instead always being the one who stood strong. 'Nothing a ham and pineapple pizza can't fix.'

Rory looked as if she'd suggested using the stick insects as a topping and laughter unexpectedly trickled out of her like a stream of treacle, softening and sweetening the accident that nearly ended so badly.

'A million pounds couldn't make me eat that,' he said. 'In fact, I've got trust issues now, so I'd better do the food ordering. The takeout's on me, as a first little thanks for letting me stay.'

Elena locked the front door and pointed vaguely upwards, to his room. Rory picked up one of his suitcases and she went into the kitchen, moving slowly, still digesting what had happened.

She ran a glass of water, downed it and wiped her mouth with the back of her hand. Elena sank into a chair at the marble-effect dining table.

I want to ring Mum. Her hugs are always the best, even now that I'm grown up. But I can't worry her or Dad. I'll tell them in a few days, joke about it. It's no big deal. The firework wasn't even live.

She stared at the glass tank in the middle of the table then got to her feet, took off the lid and put in her hand. Brandy – or Snap – lay on a twig. Gently, she picked the stick insect up and placed it in her palm, marvelling at its straight lines and sharp edges. A missing leg meant this one was Snap. She eyed its tank, not doubting it met the criteria for a big enough living space – going by human guidelines, that was. But what life was that, for any insect to be stuck in a cube of glass with no hills, no streams, no changing weather, no predators to hide from?

Did Elena's life, like theirs, lack real drama?

Carefully, she placed the insect back on a twig, put on the tank's lid and washed her hands. But drama was dangerous, everyone knew that, especially in the middle of the night, in the pitch black, wandering in your Disney pyjamas when you're only aged ten, on your birthday – and bumping into an adult with whom you made a dreadful deal. She opened the freezer and took out a couple of lemon slices, frozen into ice cubes, and put them on a plate to carry them into the lounge. Once there, Elena took gin out of the drinks cabinet and poured two glasses, dropped in the cubes and placed them on the round terrazzo coffee table, in front of the sofa. Footsteps sounded down the stairs.

'In here,' called Elena, wishing she was on her own.

Rory appeared in a white shirt and patchwork cardigan, hanging loosely, emphasising his agile athleticism. He pointed down to a pair of moccasins. 'Bought them especially. Didn't think you'd be a shoes-in-the-house type of person like me.'

Too right, she said to herself, wondering if he was making a point.

Elena indicated for him to sit down and pushed across his drink. She took another sip, hugging a cushion to her chest with the other arm. She hadn't been playing it safe all these years – no, she hadn't been playing *at all*, like an actor with stage fright who only went through with rehearsals and never truly got to fulfil their role.

'I went into the wrong room first, upstairs... Your home office,' said Rory as he skimmed the takeout menu. 'It's so tidy, with the box files and pen pots, the shelves with framed certificates of achievement, and stationery stacks. The blinds and minimalist décor really give it that office feel. There are zero distractions, what with the desk facing the wall. It would drive me crazy. I work best with music and a view – although there is that beautiful oil painting of a cottage made out of books.'

'That room has been brilliant in recent years, when I'm working from home. It really gets me into the zone if a deadline's looming.'

He looked up. 'Thought I'd spot a pile of sneaky paperbacks in there but no, so why zero bookshelves in here as well? You're always reading them during your breaks at the office.'

'I'm not like you with the collection of trainers I spotted at yours that, placed in a line, would add up to the length of a marathon.'

He gave a little bow. 'Guilty as charged.'

'I give paperbacks to charity shops and use my Kindle at home.'

'But don't you booklovers hoard novels like nuts? Did you

know, a squirrel might hide up to three thousand acorns in the winter?'

'You think I'm hiding three thousand stories?'

He stared at her for a few seconds. 'No. Just one.'

Her cheeks flushed. What did he mean?

Elena lived for stories. Books like *The Butterfly Lion* by Michael Morpurgo had kept her company when little, on the rare occasion she'd longed for the company of another child, a sister or brother who didn't exist in real life. And she loved tales about animals. Jane Austen fulfilled her romantic longings as a teen and in her twenties her mum's Jackie Collins ball-busting stories made her feel anything in business was possible. She dived into romances and thrillers, after challenging days at the office – happy ever afters and the punishment of criminals gave her faith that, perhaps, everything in her own life would come good. Her one big sadness was that Mum had sorted through her ever-increasing collection of books when she was twelve, as a surprise to create more shelf space. She'd thrown away many that were too tatty to go to a charity shop, not thinking that they'd been favourites. Mum had been mortified by her mistake. Apart from the more well-known stories, Elena couldn't remember all the more obscure ones that had been so important during challenging times – like those from 2004.

The worst year of her life.

Yet the best.

3

RORY

Rory drew the curtains closed. Whatever the time of year, he liked to sleep with the window open, but the ones in Elena's spare room were firmly locked. The rug was stuck down with gripper tape and none of the furniture had sharp edges. The en-suite bathroom had a lock on the cabinet even though Elena had no children, as if she were worried ghosts might break in and accidentally swallow tablets that would make them real. There was an anti-slip mat in the shower, bright lighting and a grab rail by the bath. These precautions likened to a dialled-up version of the uptight measures taken by the Elena he'd got to know at work this last year. She always closed the filing cabinet drawers that colleagues left open, like a messy teen's over-pedantic mother, and made sure the staff's mugs were washed up, even though evening cleaners came in to tidy up. He must have lost his mind when he'd agreed to take Elena up on the offer of her spare room. This was a posh area. Perhaps all the residents were equally hyper-vigilant when it came to doors and windows. But as for everything else... However, her fun side shouted from the walls, too, hinting at the Elena who was more chilled on a staff night out, like the abstract framed print of *The Scream* with a ginger cat, instead of a man, standing with its mouth open. Also, a human portrait with the face made up of vegetables, with pea pods for eyebrows. The bedside lamp was made from an old-style rotary phone, the handset elevated in the air and projecting the light.

Rory collapsed onto the bed. His shoulders sank. No one was watching. He could let it all out and exhale noisily; let out the fear that had ripped through his body, at the prospect of his colleague suffering a violent death. He dropped his head into his hands, palms pressed into his eyes, still seeing her terrified face in the darkness. What if he hadn't dislodged the firework in time? During those crucial seconds, in that field, whilst he'd resolved how to save Elena, random thoughts had muddied the process, random small things. Like how she bit her lip when he made her laugh, but she didn't want to let on; how she doodled whilst on a phone call at work, usually ladders or building blocks – signs of ambition, he reckoned and respected.

A notification flicked up on his phone – Izzy, from his group of mountain-biking buddies, had invited him over for a gaming and takeout night this week. Now and again they hooked up. It was a casual relationship that suited them both, when they weren't dating other people. He reached across to the bedside table, put down his phone and grabbed a pen and the journal he wrote in every night – had done since he was eight years old. The style hadn't changed. It was called *Rory's Day In Numbers* and listed things of note he'd done or seen during the day, in a mathematical way. His dad had encouraged it when his son was little. Being a plumber, he worked with numbers, calculating costs and taking measurements. Rory had always loved maths but struggled with English and writing. The teacher said journaling might help. Rory's dad, Mike, had come up with this compromise.

Saturday 9th November

1 hour packing.

50-minute drive to Elena's.

Whaaat, 2 sentry boxes?

1 burglar alarm, 1 CCTV camera.

0 seconds before I wondered if moving in with Elena was a mistake, despite my renovations hell. She and I are as different as paint and paint remover. 5 seconds after these thoughts before feeling ungrateful. However irritating Elena was, her spare room was far less dusty and noisy than my canal-front apartment.

15-minute walk through Cariswell village centre, 2 Jaguars, 1 Lotus, 3 Porsches parked up.

2 degrees centigrade.

3 noisy rockets, 2 peonies, 1 chrysanthemum, 4 comets, 1 horsetail – multi-coloured light travelling at 186,000 miles per second, noise at 767 miles per hour.

5 reckless teenagers.

THE LONGEST FEW SECONDS OF MY LIFE.

£6.50 taxi fare.

4 gins.

1 large pizza, 14 pineapple chunks on top (yes, I gave in), 1 garlic bread, 1 potato wedges, 2 pots of coleslaw, 2 cookie dough desserts. To Elena's disgust, a large squirt of tartar sauce, one of my favourite side relishes whether I am eating fish or not. She needs to live a little.

1 game of Scrabble, 235 to 224. Elena won, with the word za, a slang term for pizza. Fittingly, my last two letters were fk.

3hrs and 6 minutes of listening to background KILL ME NOW music – or gentle jazz, as Elena prefers to call it.

24:00 bedtime. Elena slid 3 bolts across the front door. 3?

1 minute killing it, singing 'Ocean Eyes' by Billie Eilish in front of my bathroom mirror, aided by a toothbrush microphone with 2,500 bristles.

4

ELENA

Elena and Rory walked out of the lift on the third floor. The marketing office was open plan. It was Wednesday 20 November, the day of a meeting she'd arranged with boss Derek, the director of marketing. Years ago, before starting her career off in HR, she'd had a Saturday job in the sixth form, thanks to her dad speaking to one of his friends. She'd worked in every department, including HR, but also production and marketing, and a passion and focus had grown for the latter. Her unusually broad experience had propelled her career forwards. Under Derek, Elena ran the marketing department at Bingley Biscuits, but this meeting was an example of how she sometimes stepped out of her strict remit, such as becoming involved in product development.

She'd had an idea on how to optimise the Bingley Biscuit brand during the current cost of living crisis. Rory had lived with her for a couple of weeks now. He was tidy, enjoyed cooking and always washed up, and didn't interfere much with her usual routine. She'd put in overtime, researching her fresh concept after work, whereas Rory had been out at some sports club, or at his dad's, and once met up with his mountain-biking mate, Izzy. The whole friend-with-benefits thing didn't do it for Elena. She and her new housemate were just different that way, she told herself.

Today wasn't a formal pitch to Derek – more of a casual chat. But it was crucial it went well. Her idea could be seen as compromising the Bingley Biscuit name and had been rejected in previous years. Derek might be very hesitant about pitching it to the board. He might not even hear her out – especially if Rory didn't back her up. She'd told him about it a few days ago and suggested he join the meeting. Elena had never been afraid of fighting her corner, not when it came to a project she wholeheartedly believed in.

At eight forty-five in the morning, most of her colleagues were already on phones or typing away. The grey walls and flooring might have lacked appeal, along with the bland desks, printers and computers, were it not for the bright mosaic of prints of the colourful tubes of Bingley Biscuits on the walls. Their chocolate-coated oatie biscuits sold best, followed by the crumbly shortcake rings and cream vanilla sandwich fingers. These family recipes went back to the beginning of the twentieth century when the Bingley family had opened a home-baked goods shop on Oldham Street, in a part of Manchester city centre now known as the Northern Quarter. Business boomed and premises expanded during the postwar economic prosperity of the fifties. By the mid-sixties, the family had bought their first factory. It was a fiercely competitive market, but the brand had held its own over the years, and more than that – at least, until the pandemic.

Gary's desk was nearest to the door. He was a well-built man with a ginger buzz cut and a goatee beard, about the same age as Elena, today wearing an Aztec print shirt. She and Rory stopped by his chair. Caz, fortyish, with a ladybird red bob and lips to match also came over. Gary sat, his fingers intermittently typing and dipping into a bag of Maltesers, acting as if the other three weren't there, until Elena hummed the first line to 'Bohemian Rhapsody'.

'Never did like karaoke,' muttered Gary.

'You've been on at me for months to organise it!' said Elena.

'Yes, and it took until Rory asked you,' he replied with an injured tone. 'We really should be allowed to bring partners next time. My husband would have smashed it with his version of "La Bamba".'

'Don't be such a sore loser. Last night was fun,' she said and pushed his shoulder. Kind of. 'Bohemian Rhapsody' had been Rory's choice. He liked a challenge and she'd wanted to prove she was equally up for it. 'Although I agree, it's a shame your Diego couldn't come. We must go out for dinner again soon. I haven't seen him since before Christmas. I could listen to his Spanish accent all night long.'

'I recommend it,' said Gary, unable to stop himself smiling.

Caz sighed. 'Competitive as I am, I'm not cross that we got booed off the stage. You two smashed it. Perhaps our choice was bad. Singing that classic "Ain't No Stoppin' Us Now" was jinxing it.'

'Watch out, Caz and I will thrash you at the next staff night out,' said Gary, breezily. He'd paired Elena and Rory together for the karaoke, seeing as they were what he called house buddies now.

'No chance,' said Rory and helped himself to one of Gary's Maltesers.

'Amazed you sang so well, though, Elena, what with your main focus being on that guy in the Italian suit,' said Gary. 'Give us the low-down.'

'Nothing to report,' she said airily. 'Andy's an accountant. Who knows where the evening might have gone if it wasn't for Rory dragging me up on stage when things were getting cosy?'

Rory shrugged. 'Sorry about that. Bad timing. But it was our turn. You should have got his number.'

'I would have but he'd left by the time we'd finished.' Andy had lovely eyes. Soft hands. A genuine smile. She imagined the comfort of skin touching skin, of kisses you could lose yourself in... Oh, how Elena longed for that physical comfort right now. But it wouldn't be fair to get close to a man, not when her thirtieth birthday was just over a month away...

'So, spill. What Christmas night out have you got in store for us colleagues, Swan, in December?' asked Gary.

Elena tapped her nose and headed off to the other side of the office. Rory had been given the desk opposite hers, when he'd joined the company permanently. The top of hers was fairly tidy, with a pen pot, file rack and wire letter tray, and a stress ball in the shape of a sloth. Gary had bought it for her last Christmas, for the Secret Santa. He'd said it was ironic as Elena was the least lazy person in the office. Her top desk drawer, deep and wide, was messier, filled with an array of dog-eared paperbacks – and a spare Kindle, kept at work, to act as a back-up. Elena would rather run out of food than stories. All genres were in that drawer – historical and contemporary, by British and foreign authors. Her current read – or re-read – was *Sense and Sensibility* by Jane Austen. Despite her party-loving image at the office, she strongly related to responsible, measured Elinor, who greatly contrasted her impulsive sister, Marianne. Closed versus open, safe versus risky... Elena knew which type she was, or, rather, what she'd forced herself to become.

'I'm not sure Brandy and Snap appreciated our tuneful

rendition when we got home.' Rory put down his satchel and took off his damp trench coat.

'Oh, *home* is it now? Don't go getting any ideas. And I seem to recall it was only *you* singing.' She made herself busy, taking off her coat, not wanting to give away that since he'd moved in, her place had felt like a real bolt hole in a way it hadn't before. Even though they hadn't spent much time together, just knowing that someone else shared her home reminded Elena of when she'd lived with her parents. She'd forgotten how reassuring it felt, how comforting, to hear someone else upstairs singing in the shower or boiling the kettle. She was very close to her mum and dad and had lived with them, happily, until starting at Bingley Biscuits four years ago, and pole-vaulting onto the property ladder with her current pad. The privacy and space were great, she'd told herself. Yet how quickly she'd grown used to Rory's evening rendition of 'Ocean Eyes' that wafted through the spare room's walls. Not to mention the conversations he had with Brandy and Snap – mostly telling them how clever they were, with their playing dead and camouflage skills, and reeling off statistics about their fellow species.

This last week, he'd even persuaded her to watch TV again a couple of times. They started a new Netflix thriller series. Her last boyfriend, from over a year ago now, loved watching thrillers too, but didn't dissect them in the way Rory did, in the way Elena loved to, looking at the plot and characters analytically and trying to work out the ending. Not that it mattered. There were so many other things she'd... liked about Darren. She'd never said loved, not when it came to boyfriends; she wouldn't let herself get that attached. In fact, she and Darren split up after ten months – the longest she'd dated anyone for years – because she couldn't commit when he'd begun talking about the future. What would be the point, when hers was so uncertain?

Elena leant against her desk. The firework. It had been a warning. It had to be.

With his unaffected dancing when she put music on, with his colourful clothes and spontaneous bursts of singing, Rory had turned out to be a good distraction from darker thoughts about the little girl who'd got lost in the wooded area of the common and made a deal with a strange woman.

Rory slid a folder of paperwork out of his bag. At least *he'd* taken the idea seriously. Their meeting was at nine but Derek was always early. They headed for his office, the only private space that wasn't open plan. Elena knocked on the door. A friendly voice invited them in. Derek stood by the window, looking across at the industrial landscape. The factory was Sharston way, a thirty-minute drive from south Manchester, up to an hour during peak traffic. He turned around and ran a hand over his receding grey hairline. He wore a dark jumper and chinos, and glasses with a bold, dark blue frame. Derek was fair and transparent, the two things Elena valued most in a boss. He also passionately believed in enjoying Bingley Biscuits' products. The chinos hugged his legs, like the jumper did his chest. A double chin lay against the top of the shirt collar. Gaining extra pounds went with the job. Elena had put on almost a stone since joining the company four years ago, thanks to the freebies and tasting sessions. Caz bemoaned her own weight gain and Gary obsessively went to the gym. Rory's life was far too physical for the daily Bingley treats to make a difference. Elena didn't mind the extra curves. They made her look even more like Mum.

The mum she'd nearly lost, a long time ago.

Derek indicated for them both to sit down and sat behind his desk – basic, white, the same as everyone else's. It was the rest of the room that reflected his status, with the Nespresso coffee machine, filtered water and the row of industry awards on a shelf. On the wall hung a photograph of Derek standing next to King Charles, who'd visited six months before, on a tour of manufacturers who were reducing their carbon footprint. His Majesty had talked, at length, with CEO John Bingley about the company's new study into the possibility of the electrification of their gas-fired industrial ovens. That was the Bingley Biscuits secret to success. It had embraced change throughout its hundred-year history, continually diversifying, experimenting, taking on board new social responsibilities, such as a reduction of palm oil in their products. Most importantly, it kept a finger on the pulse of what mattered to consumers.

'What have you got for me? I'm intrigued.' Derek rubbed his hands together, straight to business as usual. 'It's now in doubt as to whether our continued drop in profits is solely down to the energy crisis and global price increase of our basic ingredients.'

'Is the Lipstick Effect finally waning?' asked Elena.

Derek hesitated. 'Yes, I believe so.'

The Lipstick Effect reflected how, in times of hardship, consumers spent money on small luxuries, like when sales of lipsticks increased after the 9/11 terrorist attacks. When the pandemic hit, Elena had only recently joined the company, but had tracked its performance for several months whilst she worked her notice at her previous place of employment. She'd pitched the idea of bringing out individual tubes of limited-edition luxury brands of their biscuits at her interview. This concept had already been discussed by the board, previous to Derek taking her on, but her impressive, evidence-based pitch had given them the push they'd needed to run with it. Customers couldn't get enough of the Dulce de Leche cookies and double chocolate pecan shortbread fingers. They wanted comfort, they wanted an affordable treat. The rise in profits had landed Elena a big bonus in her first year. But Derek was right.

Consumer behaviour was changing again, as the financial squeeze continued to tighten.

'The time has come to backtrack on the luxury angle as a solution, Derek,' she said. 'I'd love to wave a magic wand and come up with a completely new approach, but all my research keeps throwing up the same conclusion that's been discussed on and off. The company can't delay any longer: a budget-friendly line is the *only* way forwards – with the right product. And if the board are prepared to hear me out, I've got one in mind.'

Derek folded his arms. 'Really? Not this again.' He sighed. 'Well, there's no point getting carried away just yet. Rory? What's your take on all this?'

Elena held her breath.

'Every saved penny counts at the moment,' said Rory, 'even on a packet of biscuits. Profits are down across the industry – our competitors are in the same position. It's not just Bingley Biscuits. The Lipstick Effect *has* waned. These figures back that up.' He took a sheet of paper out of his file and pushed it across the desk. 'However, for many of the companies that have introduced cheaper lines, sales didn't start well...'

Elena clenched her hands.

'...but slowly that's turning around.' Rory pushed across another sheet. 'It might just be the right time for Elena's approach.'

Eyebrows in her hairline, she stared straight ahead, unable to remember the last time Rory had embraced a pitch of hers from the very beginning.

'Oh. Right...' Derek looked up from Rory's numbers. 'But you're both familiar with the board's stance. They're worried about devaluing our quality name. That's the reason this idea of bringing out a basic biscuit range hasn't ever moved forwards.' He shook his head. 'Sorry Elena, but I can't see them going for it.

They've discussed it ad nauseam. I was hoping you'd come up with something completely innovative.'

'Derek. You're director of marketing. You know, as well as I do, it's about how you sell it,' said Elena, firmly. She put her hands on his desk and leant forwards. 'We tell the public that Bingley Biscuits cares about their struggles, and that we are acting upon them; that affordability is our priority. What's more, the phrasing we come up with can't be mere words stuck on the side of a packet, either, or in a light-hearted jingle at the end of a TV advert. The concept has to come from the heart,' said Elena, laying her palm against her chest. Once she'd decided to leave her last job at a confectionery company that no longer challenged her, Elena had quickly received several offers. But one of her reasons for joining Bingley Biscuits was their reputation for high ethical standards. 'Consumers aren't stupid. We'd need to avoid sneaky tactics like a blanket hike in the price of our whole range before bringing out a budget-friendly version that, in effect, is simply the price of what customers were already paying. We've seen that time and time again in some of the supermarkets, with other products.'

Derek paced the room, juggling a stress ball between his hands, his questions becoming louder and quicker, Rory pulling out more sheets from his folder, with graphs and numbers, with the stats from marketing surveys, showing how slowly customers were becoming loyal to competitors' more affordable brands.

Elena's mouth fell open. Rory really had got behind her.

Thirty minutes later, Derek collapsed into his chair. 'The stats are all there. Good work, both of you. It's convincing. Other companies *are* turning over a bigger profit with cheap lines. But at what cost to their reputation, in the long run? We don't want to alienate customers who see one of our biscuits as a superior product.' He reached forward to a tube on his desk and offered it to the other two, before tugging out a vanilla sandwich finger. The three of them sat eating. 'Okay. I'll pitch the idea of a cheaper line to the board again.'

Yes! Elena wanted to punch the air.

'You have a chat with the team,' he continued. 'Get their brains ticking. I'll schedule a meeting for the whole department on Friday. This pitch will need to be rock solid, and that requires teamwork. In the meantime, there's no harm in you working on your product idea, Elena. I hope it's a strong one that will at least spark the board's confidence in taking this direction, even if product development, ultimately, have to reject it.'

Beaming, Elena reached for Derek's tube of vanilla sandwich fingers and looked mischievously at him, and he rolled his eyes in an affectionate manner. She got up and closed Derek's door behind them. A notification flashed on her phone – a text from Gary.

> Your meeting's going on a bit! I'm making coffee for everyone.

'Thanks for backing my idea,' she said to Rory and passed him a biscuit.

'Just backing the stats,' he said.

Of course.

Marketers were often expected to come up with miracles, something fresh and sexy, but now and again, the answer was about going back to basics; it was about simple policies with no clever, underlying agenda, and right now that meant giving customers a genuine opportunity to save money.

They strode in the direction of Caz's desk. She and Rory were senior members of the team, underneath Elena.

A crash came from the small staff kitchen followed by a swear word. Elena hurried to see if Gary was all right. A stream of coffee flowed across the floor, out of the kitchen's door. Unaware, she stepped in it and jerked backwards before slipping, falling, falling, her face lifting to the tiled ceiling. Her phone went flying.

No!

What if she landed smack bang on the back of her head, on the hard floor? Like that soap actor who died in a random accident on an ice rink, because a bleed in his brain was missed. Having lost control of her balance completely, Elena let out a yelp and closed her eyes.

Please, let it be over quickly.

But... wait... What? Strong arms caught Elena and pulled her up.

'Nothing to see here, folks,' said Rory as people got up to look. He picked up her phone, took Elena by the hand and led her through the office doors. Hardly able to breathe, she rubbed her back.

'Reckoned you might want some privacy to, you know, nurse that injured pride and...'

'Right... thanks,' she said, and her voice hitched.

His brow wrinkled. 'Elena? What's the matter?'

Elena's breathing heaved, her hands sweaty, tingled, and a sense of foreboding consumed her. No. She was being silly. The universe, some dark force, wasn't out to get her. This silly trip-up wasn't a warning, nor was the firework.

'You can tell me,' he said in a gentle voice she hadn't heard from him before. Rory stepped forwards and brushed a flyaway lock of her normally military-neat blonde hair out of her face. Under any other circumstances she would have been taken aback by such a tender gesture.

She forced her lips to upturn and took back her phone. 'Come on. Let's help clean up that mess. I've pulled my back a bit, that's all. It'll be fine.' Elena gritted her teeth and went to go. But he caught her hand again and looked her straight in the face. Tears welled up and Elena suppressed a sob. She practically ran back into the office and headed for the toilets. She stood in front of the mirror, wiped her eyes, breathed in deeply. Okay. Armour restored. Her chin trembled.

Keeping that childhood promise a secret for such a long time, bearing the burden... It had been so very hard. But that had been the price for saving a life. A price ten-year-old Elena had been willing to pay.

5

ELENA

Radio blaring, as it had done the whole journey, Elena parked up outside her garage. She and Rory had agreed to take it in turns to drive to work. They got out and she made for the front door but had forgotten her bag. Elena ducked back into her grey Mazda to retrieve it and when she came out, Rory was by her side.

Gently, he pushed his body against hers sideways so that their arms touched. 'I'm not going to mention it.'

'What?' she asked, avoiding eye contact.

'Gary getting his revenge, this morning, on our amazing karaoke performance, by turning the fuel that drives our department into a slip hazard. My lips are sealed.' He pointed to his mouth. 'Nada coming out of here.'

'But you did.'

He raised an eyebrow.

'Mention it,' she said.

'Ah.' He gave that boyish smile.

'It was almost worth it, because afterwards Gary gave me the last of those lemon almond cakes Diego made for his coffee breaks.' She gave Rory a wry glance. 'It's no big deal. Honestly. I... didn't sleep well last night. That's probably the reason I—'

Rory held up his hand. 'You don't have to justify why you got upset. If you ever want a hug, I'm here, just saying. You only have to hug for twenty seconds for it to raise serotonin levels and lift your mood and—'

'Please. If it makes you feel better, just do it. My brain can't take any more statistics today, not after an afternoon working closely with you and Caz.'

Rory pulled her towards his chest. Oh. He smelt... nice, like fresh linen, mown grass, and a favourite book, all rolled into one, instead of the sports shoes or rubber wetsuits odour she'd been expecting. She would have closed her eyes, for a second, were it not for Tahoor's curtains twitching to the left. As rain started to spit, they headed indoors. Elena slid across the three bolts behind them, switched on the lights and heating and Rory went straight into the lounge to see Brandy and Snap. Elena had moved the tank in there. The day after moving in he'd prioritised finding the best fresh bramble branches, and a grassy verge alongside a nearby quiet road had obliged. He took the lid off the tank.

'Hello, my beauties. How was your day?' He lifted up a nearby plastic bottle filled with water and lightly sprayed the leaves. He put the lid back. 'Right. They've got *their* evening drink. Fancy that bottle of red I bought at the weekend?'

'As long as you don't put a spray nozzle on it. I'll get changed. It's a pyjamas night for me. Might grab a shower first. Meet you in the kitchen in thirty minutes?' she asked, surprising herself. 'We've still got chicken left from Sunday's roast.'

'Want me to rustle up a stir-fry?'

She gave him a thumbs-up and went upstairs. Elena threw herself on her bed and stared at the ceiling like she had this afternoon when falling backwards. If Rory hadn't been there to catch her today... He'd saved her again, like a guardian angel. Was that why he'd moved in? Was the universe using him as a puppet? Was it manipulating her day-to-day, putting her in danger, only to have Rory prevent the worst happening, to string out the torture until the grand finale? Her birthday, 21 December, was one month tomorrow. She only had to get through the next four weeks. Elena bit on her fist. She could do this.

* * *

'Elena! Where are you? The stir-fry is almost ready.' Rory stood at the bottom of the stairs. Elena came out of her bedroom, the aroma of fried vegetables wafting up the stairs. He frowned. 'I looked in there five minutes ago. You'd disappeared into thin air. The shower wasn't running. I called your name. I even checked in your office, but that was empty too.'

Her cheeks pinked up. 'Oh... I had my ear pods in.'

'Really? I didn't hear the slightest movement in the bathroom.' A timer in the kitchen pinged and he shrugged. 'Anyway, looks like you've lost track of time. You've got five minutes to get into your pyjamas.'

But Elena was already walking down. She stopped, a few steps above him. 'Love that sparkly top and its beading. Bit over the top, though, isn't it, for a night in?'

'Not at all! The gold goes well with the black jeans I'm wearing today. At least one of us is dressing up for dinner.'

Elena rolled her eyes.

'It's lovely and cool if I'm frying. I'd have been boiling in that jumper I wore to the office.' He ran a hand over the beading and stared over her shoulder for a moment. 'Don't save anything for best, I say, because you end up never wearing it.'

Elena couldn't help admiring how the sparkly metallic top hung on him as if he were a *Vogue* fashion model. Whistling, he went into the kitchen, with a natural strut that would beguile the audience of any catwalk show. The doorbell rang. Elena pulled a puzzled face and slid across the bolts. She opened the door and faced an elderly man with a grey beard, beaming with the perfect flash of white that only dentures provided.

'Tahoor? Everything all right? What on earth has brought you out in this rain? Come on in,' she said and gestured with her hand, heart sinking a little. What did he want?

Tahoor strode in looking pleased with himself, raindrops pelting down now. He pulled off his hood and rubbed his hands together.

'I've come round to introduce myself to your young man,' he said and beamed. 'Held off as long as I could, with my darling Isha's voice ringing in my head, telling me I was being a nosy old so-and-so. Yet she would be so happy for you, my dear. And for me. My prayers have been answered. This cul-de-sac is distinctly lacking when it comes to men. Finally one moves in!' He clapped his hands.

He had a point. Most of the cul-de-sac was home to women like Elena. Cherry, over the road, had got divorced and stayed put with the children. Beth had bought her long-term partner out, after they split. Whereas Julie and Sandra married each other last year. There were Deidre and Ivy too – they'd lost their husbands within months of each other. Tahoor really was outnumbered.

'Where is he?' Tahoor hissed. 'So glad that you're finally one step closer to marriage, what with your big three-o approaching.'

'We're not... Rory and I are definitely not... And in any case, I—'

'Nice to meet you, Tahoor,' said Rory, having thrown down

the tea towel, and hurried over, catching the end of their conversation. He put an arm around Elena and gave her a smacker of a kiss.

She gave Rory a glare as pointed as one of the kitchen knives. His eyes had filled with mischief and Elena braced herself, waiting for talk of weddings and honeymoons. Or comments from Tahoor about how the time was now nearing when she could finally leave her job and have children. She'd given up explaining that she'd still had many ambitions for her career. However, he'd gone very quiet and was pulling at his beard, eyeing Rory up and down. He'd pinned his hair back, whilst cooking, with one of Elena's hair grips, and Tahoor studied the flimsy sparkly top and compass bracelet.

'Oh...' The old man cleared his throat. 'My mistake. I thought you two youngsters... Jolly good. I went to Julie and Sandra's engagement party, you know. I'm all for... Hurrah the BLT community.'

'It's LGBT,' mumbled Elena, and she bit the insides of her cheeks, praying she wouldn't catch Rory's gaze again.

'BLT stands for bacon, lettuce and tomato,' said Rory in a controlled voice.

No... Elena, couldn't hold it in. Rory was trying not to laugh as well.

Tahoor rubbed his forehead. 'I suppose that means you and Elena aren't...'

'No, we're not. But not because I'm gay. I'm as straight as Elena's parking.'

'Gosh. Super straight then. It's just that top, it reminded me of my late wife's gold sari that she wore to our daughter's wedding. Very nice,' said Tahoor. 'So, Rory, m'laddo, are you watching the football at eight? City versus Liverpool. Go the Blues! It's so long since I've had company during a match. No one in my daughter's family is a fan. I used to watch with a married friend. He'd come over with his wife, and she and Isha would catch up on each other's news and cook. But I don't see him so much now that I'm not part of a couple.' Sadness had crept into his voice with those last words.

'Oh, Rory *adores* football and would like nothing more than watching men kick a ball around for ninety minutes,' said Elena smoothly. 'Please. Do stay and watch with him.' Rory stood next to her looking as if he wished he'd poisoned the stir-fry. Tahoor's face had sprung to life. Her chest pinched slightly. Perhaps she should have done more since his wife died in the spring. She'd taken his daughter Yalina's number, agreeing to act as a go-between in emergencies, and Elena went round once a week, to check he was okay. But she'd never actually invited him in for a drink, despite lovely Isha often insisting she went into theirs for her homemade cardamom tea cake.

It would be fine, him staying for the match. She'd have no regrets over this, despite his attitude to her career and insistence that it must be terrible for her having to work until a man gave her a ring and got her pregnant. 'A fizzy drink, Tahoor? Or juice? Coffee? Have you eaten? Rory, do take his coat...'

'Thanks, my dear. I won't get in the way. You get on with your housework or cooking, whatever you were doing. Right, after you, Rory, and let's hope we're not subjected to any of those bloomin' woman commentators...'

6

RORY

Rory collapsed onto his bed. *Please, if there's a god out there, never make me sit through another football match.* A smile waved across his face, like the City and Liverpool fans in the crowds. He rolled onto his side and stared out of the window. The moon shone brightly as if smiling too, happy that rain clouds had cleared. He'd walked Tahoor home. Rory let out a groan. The old man had been so delighted with a bit of male company that he'd invited himself over to watch another match next week. It was the stick insects all over again. When was Rory going to learn to say no?

Elena had disappeared upstairs during the match. It had been odd how, earlier in the evening, whilst he was cooking, she seemed to have completely vanished. She definitely hadn't been in her bedroom or its bathroom, nor her office. Her blushed cheeks had given away that, for some reason, she hadn't wanted him to know what she'd been up to.

Elena Swan seemed easy to read at work – hardworking, organised, popular with the staff. So what had she got to hide at home?

Tahoor had asked Rory in as he was having trouble bleeding a radiator in the bedroom he slept in, the biggest at the front of the house. On the way out, Rory had noticed the elderly neighbour had a burglar alarm, but not a single bolt on his door, nor a CCTV camera either, like Elena's. They clearly weren't standard fittings for each house in the cul-de-sac. Since moving in, Rory was increasingly struck by how safety-conscious Elena was. Their sporadic chats, away from the office environment, had revealed that she'd never got blind drunk, nor even flown on an aeroplane. Nothing especially unusual about that – unless, like Elena, you mentioned those things with a voice tinged with regret.

Yet she wasn't shy. Her rendition of 'Bohemian Rhapsody' at the karaoke, last night – well, a duet, in fact – had proved that, although she had looked awkward at the start and shot off the stage as soon as the last note played. Elena held her own with colleagues, never afraid of a heated debate. On a department night out, in the spring, when a youth stole Caz's handbag, she was the first to give chase. In the summer she'd asked the manager of the coffee shop next door to work, out for a drink, but he was taking a break from dating, she'd explained to Gary one lunchtime in the staffroom, when Rory was in there making a coffee. She'd been fine about it, so rejection didn't scare her either. Yet during the last couple of months, now that he gave it some thought, Rory had sensed a change. Elena had been late to work a few times, until she got used to a new route to the office. She'd muttered something about avoiding an accident hotspot. She'd stuck down a rug by the department's entrance with double-sided tape, even though no one had ever slipped on it. As for the milk she used to drink a couple of days past its use-by date if it smelled okay, Elena now took her coffee black. Elena's careful modus operandi at home looked new, too. The bolts shone as if recently screwed on, and she'd mentioned in passing that she'd only got the CCTV installed a few weeks ago.

Unless he was over-thinking. He ate ham a week past its use-by date and would use any rug to surf across a smooth floor. As for taking an aeroplane trip, he'd once enjoyed a wing-walking experience. Who was to say which one of them, he or Elena, was more out of the ordinary? But imagine living your life according to so many rules. He leant against the bed's headboard. It was none of his business why Elena had been so upset at work, why she erred on the side of caution, nor where she'd disappeared to earlier.

It wasn't.

Even though he couldn't forget the terror on her face, when she'd slipped.

Rory rolled his lips together, got changed into his pyjamas and sat in bed. He reached for his journal.

Wednesday 20th November

15-minute morning shower singing 'Ocean Eyes' aided by a 385ml shampoo bottle microphone.

2 checks by Elena that the front door is closed. Seriously, she needs to loosen up.

50-long-minute drive to work listening to a CD of her KILL ME NOW music.

Heart thumping more quickly than its normal 62 beats per minute, as Elena slipped and almost fell.

The expected gag reflex from her when I took out my gherkin jar and ate two, each one containing 0.035mg copper and 0.245mg iron – keep magnets away!

The daily pickle *joke* (using that word loosely) from Gary, asking if I'm pregnant.

0 words spoken on the way home.

As long as it took to cook a stir-fry for Elena to go missing without leaving the house.

THE MOST BORING 90 MINUTES OF MY LIFE (and that's saying something, having sat in the lotus position for one hour, trying to meditate, as a *fun outing* on a quad biking trip to Cambodia), with 3 goals, 1 red card and 3 penalties.

2 expletives in Urdu.

1 celebratory coffee after City won 2 to 1.

1 radiator bled in Tahoor's bedroom, that had 4 photographs of his wife on a chest of drawers, 1 half-empty pink perfume bottle on a bedside table, along with 1 well-thumbed women's fiction novel. 1 purple sari hung on the front of a wardrobe. 2 pairs of slippers, 1 brown and large, the other floral and small, lay on the carpet by the radiator. On 1 pillow of the double bed lay what looked like 1 neatly folded, pastel nightdress, along with 1 little teddy bear holding a red heart.

0 of the football bravado as Tahoor stood quietly and ran a hand over the purple sari whilst I fiddled with the bleed key. I wanted to hug him, especially as the rest of the house looked less well cared for, with dust and a frozen meal carton on the kitchen unit, amongst a pile of unwashed cups and dishes, and crumbs on the floor in the lounge, which needed a good tidy.

5 minutes, near midnight, putting the world to rights with Brandy and Snap, as they lay on my hands and conducted my words by waving their baton-like front legs.

7

ELENA

Humming, Elena walked into the lounge and yawned before peering into the glass tank. She'd placed it by a wall, on a natural oak chest of drawers – away from direct sunlight but close enough to the radiator to keep Brandy and Snap warm. Elena had done her research by going into chat rooms occupied by stick insect owners, scrolling through their friendly conversations, whereas Rory would have searched for surveys and statistics that supported the best place to locate it. Like Rory, she'd never owned a pet – wanted to, maybe a dog or a cat, but as she got older, Elena worried she wouldn't be around to look after it for its whole life. Although, she did secretly adopt next door's black cat when she was little. Without the grown-ups knowing, she'd fed it processed cheese and played with it on the common near her house – until the terrible thing happened and she'd got talking to the stranger there. After that, she never visited the common again at night, and went through a phase of believing in well-known bad omens, like never to cross paths with a black cat, as she'd been doing; like running from a blue butterfly in the park, and being overwhelmed with fear when she accidentally trod on, and killed, a ladybird. Young Elena sobbed the time she'd dropped and cracked a hand mirror, and told her dad off when he left shoes on a table. As for that afternoon a visitor had opened an umbrella in their house...

But Elena was an adult now.

She crouched down and spotted Brandy, with six legs intact and antennae so long they probably picked up messages from distant aliens. Stick insects might hold all sorts of secrets and answers to the big questions.

'Will humans ever live in outer space?' she asked Brandy. 'Is there life after death? Most important of all, are Jaffa Cakes really biscuits?'

Footsteps sounded and Rory stood in the doorway. He wore tartan pyjama trousers with a navy-blue T-shirt, underneath a silk, cerise dressing gown. He'd taken to wearing it, to take off the morning chill, having found it hanging on the back of his bedroom door. He'd forgotten to pack his own bathrobe and acted as if silk was as warm as thick wool. Idiot. Elena had only ever put it on if a boyfriend slept over – a bit of glam in contrast to the usual dark grey, woollen one she'd pulled on this morning. Anyway, Rory being Rory, it suited him, and quietly she admired his indifference to fashion norms.

'How about coffee? I've a new Mexican grind? It has notes of jalapeno apparently.' He about-turned and headed for the kitchen. Rory had also bought chocolate croissants the day before, and they sat in the lounge, eating and drinking. Yesterday they'd driven to the office in separate cars as she'd had a cervical screening test with the nurse – Elena never missed health checks. Thank goodness Rory had done his weekly food shop, as the granola Elena usually enjoyed had run out, meaning it would have been plain toast for her breakfast.

Ah, Saturday. Bliss.

'Got much planned today? If not, fancy a swim?' he asked after the last mouthful of pastry. 'There must be a pool nearby. I haven't taken a dip since I did that underwater rugby session, back in August.'

'It's the middle of winter?'

'This *is* 2024, a couple of centuries since the industrial revolution began.'

'I'm trying to reduce my carbon footprint and swimming in a heated pool won't help that,' she said breezily.

'The pool will be heated regardless of whether you're in it,' he said smugly.

Damn. He won that. Their relationship skated nicely on the surface, as if their words moved on smooth boards and not jagged blades, with banter to determine who could be the cleverest. It kept them dynamic at work, producing their very best; it kept Rory, like everyone else, away from her hidden depths. Perhaps a dip in the pool would get rid of the tension, still in her shoulders, after the rogue firework and coffee spill.

'Okay. If I can find my swimsuit. A leaflet came through about a pool being opened to the public only a couple of streets away, at a local school. It's a private one.'

'Of course it is.'

She threw a cushion at his head and got up to change. 'After lunch I'll make a roast, unless you're going out?' she said, feeling obliged to return the favour, after the breakfast he'd thoughtfully bought for both of them. It can't have been much fun for him, living away from his own personal comforts. Like his air fryer, hot chocolate machine, and the souvenirs from the countries he'd visited doing extreme sports, such as the Alpaca blanket he'd brought back from the bungee jump in Peru. And fancy gadgets and travel mementoes were all very well, but home was where the roast potatoes were.

An hour later, she stood by the edge of the pool, in her blue and gold chain-print one-piece, and breathed in chlorine. It took her back to her childhood and swimming trips with Mum and Dad. The three of them would race widths, throw balls and swim through each other's legs. Elena eased herself into the water, her waist shrinking as if it could fit into a Bridgerton corset. She'd loved those books and hadn't bothered with the TV series. Elena bobbed up and down, acclimatising herself slowly to the temperature. She lay on her back, star-shaped, feeling as light as one of those pops of colour from the firework display, floating through the sky. Brushing her hair off her face, she stood up again and smiled at a small child paddling past in an inflatable ring. Elena was about to swim a length when Rory appeared on the pool deck. She did breaststroke over to the side and looked up.

'Nice trunks,' she said and sank into the water. Very nice. They clung just tightly enough on his slim but muscular legs. She forced her eyes to his face, ignoring the heat in her lower body that must have been caused by the pool's heating system.

'A gift from my granddad. He's always dreamed of going to Hawaii. Nearest he's ever got is drinking a canned Mai Tai on Blackpool beach.' Rory strode to the end of the pool and easily dived in, with the grace and style he radiated on dry land. He popped up by Elena, breath even, as if he survived as much on chlorine as oxygen. They both hung on to the side and Elena reached out towards his chest and a silver necklace. She pointed to the pendant.

'A shark's tooth?'

'Found it on a beach in Florida, last year. I went on a last-minute surfing holiday with mates. It was shortly before I started doing contract work for Bingley Biscuits.'

'Fun memories, then.'

Rory fingered the pendant. 'Sure...'

He went to swim away but something in those eyes, chestnut and flicked with hazelnut, like a warm, inviting mug of hot chocolate, made her touch his arm. 'What else?'

He ran the tooth along his bottom lip. 'Sharks are misunderstood creatures, made out to be ruthless killers of humans. Yet you can probably count their fatal attacks on us, each year, on two hands. Them going for us is rare, whereas we slaughter almost one hundred million sharks in the same time period, for their fins, or oil for cosmetics...'

Elena's mouth fell open. 'That many?'

He nodded. 'It's relatable, that's all. Appearances can be deceptive. Show me a human who says they don't feel misunderstood and I'll show you a liar.'

Before she had a chance to reply, he disappeared under the water and swam down to the deep end. Elena followed. Was there more to Rory than his dangerous hobbies, the wisecracks, the enviable fluid, easy-going approach to life?

They did several lengths and raced the last, Rory winning, despite Elena grabbing hold of his feet and tickling one. She couldn't remember the last time she'd laughed quite as loudly. A bodybuilder type walked past on the pool deck. He must have been six foot tall and built as if he lifted weights as often as Elena lifted her coffee cup. Rory got out and stood on the side, doing stretches. Today's swim must have seemed tame to an extreme sports enthusiast like him. Well, Elena could be daring too. Like when she was a teen, she'd try to swim a width, underwater, as close to the bottom as possible. The pool had almost emptied out as lunchtime approached and she trod water against the far concrete side of the pool. She closed her eyes, bobbing up and down, mentally preparing herself.

Elena took a deep breath, ducked under the surface, propelled herself downwards and touched the bottom. Victory!

But the tricky bit was staying as low as you could, until the far side loomed into view. Searching, her eyes stung, and as an automatic reaction, she opened her mouth with discomfort and took in an unexpected gulp of water. A gag reflex kicked in and Elena kicked her feet furiously, to reach the surface. She was almost there when a swimmer appeared out of nowhere, grabbed her by the waist and dragged her back to where she'd started, skimming the water strongly with their other arm. Behind them, a resounding smack hit the surface of the water. Its impact rippled across, creating turbulence. Elena wriggled free and shot up to the surface, spluttering. She placed her hands against the person's body and shoved it away, with all her might.

'What the fuck are you doing?' she said, heaving, eyes and nose streaming, vision finally clearing. 'Oh, Rory?' She had a coughing fit and he gently guided her over to the side. 'If you think that's funny...' she stuttered, still struggling to breathe.

A bald lifeguard appeared by them, standing above them on the tiled floor in red shorts. 'Are you okay?' he asked Elena and crouched down. His colleague was talking firmly to the body-builder, on the other side of the pool, ordering him out of the water.

Rory pointed. 'That guy didn't check the water well enough before diving in. You were already underneath the surface as he did a run up. I yelled but he must have assumed I was shouting at someone else. I was in the water by then, so I pushed myself off the side with all my strength and—'

'Fortunately for both of you, the diver stopped and did another run up, still not understanding anything was wrong. It gave you just enough time to get her out of the way.' The lifeguard shook his head. 'It won't happen again once Judy has finished with him. He should have been more careful.' The lifeguard sucked in his cheeks. 'I once witnessed a very bad, freak diving accident, similar circumstances, about ten years ago. Bad neck injuries, the pair of them, one of them life changing. They almost died. You had a lucky escape, miss.'

Elena gulped again, but this time fear entered her chest instead of chlorinated water. At his words, the water felt as chilly as when she'd first got in.

'I'll get the accident book.' The lifeguard stood up and jerked his head towards a sign before walking away.

Elena stared at the wall ahead of her and the big red and white sign with the words 'Careful in the deep end! Swimming and diving!'

'I saw the man but thought he'd finished and was heading for the changing rooms.' Her voice cracked. 'That's three times you've saved my life,' she whispered.

'That's a little dramatic, but I'll take it,' he said and gave her a curious look. 'Come on. Race you to the shallow end. Let's get out, help the lifeguard with the paperwork and then head for the coffee machine.'

But Elena didn't race and she had no stomach for a drink. She hardly said anything as they walked back to her cul-de-sac. It was coming true, all of it: the terrible thing she'd promised, aged ten, to the stranger amongst the trees, who'd kept their side of the deal. Now it was Elena's turn to repay the favour.

Oh, over the years, on a good day, she'd pretended that the promise would never be called in. But there was no denying it now. Her mind raced over the incidents of the last couple of weeks and she took a sharp intake of breath.

Everything happens as it should... Everything happens for a reason... These were phrases bandied about, as if fate had tangible power. What if there *was* sense in them? What if the universe was on the stranger's side, out of fairness, out of a belief that once a deal is made, *both* parties must fulfil their side of it and to hell with the consequences?

The universe would know that Elena had worked in HR. Perhaps it had sent her one verbal and two written warnings: the voice shouting 'Watch out!' at the firework display. The text Gary had written about him making coffee. The big red and white swimming sign with writing saying to be careful in the deep end.

This meant only one thing.

Termination was next.

Elena's house came into view. No. She was being ridiculous. The universe, some force, intervening? What an impossible idea.

Or was it as possible as the reality of what had happened in 2004 – that because of the promise young Elena made, a woman with an unfamiliar accent, living in a tent, in the woods, had saved a life that the doctors had written off?

8

ELENA

Whistling greeted Elena as she walked into the kitchen, its windows steamed over, the air fragrant with pesto and garlic.

'Took you forever to wash your hair,' said Rory, and he passed her a glass of wine.

They'd grabbed a burger after the pool before heading to the cinema, his idea. She'd done her best to focus on the latest Marvel movie. Elena was no movie snob and, like her books, she gave every sort of film a go: literary, commercial, adult, teen. No surprise that Rory was a huge fan, what with the movie's daredevil action. He'd insisted on buying a bucket of popcorn and two bright-blue slushy drinks. She caught him giving her worried glances during the screening, perhaps concerned she'd get bored, despite the jump scares.

'I came to look for you but your room was empty and the shower wasn't running, just like last time,' he said and sipped his drink.

Elena's phone rang and speedily she answered it, glad to walk away from the inquisitive look Rory had shot her. Ten minutes later, she returned to the kitchen.

'Mum and Dad have invited me to dinner, tomorrow night. They said to ask you along. It's Moussaka Monday.'

'It's *what*?'

'On their first holiday together, back in the eighties, in Kos, they wanted to go somewhere fancy for their first proper meal out together. Back home they'd only ever had takeout as a treat. So they sat down in this restaurant and without a word of Greek, simply pointed to a moussaka dish other diners were eating. It was only when they asked for the bill that they realised they'd gate-crashed a wedding.'

'Way to go!'

'To add to the celebrations, Dad got down on one knee and proposed!'

'Wow. What a story. Remember our first meal together?'

Her brow furrowed.

'I'd just begun my first ever contract job with Bingley Biscuits and you insisted on taking me out after work, for food. We'd brainstormed, for fun, during our lunch hour, over the concept for a new stuffed cookie range you'd heard about from Mary in product development. Neither of us had eaten a thing since breakfast.'

Elena always took new team members out to get to know them, whether they were temporary or permanent. Going the extra mile had become a way of life. Sometimes it wore her down, but Derek approved and Mum and Dad showed off about her to friends, mentioning her commitment to her career, her fancy house. 'Yes, I remember. You researched the figures – the jump in stuffed cookie sales during the pandemic had been sustained and they were still tracking well. I thought we could pitch them as being stuffed with love and comfort. It was a shame the product was never taken forward.'

'It had been a long day so I suggested takeout back at mine,' he said. 'We picked up fish 'n' chips on the way, your treat. You asked the guy – he wasn't English – to shake your fish free of excess batter before frying. It was noisy. He gave you a really odd look. Our order took forever and when we got back to mine and opened the food, we understood why.'

'He must have only heard the words *free* and *batter*, taking free to be the word number three, so frying the cod that many times, each with a new coating of batter. That fish would have made a good rugby ball. Talk about a thick, leathery coating.'

'Yet you ate it. No complaints. I've never forgotten that.'

A flicker of something pleasant tickled her insides.

'Moussaka Monday sounds good. It's great that your parents are so romantic. That's the dream, isn't it – finding someone to spend your whole life with?'

Was it? Elena had never allowed herself to contemplate that.

She wanted to ask about his parents. He only spoke about his dad, who lived on the outskirts of Manchester, was called Mike and worked as a plumber. Rory drove over there every now and again for dinner, and his dad caught the train into town and they'd get lunch and go to the cinema. Rory was a talker, a doer, as vibrant as they came – yet, on the subject of his mother, he closed down like a funfair that had suddenly lost its electricity supply.

'Tahoor's wife, Isha, made a mean moussaka,' said Elena. 'She'd often bring me round a portion of their dinner – dishes from around the world, though the biryanis from her childhood were the best.'

Rory told her about Tahoor's bedroom and a sense that he was struggling to keep on top of managing the house.

'Nine months isn't that long, I suppose,' said Elena. 'Not when you've been with someone most of your life.'

'But her nightdress is still on the pillow next to his.'

Elena sat up at the breakfast bar and put down her phone and glass. She rubbed her forehead. 'I should have gone around more often; should have realised how lonely he felt. On reflection, his shirts always look un-ironed, his lawn overgrown, and often, when he opens the door, there is a pile of unopened mail at the side.'

Rory left the pan and went over, squeezed her shoulder. Out of nowhere a lump appeared in her throat. No one ever comforted Elena because she'd learnt so long ago to hide any worries. 'You aren't responsible for everyone's happiness. But maybe I'll pretend to enjoy myself more when he comes around for the football on Wednesday after work.'

'When he *what*?'

'Didn't I mention it? I found it hard to say no.'

She pictured the unworn nightdress next to Tahoor every night. 'Let's have him over to dinner as well, then? Isha once said, out of all the complex recipes she made, he was like an excited schoolboy whenever she dished up fried eggs, baked beans and chips.'

'I'm in. His wife sounds pretty cool.'

'Isha would come over for coffee, before she got ill. She grew up in a residential area, in Karachi. Her family lived in the same street as friends who knew Tahoor's family. As a young boy, he'd visit often and play tag outside with a group of lads. Isha was a bit of a loner and enjoyed kite flying. They were too shy to talk to each other, until their late teens. She showed me photos of the harbour, Mohatta Palace, fantastic parks. They both had siblings there and used to visit once a year.'

'I did cliff diving in Southern Pakistan, one summer holiday whilst I was at uni. A group of us went backpacking. An incredible holiday. I only spent one day in Karachi, but I loved it.'

'Is there any country you haven't visited?' she asked sceptically. 'How do you find time for all these holidays?'

'Contract work is something of an enabler.'

'So why sign up to Bingley Biscuits permanently?'

'Maybe it's time to grow up,' he said and gave a wry smile.

He'd taken the words from her mouth. Or so she thought.

Don't say that, Rory. Don't stop being everything I want to be – brave, daring, living life spontaneously, more afraid of missing out than of things going wrong.

'Isha wore the same charm bracelet every day,' said Elena. 'It had a kite on it. Tahoor bought it for her the day they got married. If the wind ever got up, I'd see them sometimes, in their back garden, flying a kite.'

'I got invited to a kite fighting session once,' said Rory. 'But it didn't appeal. I love kites because they look so carefree. They're a bit like guppies splashing amongst ripples of water.' He gave a sheepish smile. 'Saw a shoal of those whilst big-wave surfing in South America.' They sank into silence and he opened the oven door to check on the garlic bread.

'Sorry I didn't feel up to making that roast after all, what with... what happened at the pool,' said Elena brightly, as if she were over it. 'But you didn't need to make dinner again. I don't expect you to "earn your keep", so to speak. Weren't you meeting a friend... Izzy, tonight?'

'Change of plans. She's come down with that flu bug going around. It's only pasta and you haven't tasted it yet.' He cocked his head. 'Let's do the maths of who's made the most meals since I moved in. We've not eaten together every night, for a start, and—'

'Let's not,' she groaned, and he gave a soft laugh. She liked that sound. 'And fair point. I've kept to myself a lot, working on my pitch to Derek for many evenings, and you often eat out with friends, like after that axe-throwing event. Still can't believe I lost that bet about you hitting at least one bullseye at it. It can't be nearly as hard as your other extreme sports, like skydiving, and you do those easily enough.'

'Firstly, axe-throwing is not an extreme sport...'

'Said no sane person ever.'

'Secondly, what makes you think I'm good at my hobbies?'

'Er, because you're still alive?'

He shrugged. 'No. I always find it hard to hit the exact landing target when skydiving, I fall off my surfboard more than most people, and am never the fastest at mountain biking.'

'Then why do them?' she asked.

'I'm not taking part to win,' he said and jumped up to check the pasta.

He turned back to Elena, and she raised an eyebrow.

Rory went to talk but then twirled the fork between his fingers. Finally, he spoke. 'It sounds cheesy, but I'm chasing... a sense of being alive, I guess. Modern life anaesthetises, suffocates... what with us all spending hours in front of screens, typing or scrolling, boxed in a building that's centrally heated and free from risk, away from strangers, away from the elements. Those two things have been given bad names – "beware that person looking at you", "watch out for the wind and rain, heat"... but surely we've been put on this earth to cross paths with things like those as well?'

Elena listened intently.

His eyes shone. 'I want to talk to people I haven't yet met. I want scorching sunrays or freezing snow on my face.' His hands became animated. 'I love Netflix, love a good session on my phone, but I want a life that gives me more as well. I haven't got the physical powers of a Marvel hero, but I've got common sense and a desire to exceed the limits that most people allow to imprison them. Above all else, I'm building memories that are all mine and not down to something I've only experienced through watching others, on a screen...' He gave a sheepish look but she nodded, wanting to say something, but how? Her life had been on the sharpest edge in recent weeks and she'd do anything to change that for banality.

Elena insisted on washing up, carefully putting the knives away, hiding them at the back of the drawer. She made sure the hob was off, checked the bolts on the front door several times, and went around the ground floor to see that all windows were closed. Rory offered to set the burglar alarm and she made sure that the battery of the personal alarm in her room was working. They said goodnight and she followed him up the stairs. Elena cleaned her face and brushed her teeth, listening to Rory singing 'Ocean Eyes' through the wall. It felt comforting, until it didn't, when he eventually stopped and the house went quiet, dark. She lay there for an hour, but sleep wouldn't come.

The firework. The spilt coffee. The diver.

Her whole body twitched as a loud creak came from downstairs. She sat bolt upright. Elena got out of bed and put on her dressing gown. She paused outside Rory's room. Elena wouldn't bother him. The noise was probably nothing. Pulse racing, she crept down the stairs. The creak sounded again, she sensed it was near... But the hallway looked exactly the same as usual. So did the empty kitchen, lounge and dining room. She exhaled.

Of course. They'd had the heating on late. It must have simply been the wood in the house contracting as it cooled back down. Elena went into the lounge and flicked on a table lamp. For several minutes she sat with her head in her hands. She looked up at the curtains, to the left of the glass tank, tightly pulled to keep potentially sinister eyes out. A movement caught her attention in the tank. What if Brandy and Snap wanted to look at the night? She got up and drew the curtains open wide.

She would be safe. She was locked in the house. The door had been bolted.

Elena gazed up at the stars. Tahoor's light was on, in the bedroom at the front of his house. He stood staring upwards too. The night sky was clear, crisp, and a satellite flew past. He wore Paisley pyjamas and an expression that couldn't look more opposite to the one he'd worn when celebrating City's win.

A rustle sounded from the tank. She took the lid off and put in a hand, waited and finally Snap climbed on board. She put the lid back on and sat on the sofa with the insect. Its front legs waved in the air. It moved from side to side. Rory had told Elena this meant it could be scared as it was pretending to be a twig swaying in the breeze.

'I'm not going to hurt you,' she whispered. 'It's nice to have a couple more females in the house. Do stick insects swim? I went underwater today. But this diver...' In a shaky voice, she told Snap what had happened at the pool. Eventually, its swaying stopped. 'You're amazing, you know that?' she mumbled. 'Rory treated me to some more facts about you tonight. Next time you moult, that's when you'll regenerate a new leg.' Elena sighed. 'I wish I was able to shed my past.' Gently, she placed Snap back in the tank on an especially green leaf, put the lid back on and then she peered outside again. Tahoor's light was off now. Another satellite went past. Rory would have ridden it bareback, given the opportunity. The thought of him taking on yet another mad activity didn't irritate her like it had, before he moved in. She used to wonder if he did extreme sports to impress. However, recently, she'd got the feeling there was a deeper purpose.

For several minutes, she stood as still as Brandy and Snap playing dead.

Rory's life was all about stepping out of his comfort zone. A determined look crossed her face. Elena's fingers curled into fists. Before she knew it, she was talking to a deep-seated fear that had tightened its grip on her in recent months.

'I'm sick of being scared, of you always making me look over my shoulder, risk-assessing my every move.

'No more!

'I'm Elena Swan, the ten-year-old girl who gave up her life for another, and who for twenty years hasn't burdened a single soul with that knowledge; the teen who got beaten up, protecting a friend from bullies; the young woman who reported a senior colleague for inappropriate behaviour. I'm the worker who admitted she'd made a mistake going into HR, and started her career over, pretty much from scratch, in marketing. I'm the train passenger who once intervened when a bunch of lads were shouting racist abuse at an old man and no one else said anything.' Her breath hitched. 'It's the very last months of my twenty-ninth year, when I should be making the most of my life...' Her jaw tightened.

'Just like Snap will shed her old skin, I *will* shed my fears. For fuck's sake, I'm an adult, not a primary school child. Finally, I can see that being terminated isn't the worst outcome. The worst is already here and it's me tiptoeing my way through my existence, and to a much greater degree lately, listening to that voice in my head making me question the safety of everything. I've never gone abroad, for God's sake, kidding myself I was happy with that, when I love foreign food, and speaking French for my GCSE gave me such a buzz in my stomach. I've kept boyfriends at a distance, afraid of commitment, for their sakes, not that they'd ever guess it. Rory's shown me how *my* life has always felt anaesthetised and suffocated.

'I can't worry any more. I can't keep hiding in the shadow of the person I could and should really be.'

She waited for the sense of doom to wash over her, to drown her in despair.

But instead... Elena raised her eyebrows... A weight lifted. She felt as light as Snap had, on her fingers. It was time to be less like fictional, cautious Elinor, and more like that character's rash sister, Marianne – less sense and more sensibility.

She stood up. 'I'd do it over again, you know? In order to save that precious life. It was worth it.' Elena put her shoulders back and lifted her chin. 'It really was – even if I never make it to this Christmas.'

Elena strode into the hallway and moved the three bolts across, then went into the kitchen and opened one of the windows. Ignoring the hob, she went up to her room, as wispy and light as a feather that could waft up into the air, carefree as a kite.

In these last few weeks before her thirtieth birthday, Elena Swan would make up for the fun she'd missed her whole life.

9

ELENA

Five thirty. Almost time to head to Mum and Dad's for dinner, but Elena rang to ask if it was okay if she and Rory turned up a little late. An idea had been growing in Elena all day, a fleeting thought at first that had eventually taken root and rapidly grown. This suited her parents as their golf game had gone on longer than expected. She pictured them in their diamond-patterned jumpers, as colourful as those of that pop group they used to love, Bucks Fizz. A wave of affection swept over her.

Gary came over with his coat on and threatened to press the off button on her computer. 'I know that look, Swan,' he said. 'Which reminds me, what genius plan have you come up with, for our department night out in December, then? A festive-themed silent disco? Another evil Santa Claus grotto escape room like last year? I'm secretly hoping it's a Christmas bake off. But whatever it is, go home, gal, it's time to chill.'

'I'll fix the date soon but as ever, I'll be keeping the details top secret until the week before,' she said, without stopping typing. 'Mind you, make me a coffee before you go and I might give you a hint.' She looked up and grinned.

'Would love to, chica, but I'm off for drinks with Diego at our fave salsa bar. His boss has closed the restaurant tonight. Deep cleaners are coming in before next week's celebration of it being open five years. There's even an actor from Corrie going. How about a mint instead?' He held out a packet and Elena helped herself. Gary headed across the office and disappeared out the door, but not before treating the room to a Latin dance move. She signalled to Rory and he ambled over, already dressed to leave, in his red leather jacket with black trim.

'I... we... need to see Derek. It's important,' she blurted out.

'*Now?*'

'Something's come up regarding the budget biscuit plan. The product idea I had – I've seen it through different eyes and am even more excited about how it could take off, and how it could persuade the board to take this pitch seriously.'

'With me desperate to sink my teeth into mouth-watering moussaka? And Derek hating unplanned meetings? Especially at the end of the day?' Rory stretched out an arm. 'Lead the way.' Elena jumped up, brushed down her trouser suit and walked over to Derek's room. She knocked on the door. A tired voice said, 'Come in.' Heart racing, she entered, Rory close behind.

'Elena? Rory? What's up? You've got five minutes. Family party.'

'The details of the budget biscuit plan that we firmed up in last Friday's meeting – we need to include my idea,' she said. 'I can't hold back on it any longer. It's – better for us, better for the customer. A budget biscuit that won't be higher in trans fats because of the cheaper ingredients we'd be forced to use, that aren't up to our usual quality. Rory's view on this would be useful too. Mentioning my product idea to the board, at this early stage, might just swing it for us.'

Derek consulted his watch and begrudgingly smiled. 'Okay.

Never could say no to enthusiasm, and compromising our principles hasn't sat well with me either. I'm listening.' He pushed up his jumper's sleeves, leant back in his chair and took off his glasses. Rory sat down on one of the chairs opposite.

Elena pressed her palms together. 'Bags of broken biscuits used to be very popular. Biscuits get broken in transit, and during the manufacturing process, less-than-perfect products are binned for many reasons – such as being misshapen, or having crumbled edges, due to fillings leaking, coatings having gaps or flawed patterns. As you probably know, and I learnt from my research, Bingley Biscuits stopped selling these in the eighties, with the evolution of a society all about image and materialism. You were what you bought – broken biscuits didn't fit in with eighties aspirations. But times change and I'd say, during a cost-of-living crisis, us saving wastage fits in perfectly with our vision.'

'My mum used to buy them from Woolworths when I was a kid, and at the local market.' Derek frowned. 'But what would make our broken biscuits stand out? Broken biscuits are broken biscuits and even less sexy than a budget line, surely? They're effectively the manufacturing process's leftovers.'

'Which means you've got a story you can tell, to sell them, right, Elena?' asked Rory.

She did! There was that flicker inside her, again, Rory had her back.

'Spot on,' she said and beamed. Elena had entered the office this morning full of determination that she would no longer be broken by a twenty-year promise. To her surprise, using that word – broken – brought a revelation: that the difficulties over the years, caused by that night in 2004, had somehow made her stronger. They had. She was still standing, still achieving and hadn't allowed the prospect of a bleak future to steal her whole life away.

Broken but put back together, more robustly than before.

That was the story: being broken wasn't The End.

She stopped pacing and faced the other two. 'Feeling broken? Bad day at the office? Depressed by world news? Struggling with bills? Enter a fun bag of broken biscuits, living their best life, diverse but side by side, the shortcake rings, the vanilla sandwich biscuits, the chocolate-coated oatie ones, broken but partying together.' She waved her hand in the air. 'In the commercial, I see a diverse bunch of friends, going round to a sad mate's house, with bags of our broken biscuits, all of these people laughing together, cheering their friend up. Those biscuits shout friendship, inclusivity and overcoming hard times. I can picture the advert already – the empathetic smiles, bright colours, the dance music, interspersed with hugs, all of it held together by Bingley's broken biscuits being passed around and enjoyed.'

She held her breath.

Derek didn't blink at first. 'Christ,' he said eventually. 'You might be onto something. I love it! Modern, fresh, relevant... This could really work.'

'We *could* come up with a clever name for them, inspired by the idea of taking a break – but, actually, keeping it simple might work best,' said Rory, leaning forwards. 'How about *Not-so-Broken Biscuits*? Part of the bag could have a transparent window to make it clear the contents aren't actually whole, to avoid being accused of misleading customers. The o in the word broken could have a smiley face in it.'

Derek was writing notes. He looked at his watch again, swore and closed the notebook. 'I've really got to leave, but well done, Elena. I'm impressed. Let's talk more tomorrow. Keep going with those name ideas, Rory. I won't get much sleep tonight. My brain's already twitching.'

Elena and Rory left his office and talked non-stop about the meeting, all the way down to the car park. Tomorrow they'd research which competitors were selling broken biscuits, and analyse their marketing campaigns.

'You're a genius, Swan,' said Rory. He clapped her back and without thinking, she gave him a hug, before pulling away and breaking eye contact. Rory got into his yellow Volkswagen Beetle.

'Finally, you notice my huge talent,' she said and clambered in the other side, hoping the banter made light of her throwing her arms around him. Rory turned on the engine to clear the windscreen. 'Mum's asked if you'd like sushi to start tonight, by the way. It's as much a fit with moussaka as oysters with pizza, but my parents love it, and the supermarket had a special deal on.'

'Sounds great. What will you have?'

'The same.'

Rory stopped putting on his seat belt and looked sideways at her. 'But you always say raw fish is way too risky if someone brings it in for their lunch.'

'I can change my mind, can't I?'

'Go for it! Fun fact: as a general rule, chefs have to freeze the fish down to minus forty degrees anyway, to kill off bacteria.'

'Whatever. Let's face it – I probably consumed more germs at the swimming pool yesterday.'

Rory switched on the radio and tuned it in to Elena's favourite station.

'You hate Kill Me Now FM, as you call it,' she said.

'A guy can be nice, can't he?' he said, in an unexpectedly gentle voice.

Elena paused and glanced at him sideways. 'I'm okay, you know,' she said quietly. 'In fact, what happened at the pool has given me clarity.' She pointed to the car roof. 'Put it back.'

'Elena, the frost hasn't lifted all day!'

She tightened her scarf. 'I want the rush of winter in my hair.'

'You do?' Rory looked puzzled.

She gave him a determined look. Rory put back the roof, released the handbrake and drove onto the main road. Five minutes later, down the broad bypass, despite the rush hour traffic, despite the horns of impatient drivers, the loudest sound was Elena whooping and laughing as her blonde hair rippled in the breeze, more wildly than any whitewater rafting waves.

10

ELENA

Unable to stop smiling, Elena stood, hair windswept, whole body invigorated, outside her parents' house, an unassuming three-bed semi on a quiet road in Bridgwich, thirty minutes away from her home. Her mum and dad were teachers and had met at university in the eighties. As their names were Don and Melanie; it had been a joke amongst their friends that they were the Mancunian version of Hollywood couple Don Johnson and Melanie Griffith. Elena's dad had been thrilled, as a huge fan of *Miami Vice*, in which Johnson starred. He still dressed the part and opened the door in pleated linen trousers and a navy shirt, loafer-style white slippers with no socks and sporting blow-dried high-lighted hair. The only thing missing was the tan – and the American accent.

'You look dead freezing, love. Fancy a brew?' Don opened the door wider and gave Elena a hug. He held out his hand and gave Rory's a firm shake. 'Good to meet you, lad. Cool jacket. Reminds me of the one Michael Jackson wore in the "Thriller" video.'

Melanie appeared, wiping her hands on a tea towel. Strangers had often made a point, over the years, of saying how much Elena looked like her mother. The same blue eyes with slight shadows underneath, the nose that raised slightly at the tip, the bow-shaped mouth with the fuller top lip. Melanie smoothed down Elena's hair and gave her a tight side hug. 'Come on into the warm, both of you. Rory, take off that jacket before my husband asks you to do the moonwalk.'

Don proceeded to attempt that famous dance move, succeeding only in making Elena grab Rory's arm and lead him swiftly into the kitchen. A cup of tea later, they sat at the table in the cosy dining room, walls filled with photos from family holidays, golf tournaments and Christmases.

'Are you sure sushi is okay, El?' asked Melanie. 'Happy to rustle up some garlic bread or a bowl of the leek soup I made at the weekend, instead.'

'I can't make a fuss, not when we've got guests.' Elena reached forward, picked up a salmon sushi roll. Without studying it, she popped the fish straight into her mouth. The unfamiliar texture almost made her gag, until the freshness of cucumber and avocado cleaned her palate, before the crunch of the fried onion on top hit. Three pairs of eyes stared at her.

'Well I never,' said Don. 'You'll be joining me for a Guinness later, at this rate.'

'That's never going to happen,' she said and picked up a square of spiced tuna, proud of herself, despite needing to chug back half a glass of water when the chilli set her tastebuds on fire. She hardly had room for apple crumble after the moussaka, but helped herself to a large portion as it was her favourite. That's why her dad had made it. She drank back her coffee and sighed. 'Delicious. I'm stuffed.'

'Me too,' said Rory and patted his stomach. 'Was that cinnamon in the crumble topping? And I swear I tasted orange juice in the fruit.'

Don almost choked on his coffee. 'You get my daughter eating sushi, when I've tried for years, you wear a jacket more eighties than any of mine, and now you suss out my secret ingredients? What's more, announce them out loud? You're one brave man.'

'He is indeed. A bit of an extreme sports expert,' said Elena. 'Tell them about your skydiving, Rory. Also, he's taking me on a bungee jump this weekend coming.'

'He is?' chorused Don and Melanie.

'I am?' asked Rory and put down his cup.

'Well, you did challenge me to do one, in the summer – explained how a mate of yours ran a club at that National Trust park near where you used to live, Knutsford way? He said he could fit you in anytime as you helped him set up the website and market his business.'

'Yes, I challenged Gary as well and you were even more adamant than him that the answer was no – which was saying something, as Gary declared he'd rather give up chocolate forever.'

Melanie exchanged glances with Don. 'Sounds exciting, love,' she said in an unsure tone. 'Scrambling to duck when someone shouts "fore" is about as risky as our sporting endeavours get.'

Rory was grinning. 'Okay, Swan! Let's do this! I'll ring Tim tomorrow. This is very late notice. It depends on the weather forecast though, and he doesn't run as many jumps at this time of year. But this is ace!'

'I've checked,' she said. 'No fog is forecast, no wind either, nor rain!'

Rory rubbed his hands together. 'Great! You'll love it. Honestly.'

Elena beamed.

They got to their feet and Rory turned to one of the walls and studied the photos. 'That's an incredible view,' he said, pointing to a mountain range.

'Scotland 2008,' said Don. 'Best whisky I've drunk in my life.'

Rory moved to the next shot of a teen Elena and her mum on a big wheel.

'The Nottingham Goose Fair,' said Melanie. 'We went there every year when El was at school. I never got used to the spinning drum ride but, when she was younger, El loved it. She was always such a sensible child, but the fair brought out an impulsive, adventurous side. She'd insist on going on the Ghost Train several times – until she got a bit older and then preferred just to wander through, eating candyfloss.'

A quizzical look on his face, Rory glanced at Elena before pointing to another photo. She was wearing Disney pyjamas, sitting by a Christmas tree. 'You look as if you've come down in the morning to no presents,' he said and pushed her shoulder.

'That was... a very difficult Christmas,' said Don and rubbed the back of his neck. 'El was only ten. Mel was still in hospital after... a bad accident. Elena insisted we put the photo up, even though she looked unhappy, as her gran was in it too. My mum had moved back to Canada the year before. She didn't return to England often and flew over to surprise us on Christmas Eve, having heard about... about what happened to Mel.' He stopped for a moment; gathered himself. Rory gave him a sympathetic glance. 'We had a family trip booked to see her the following year but... for one reason and another, it didn't happen.' Don cleared his throat. He put an arm around Rory's shoulders. 'Now, tell me, lad, which team do you support – the blues or the reds?' Don guided him towards the lounge. 'Great eyeliner, Rory, by the way. Or guyliner, as it's called, according to one of the kids at school. You'd think they were being paid to keep me current, the number of times I get corrected. Only yesterday one kid asked me what my Roman Empire was. And a cheeky lad told me not to have a Menty B when he got something wrong. As for the phrase "rizzing someone up", a Year Eleven told me to google the meaning...'

Elena would have burst out laughing at that but was lost in the past, staring at the Christmas photo. Dad had travelled to Canada, to see Gran on his own. Elena had refused, point blank, to get on a plane. In hindsight, that had been selfish. If only she could go back in time and fly to Ontario. It was too late now; Gran had passed. She exhaled and became aware of her mum watching her.

'Come upstairs a minute, love,' said Melanie. 'I've got something to show you.' She linked arms with Elena and they went up, into a double bedroom done out in warm pastels. She'd loved coming into her parents' room as a little girl, sifting through her mum's jewellery box and Dad's coin collection. He'd always collected unusual fifty pence pieces. Only last month he'd been thrilled when she brought over a Paddington Bear one that had ended up in her purse. She sat on the bed and Melanie opened the wardrobe. She took out a stunning blazer. It was sage green, with a slate and gold trim on the cuffs and around the bottom, with slate swirls of leaves going up one side and across the back. It was practical too, with pockets and large buttons.

'I found it in a pop-up shop in Stockport. They had a sale on. It'll go with those grey trousers you wear to work.'

Elena's eyes widened. It was... different and nothing like her conservative style. But 'conservative' wasn't a word Elena wanted to embrace any more. 'Mum! I love it.' She jumped up to hug Melanie before trying it on, turning from side to side in the mirror. 'What have I done to deserve this?'

Melanie took her hand and they both sat down on the floral

duvet. 'You haven't seemed yourself the last month or two. We're worried, love. You can always talk to us, if... say... there are problems at work? Or—'

'I'm fine. Honestly.' Since her mum's accident, Elena had always tried oh so hard not to upset her parents. They'd been through enough. She'd taken care over the small things, when she lived at home: being careful not to swear, her mum hated that; or not coming in really late, as Dad would always wait up; or silently gritting her teeth through ailments such as head or earaches. However, her mum had always seemed to see straight through the deceit.

Melanie folded her arms. 'Don't make me put my cross-parent voice on.'

No reply.

'At times, growing up, and into adulthood, you've gone through spells like this, and they've always taken me and your dad back to 2004, that week before the Christmas that photo was taken, and the months straight afterwards. How—'

'You're right. It's work. I need to take more time out. Really, there's nothing to worry about. Also... Rory's good for me. It's great having company in the house.' Saying those words out loud made Elena realise that, actually, they were true.

Melanie stared at her. 'A bungee-jump does sound... fun?' Elena went to get up but her mum pulled her back. 'El. It's me.'

Elena broke eye contact first. She'd have drunk a hundred pints of Guinness if it meant she could open up to Mum, tell her everything, without her being hurt.

'We used to have sleepless nights when you were bullied at primary school. Thank goodness the headteacher changed and the new one took our concerns seriously. By the time that photo was taken, you were much happier. That's why we were surprised... I mean, I know my accident was a shock, but ever since then... That's when you stopped riding the scary rides at the Goose fair and it coincided with when we finally had money enough to fly to Canada – but instead of being excited, you'd become so afraid of the idea of aeroplanes...'

'I outgrew my lisp. That helped a lot with the bullying. But yes, Mrs Driscott was brilliant. As for the accident, that's two decades ago now, Mum. I'll never forget it but...' Elena put on a brighter tone. 'We've all moved forwards, right?'

Melanie paused and then gave a sigh. 'Okay. I won't push you to talk about it, love, but I hope that one day you... you'll find someone you *can* talk about it with. It's like me, when I got together with your dad... Finally it felt safe to tell someone my... big secret.'

Elena shuffled to face her mum.

'I... I've never told you this before, the time never seemed right, and then I wondered if it really mattered. When I was sixteen, I... got pregnant.'

What?

Did Mum keep the baby?

Did Elena have a sibling out there?

And poor Mum. What a shock for her.

Mel's face flushed. 'I didn't even know until I had an early miscarriage. I never told the father; he dumped me after the first time we slept together, having spent ages trying to get me into bed.'

Elena took her hand. 'That must have been so hard.'

'I didn't tell Gran and Grandpa either. They'd have gone mad and given some long speech about how I could have jeopardised my whole academic future.'

Elena hadn't been Mum's first pregnancy. And what an ordeal to go through as a teenager – and alone. She took a few minutes to let the news sink in, then tentatively asked questions about the father – who he was, how her mum had met him, and then how she'd managed all on her own, with the miscarriage.

'Dad proved himself time and time again whilst we dated, being there for me, always supporting me. I trusted him completely,' said Mel.

It reminded Elena of Gary at work. He'd suffered an eating disorder at a teenager, and now and again binge-eating problems still struck. Elena never knew until he dated Diego. Eventually, Gary opened up to him; said it took a lot of guts because his illness had been dismissed so many times as a teen, him being told that boys didn't get eating disorders. Same when he was older. What with that and his confusion over his sexuality... it wasn't until he'd started trusting and confiding in Diego that he became more confident of discussing his past issues with other people.

She hugged her mum tightly. 'I'm so sorry you went through that. I'm glad you had Dad.'

'One day you'll meet someone special too, and open up. What's more, I think you'll find that means you're in love.'

'Mum!' said Elena, and she rolled her eyes. *'Please! I'm perfectly happy as I am.'* Elena tilted her head. 'It can't have been easy, telling him such a big secret.'

'No, but what a relief. It made me realise what a burden it had been, not telling a single soul about it.' Mel rubbed Elena's arm. 'Whatever it is, darling, that's cast a shadow over you when you were ten...'

'Seriously, do we have to do this?' Elena got up.

Melanie got to her feet too. 'There were positives about that time. The doctors had written me off, warned Don that the worst was going to happen. But then, against all the odds, I came back from the brink of death and was rapidly, miraculously, declared out of danger.'

Elena stared passed her mum's shoulder.

'What I'm saying, is... there is always hope, and problems tend to work themselves out. You'll get through, I've no doubt about it, like I – we all – did after that traffic accident. However bad things are, trust in time. Don said the doctors' faces showed they'd given up, but then bang on midnight something changed. What a transformation. I just came round. They couldn't work out what had saved me.'

Elena bit the insides of her cheeks, like she used to as a little girl when she worried that pent-up words might tumble out. The doctors might have been baffled, but Elena knew exactly what – or rather *who* – had saved her mother.

11

RORY

Rory lay in bed and sank into the mattress, happily sated after the meal at Elena's parents and a little drunk. He gave a soft burp. When they got back, she'd pulled out a bottle of Dom Perignon champagne, part of her leaving present from her former employer. She hadn't drunk it for four years – and now she was drinking it on a Monday night, for no good reason. Elena toasted simply being alive, in the spirit of Rory wearing that gold top and not saving things for best.

'You've woken up a different woman today,' he'd joked, 'driving with the car roof down, eating sushi, agreeing to bungee jumping.'

Elena had taken another large mouthful of champagne. 'If you must know – it's your fault. This last year you've made me realise that perhaps I've not made the most of my twenties.'

He'd basked in the compliment whilst she'd topped up his glass. Rory had always assumed that she, that everyone, thought him a little crazy.

He stretched out under the covers and closed his eyes.

Downstairs he'd put on his favourite Spotify dance playlist and held out his hand. Elena swigged back a mouthful of the Dom Perignon, stood up and took it. Laughing, they'd danced rhythmically, twirling each other around, step to the side, step to the side, hands clapping at one point, lights dimmed, cheeks aching with smiles. They'd done this occasionally whilst out on staff nights, clubbing or singing karaoke, but this felt different.

For sure he'd got to know her better since moving in, surprised how quickly her place felt like home. Despite living more by the rules than Rory, Elena was easy-going and welcoming. A week in, they both began to relax, and boy, was she funny in a spontaneous way he'd never seen in the office! Like the time she'd tickled his foot in the pool, and when she'd put that mud pack on her face. Elena had tapped Rory on the shoulder. The kitchen lights were dimmed and he'd got the shock of his life when he'd turned round. Elena couldn't stop chuckling, but then the joke backfired and the face pack cracked.

For a large part of the early evening, at her parents' house, Rory had picked Don's brains about football. Don was a Blues fan like Elena's neighbour. As a lad, Rory had known what it was like to be lonely, and he didn't want that for Tahoor. Maybe he could get into football after all. Rory opened his eyes. Despite Don's and Melanie's laughs, and Elena's obvious pleasure at seeing them, Rory had sensed a darkness within the Swan family – especially when he'd browsed the photos. Pub quiz facts about swans came to mind, about how those birds were devoted partners, how they were over-protective of their offspring, and he reckoned both of those facts applied to Elena's parents.

Rory's own dad was a bit of a swan too, in that if a mate of one died, the males tended not to re-pair. Rory didn't talk about his mum not being alive and if people just assumed he didn't see her much, that was easier. Dad had enjoyed relationships over the years but had never found a special someone, not until recently. Seeing Melanie, and the way she was with Elena, made him wish for the millionth time he could remember his mother. Dad had kept her perfume behind their wedding photo, in the lounge, for several years. During his childhood, Rory would sneak it out, close his eyes and sniff the bottle, hoping for a reminder of a maternal hug. Nothing. But then she had passed when he was two. He'd never forget the day he'd found out why exactly she died. He pushed the memory away, like he had so many times over the years. Instead of brooding, Rory opened his mouth and sang 'Ocean Eyes' at the top of his voice. Elena joined in too, through the wall. When they stopped, her laughter sounded quite beautiful. Well, he meant it was okay. Rory shook himself and sat up and reached for his journal and pen.

Monday 25th November

13 minutes of our 20-minute coffee break spent with Gary – unlucky number for some, lucky for me. I won this round of our year-long argument, since we first drank coffee together, over which is the best movie – Barbie or Oppie, and it was a debate over fashion this time. Reluctantly, Gary had to concede that Ken's giant fur coat was far more iconic than Oppenheimer's brown trench one.

4 hours – the whole afternoon – finding stats about budget biscuits and how competitors had made them appealing. Fun fact – the popular Rich Tea biscuit came about in the seventeenth century when it was just called a Tea biscuit and given to the upper classes to keep them full in between meals. A clever name reinvention later made that simple biscuit sound aspirational.

4 hours wasted because then Elena comes up with the fresh, stupendous idea of broken biscuits.

1,000 butterflies in my stomach at the prospect of this new direction.

5 strange looks from other drivers, on the way home, as Elena and I pass them with the roof of my car down, Elena waving her hands in the air and singing. Love it!

3 misguided attempts by her dad to do the moonwalk.

2 awesome helpings of moussaka that had 2 layers of aubergine and 2 layers of potatoes.

45-minute chat, over champagne, about the bungee jump, and how Elena was determined to fit it in before turning thirty. She looked buzzed. Maybe people really do assess their lives as they approach a big birthday. Bravo, Elena! Perhaps when I hit my big 3-0, I'll start wearing beige. Ha! Journal, you know me better than that.

1 single tear, just now, about Mum – Linda. 28 when she died, must visit the cemetery again soon, Stockport winter weather obliging. 25 when she and Dad married. 7 years, after leaving school, spent working in a video store. She became its manager. 1000s of times I've wondered what she'd make of streaming services. Reckon she'd have loved them and the two of us would have spent many Netflix-and-popcorn nights together. 1 solitary, precious memory from after she'd passed, years later at high school. A teacher, Mrs Norris, recognised my surname, Bunker – not easy to forget. My classmates used to call me Golfie. Mrs Norris said she and my mum had been pregnant at the same time, and gone to the same baby group. According to her, Mum said having me had made her the happiest woman ever, made her life complete, even though she was ill. Mum said she wouldn't change a thing, given her time again.

1 nose blow. Time for lights out. Sending 100 big kisses to you, Mum. If you're there, I'm doing another bungee jump this weekend. Elena and I will be hurling ourselves off a bridge on Sunday. I can tell you beforehand, unlike worrywart Dad. I promise to visit Stockport again soon and leave another bar of your favourite chocolate by your headstone.

12

ELENA

Whistling, Elena opened the oven and took out the oblong cake tin, heat whooshing into her face. She squinted and placed it on the cooling rack, then prodded the sponge. Cardamom tea cake, Tahoor's favourite. She'd never baked it before and its spicy aroma Bollywood-danced through the ground floor of her house. Rory had set up the lounge with drinks and bowls of crisps. The pre-match commentary on the television had begun. The game would kick off – literally – at half past seven.

Despite still being slightly hungover after spending last night in the pub, Elena took a large mouthful of wine. She yawned after another busy day at work, out of adrenaline now. Derek was pitching the broken biscuits idea, informally, to the board tomorrow. Every member of the marketing team was fully behind her concept. Spontaneously, last night, the department had gone to the Three Horseshoes, nearby, and the team spent the first hour debating whether the pub had put its Christmas tree up too early. It was also already advertising a festive quiz night. As a marketing team, they should have approved of the pub getting customers in a nostalgic mood so promptly, this hopefully translating into bigger booze sales. Yet decking the place out with Christmas decorations, before December, risked a consumer festive fatigue.

A couple of drinks later, the team had chatted about Elena's new product idea – and so very much more, each sip of alcohol heightening honesty. Each and every one of them felt broken in some way. Julie worried day and night about her mum, who had long Covid; Pete's mortgage had gone up to a rate he couldn't afford and he had no idea how he was going to budget for the festive season. He'd suffered panic attacks. Heartbroken Sanjay had been sending email after email to his son's school, trying to get to the bottom of some vicious online bullying; Gary's dad still refused to meet Diego and made pointed comments about his son one day 'manning up' and settling down with a nice girl. As for Caz, her husband's family was stuck in Ukraine, and Tony's hospital doctor wife was chronically overworked and underpaid. All of them reckoned friends carried them through difficult times. They loved the idea of a share bag of broken biscuits that were still deemed sturdy enough to sell despite a challenging transportation or production process. It felt relatable, they said, and inspiring. Derek had turned up late to the pub, for a swift one, before hurrying home to his wife. A flyaway comment, a look between him and Elena, gave her the impression that maybe his marriage was in trouble.

'There comes a point when you're chipped and cracked, when you've lost parts of yourself that leave deep-seated scars, when resilience kicks in, along with a desire to fight those battles and stand taller,' Elena had said in a full voice, and everyone had clinked glasses. A couple of her colleagues had tears in their eyes. This campaign was about more than raising profits.

Elena removed the cake from the tin. Unlike everyone else, Rory hadn't talked about problems, nor had she. Perhaps his wounds, from the past, from the present, were as big as hers – or more likely, her cheerful, carefree housemate simply had none. She wiped her hands as the doorbell rang.

'Tahoor! Come on in.' She opened the door and the dark night released its embrace as he shuffled into the light and she held him in her arms instead. Elena took his anorak. Underneath he wore a Man City shirt and matching blue cardigan.

'Thank you, lass. I've been looking forward to this all week. An easy win for us, it'll be. Luton Town shouldn't even be in the Premier League, playing with the big boys.'

'Hasn't Man City been seen as a small club, against United?' she said sweetly.

She almost laughed at the indignation that crossed his face, and Tahoor was about to reply when he stood still and tilted his head. He sniffed and a look of recognition spread across his face, followed by a wave of something sadder. 'I haven't smelt cardamom cake for so long,' he said in a scratchy voice. 'When Isha stopped baking, that's when I knew she was seriously ill.'

Elena squeezed his arm. 'It's for dessert, after fried eggs, beans and chips.'

His eyes widened. 'Can we eat it in front of the telly, on our laps?'

Oh, Tahoor. She wanted to hug him again. 'I don't see why not. You go through and I'll bring the food in when it's ready.'

Tahoor beamed. 'You're going to make someone a wonderful wife.' His voice lowered. 'A bit of advice though. Isha never let herself go and would refresh her make-up in the evenings and change into a new sari.' He looked Elena up and down, eyeing the baggy joggers and oversized jumper. 'With a bit of effort, you'd bag that young man, Rory. Borrow that gold top of his. Trust me.' He winked and strode into the lounge, leaving Elena staring after him, mouth agape. He sat down next to Rory and glanced back at Elena. She turned away and went into the kitchen.

When she returned, carrying the cutlery, napkins, and magazines to lean on, Rory was talking to Tahoor, slipping in the facts Don had passed on. For the first time, it struck her how deep the shadows were under Tahoor's eyes, and there was a stain on his jumper.

'Every game I pray it's going to be like that 2011 blinder, when City beat United 6–1. What a derby. I was walking on air for days afterwards, especially in the office,' said Tahoor, in a lively tone. 'My boss supported the Reds and for once couldn't call my team Manchester Shitty. I went out on a high, it was shortly before I retired.'

'But nothing will ever beat the all-time classic against Liverpool Stanley,' said Rory.

Tahoor's face lit up. 'You mean back in 1890, when the City team was called the Ardwick Association Football Club?'

'Yep. 12–0, the score. Did you know they founded the club to attract men who might otherwise have joined criminal gangs and...' Unsurprisingly, Rory had done extra research as he spoke about violence on the streets in the 1800s.

Why had Elena always assumed Rory shared facts with people to boast of his knowledge? Since he'd moved in, it had become clearer that he was simply passionate about diving into the detail. Tahoor sat rapt.

'It was also the first team, in the northwest, to have a proper women's squad,' added Rory.

Tahoor tutted in a disapproving manner. 'Lasses aren't as... robust. There's no getting around that, when it comes to height and muscle. The sport can be dangerous. Most unsuitable. The FA should never have lifted their ban on women's teams in the seventies.'

Rory shot Elena an apologetic glance. 'I'm not sure about that,' he said.

'I'm very not sure about it, either,' said Elena. 'It's a sport about skill, and there are safety regulations. *Both* sexes need to be careful about injury. And what about the Lionesses' championship victory in 2022?'

'Pah, it's all very well for a man to get into scrapes and have a broken nose or a cauliflower ear. Such injuries are a badge of honour, even,' said Tahoor. 'Whereas a woman's looks are important if she wants to do well in the world. Leave the dangerous sports to the men, I say.'

'Then you won't approve of me doing a bungee jump at the weekend,' said Elena, excited for jumping off that bridge and sticking two fingers up to the past. She should have done that a long time ago.

Tahoor looked horrified. 'Certainly not, and I'm sure Rory agrees with me.'

'He's the one who suggested trying his hobby,' she said.

'No reason why Elena shouldn't do exactly the same as me.'

'But it's not... right,' Tahoor spluttered.

Elena folded her arms and raised an eyebrow.

Tahoor's cheeks reddened and he pulled at his beard. 'Oh dear. I've done it again, haven't I? When I talked about Isha dressing up at night, the same look came over your face. It's a look that crosses my Yalina's sometimes – and now she's a teen, my granddaughter Sharnaz's, too.' He sighed. 'We'll have to bring in the card system.'

Elena frowned. 'The what?'

'Seeing as I'm such a football fan, Sharnaz made three cards – two yellow and one red. She or Isha hold them up if I've said something inappropriate. A yellow is more like a warning. Two yellows or one red means I mustn't speak about women for the rest of my stay.'

Genius! Should have been introduced years ago, although Elena would never have needed them at home. Her dad's expectations had always been high for his daughter – like when, in the sixth form, he'd landed her that job in his friend's cosmetics company. It gave her work experience and a degree of responsibility that looked great on her CV. He'd also give her a lucky silver sixpence from his coin collection, to put in her pocket for every exam. 'Love it! That's brilliant,' said Elena, giving a thumbs-up.

'Isha ran our household. I always saw her as an equal, but I've got certain views, with good reason too...' he waffled, and sat quietly for a moment. 'It's one of several reasons why I could never move in with Yalina,' he said eventually.

'She's asked you to?'

'Oh yes. But her family are a busy bunch and she has her accountancy job. I wouldn't want to be a nuisance. What's more, I'm not ready to give up my independence. I... I'm just waiting for that moment to come, when I get over Isha's death, and am able to rebuild again.'

Rory sat listening.

'Watch out then,' said Elena. 'I'll make those cards for your next visit.'

'I'll still be invited around?'

'Who else am I going to share my fun facts about football with?' asked Rory.

Humour was restored to Tahoor's face. 'I do love a football fact! Did you know most footballs are made in Pakistan?'

'Are they? I've been to Karachi. Elena said you come from there? Best kebabs in the world.'

'You should have tasted Isha's! Did you go to Clifton Beach? She loved the seafood there.'

'It was a brief day trip. We focused on the markets and drove past Mohatta Palace. Stunning.' He smiled. 'Now it's my turn for a fun fact: Gary Lineker didn't receive a single yellow or red card during his whole career.'

Elena hurried into the kitchen to get the egg and chips, leaving them talking about other well-known players. When she went back, they were both absorbed in the game. Or that's how it looked. Perhaps Rory was a good actor, but then he punched the air and almost knocked his drink on to the floor when City scored. Keen to seek peace after eating, she left two slices of cake in front of them on the terrazzo coffee table and went upstairs. The imminent bungee jump, tomorrow's pitch to the board, the hangover from last night, the lack of bolts at night... All of this left her wanting to get off the excited spinning top of life for a while, to take stock, to recharge.

Elena reached the upstairs landing and took a deep breath. Five minutes later, there was no trace of her.

13

ELENA

Elena sat at her desk and stared at the clock, as if it would help her time-travel forwards to the end of Derek's meeting. She hadn't even been able to focus on the last chapter of her current read by her favourite uplifting fiction author. For the last two hours he'd been on the top floor, with the board. It was lunch time now. Rory had gone to the staff gym for the first time, with Gary. It had only taken Gary a year to persuade Rory that you also get a buzz from pushing your body in an environment that wasn't ten thousand feet high, or under threat from cascading water.

The door to the office opened. Derek came in, jumper sleeves rolled up, glasses off. He headed straight for her desk, sat on the corner of it, mouth downturned.

'They rejected the idea?' she said and put down her book.

'We need to get our act together, need to raise our game, because the board said if we don't' – he paused and then punched the air – 'then this brilliant project won't hit the heights it deserves! They love the idea and want us to move forwards, full pelt!' Derek's face split into an axolotl smile and he held out his palm. She high-fived it back. Cheeks sweaty, hair ruffled, and wearing bright yellow trainers, Rory walked in with Gary. Elena waved them both over and Derek stood up.

'Well done on those figures you collated on competitors' broken biscuit sales, Rory,' said Derek. 'The number of consumers for those items impressed the board. As did the fact it's not a widely pushed product at the moment. The market is crying out for another brand to jump on board. That's us.' He looked at Gary. 'I conveyed how the whole team has got behind this idea. The enthusiasm is contagious – that boardroom was buzzing when I left. Right...' He rubbed his forehead. 'In the first instance I need to speak to product development and—'

'First coffee more like, the oil to our engine,' said Gary.

Derek followed him into the staff kitchen to help, the two of them talking in an animated fashion.

Rory held out his hands.

'No,' Elena said. 'Not doing it.' She shook her head. 'Nuh uh.'

He raised an eyebrow and she gave a mock sigh, stood up and slipped her hands into his. He did a quirky dance and she joined in, laughing.

'We've not shaken our stuff and done the Good Times Dance since September, I reckon, when that change to more sustainable packaging paid off,' said Rory. 'And it's good times, for sure. I actually survived that drive to work this morning.'

'What do you mean?' she replied, catching her breath.

'We might have been on the motorway, but eighty-five miles an hour?'

'Everyone does that.' Elena had cruised along, overtaking car after car, when normally she'd have stuck in the inside lane and to the speed limit. She'd insisted she'd drive every day this week, keen to press ahead with her carefree attitude. She made up an excuse that something had felt wrong with the car's suspension and she'd wanted to test it. God, how good it felt to drive without worrying about every potential hazard, not feeling she had to take the longer, safer route, on quieter roads.

'I don't speed,' he said.

'Says the man who put his foot to the floor during his rally car experience in the spring.'

'That was under controlled conditions. There were no other cars I might have hit.' He cocked his head. 'You're really going for it, aren't you? Throwing caution to the wind as you approach thirty.'

'A firework almost exploding in your chest gives you enormous perspective,' she muttered and pretended to type on her keyboard as Rory headed off to fetch their coffees. He was right. Speeding hadn't been cool. It didn't matter about endangering her own life, but it did about Rory's and other drivers'. She quickly googled a rally drive experience website and added it to her mental list of daredevil activities.

Halfway through the afternoon, when it was time for another caffeine hit, Derek ordered in donuts from a favourite bakery around the corner – a Bingley Biscuits tradition when there was a work event to celebrate, a nod to the company's roots and how far it had come. The jam donut had been one of the company's most popular items, before they'd gone into mass production and focused on biscuits. Back in the fifties and sixties, they used to be iced in blue or red and sold outdoors at Maine Road and Old Trafford. Normally Elena would stick to a humble glazed ring, and she certainly wouldn't eat any Christmas fare until the week before. But today she snapped up one loaded with cinnamon cream, covered in dark chocolate and freeze-dried cranberries. Rory grinned as she took a bite and cream spurted down her chin. When it was finished, she reached for another, with blonde chocolate and a mini gingerbread man on top, filled with ginger and pear jam. Elena never worried about calories, least of all now when she might only have three weeks and two days left on this planet. She brought up the online calculator, channelling Rory. In other words, twenty-three days; five hundred and fifty-two hours; thirty-three thousand, one hundred and twenty minutes.

How her goal had changed, from simply surviving her remaining weeks, simply going through the motions in order to be safe, to sucking them dry of every single drop of life. There were so many things she'd missed out on, like... like hot air ballooning, edge-of-your-seat wild nights out, like eating oysters, like travel, like... love. Love, the thing she wanted to experience most – yet the hardest to tick off any list because you couldn't just book or pay for it.

'Let's go to this great bar I know near here and celebrate properly,' said Elena as she pulled up on her drive after work.

'I'm in,' said Rory. 'First I need a shower. Leave in twenty minutes?'

Whilst he raced upstairs, Elena knocked back a glass of water and headed into the lounge. She took the roof off the glass tank and put in her hand, coaxing Snap to climb on. The two of them sat on the sofa.

'Shedding my skin is fun,' whispered Elena, holding up her hand, admiring Snap's flexibility. 'What does it feel like for you? Liberating, to start anew? Because that's what I'm experiencing. I've got nothing to lose by shedding my fears and inhibitions.' She eyed the tank again. 'In case... the worst happens, on the twenty-first of December, before then I'm going to get you and Brandy a bigger living space. I'm sure Rory will agree. Your universe should have sides longer than thirty centimetres.' Gently, Elena placed Snap back in the tank, said hello to Brandy, and then sprayed the bramble leaves with water and put on the lid.

Rory appeared in a black leather trench coat, wearing drainpipe jeans with boots, and a Manga sweatshirt – *The Matrix* with a Japanese twist. They set off, without Elena going back to check the front door was locked, and waved to Tahoor as they passed his house. After a brisk walk they entered a bar called Boujee and took a bottle of Merlot to a table. Elena poured out two glasses, nestling back in the velvet armchair, admiring the room's twinkling fairy lights. A Christmas tree was already up in the corner, tastefully ornate with colour-coordinated baubles. Normally she'd have cringed at decorating so early, but somehow, this year, she felt the need to appreciate it. Rory sat opposite her, candles between them flickering in the dim light, R&B music playing in the background.

'Cheers! Here's to not being broken!' She knocked the drink back in one. Rory did the same. The first bottle soon emptied, accompanied by chat about the bungee jump this Saturday. Rory took her through the safety procedures and Elena tried to look interested. She ordered a second bottle.

'How does your dad feel about you doing extreme sports?' she asked, slurring her words slightly, not caring that it never suited her to drink on an empty stomach.

'I never tell him in advance.'

'Wise. Mum and Dad messaged me last night, asking if I was still doing it, said they were excited for me – but the lack of usual emojis spoke volumes.' She raised her glass to her lips. 'Has he ever wanted to do one of the sports with you?'

Rory shook his head.

'How about your mum?'

He ran a finger around the rim of his glass. 'She can't. She isn't with us any more.'

'She's moved away from Stockport?'

'No, I mean...'

Elena put down her wine, unable to swallow for a moment. Had a big family fallout happened? 'Ignore me. Being nosy.'

'She doesn't live in Stockport. She's buried there,' he blurted out.

Elena sat very still. 'Oh, Rory, I'm so very sorry, I always thought...'

'My fault. It's easier to let people assume the best.'

'Did it happen long ago?'

'Long enough,' he said before clearing his throat and grabbing the menu. 'Right. Let's order. I don't know about you, but I'm starving.'

Elena tried not to stare at him. That's how Rory was broken – his mum must have died relatively young. Elena had dated a therapist once. He told her that his job was to find out what made a client cry and then to get them to talk about it. The things we strove to hide did the most damage, he'd said, like a kind of mental dry rot. She studied Rory more closely, as if he were one of her books that had a misleading cover or title. Up until now, with the bright clothes and boyish smile, he'd been a light-hearted genre, nicely easy to read, with a happy ever after ending – eventually he'd meet someone, settle down and swap parachutes for nappies. But now a darker subplot had emerged. It created an ache inside her chest. She didn't know why. Rory was only a colleague.

He suggested they order two Boujee Burgers – with satay and hoisin dressing on the side for him. She'd never understand why he enjoyed mixing flavours so randomly. She went to pour herself another glass.

'Slow down, Elena! I'm not carrying you home.'

She ignored him, having already forgotten her recent hangover. She was owed a few evenings with hazy memories, after so many years of being cautious. Her colleagues often got sloshed on a night out. Gary would break into Salsa moves, Caz would put the world to rights, Derek would talk about his stamp collection and the whole team would get more affectionate. As for Mum and Dad, they'd get silly, duetting their favourite songs by Rick Astley.

Now it was Elena's turn. She raised her glass to his bemused expression and carried on drinking. They ended up getting a taxi back. Rory helped Elena upstairs and into the bathroom just in time. She threw up into the toilet bowl whilst he rubbed her back. He fetched her a glass of water and took off her shoes and coat, before helping her onto the bed. She lay down and he slipped an extra pillow under her head.

'Stop fussing, I'm fine,' she said, throat burning.

'I'll remind you of that sentiment tomorrow morning, Ms Swan. Good night. Bacon and eggs, first thing?'

She gagged. *Yet*, she thought, *look at me, no holds barred, doing exactly what I want*. She waved two fingers in the air at Rory as he chuckled and departed. Elena was living her best life, she was. Holding that thought, she rushed into the bathroom and once again threw up.

14

RORY

Rory stood by the window, journal in his hand, transfixed by a fox trotting across the lawn in the moonlight. It sat down at the bottom of Elena's garden and cleaned a paw. A distant car revved its engine and the fox lifted its head. It jumped to its feet again and, at top speed, spun around, snapping playfully at its own tail. A leaf blew in its way and the fox chased it across the grass, as if in flight itself. A few months ago Rory had spotted a hedgehog in Dad's front garden and the two of them had spent an hour watching it. Of course Rory did a deep dive online and discovered that the average hedgehog had between five and seven thousand spines. His dad had put out a bowl of biscuits he'd bought for Coco, the stray cat Dad had adopted a few years earlier – or rather, Coco had adopted him, and Dad adored her for it. Mike loved his job, had mates at the pub, but there wasn't that special someone. Coco was the nearest thing he had to a companion – until he met Jenny.

Dad was moving on.

Easier said than done.

Rory closed the curtains. Like the fox, Elena hadn't a care in the world this evening. Christ, it was good to see. She'd even kicked the front door shut when they got home, not bothering to lock it. Her behaviour reminded him of Uncle Tony, Dad's brother. He'd turned forty and got divorced when Rory was fifteen. At the time, Dad had teased Tony about the new haircut, the pierced ear and electric guitar lessons. Yet, in the long run, Dad became so proud of his brother and said it took a lot of guts to dramatically change your life. Uncle Tony had always hated his job in investment banking, but it had already paid off most of his mortgage, despite the cost of his divorce. He'd always dreamed of becoming a roadie and, twelve years later, was doing exactly that. He'd encourage Rory's dad, Mikey, as he called him, to follow his dreams too. At the time, Rory had asked his dad if he had one. Dad had given a wry smile and said to grow old with Linda was all he'd ever wanted – and to annoy his son for as long as possible. 'Mission accomplished so far,' Rory had replied with a smile, and they'd hugged. Dad reassured Rory his life was great as it was. He had food on the table, a roof over his head, and six seasons of *Peaky Blinders* in a box set.

Rory was glad Dad had finally managed to move forwards. He'd been dating Jenny for eighteen months now. She'd found the number of his plumbing business online and called him out to fix her low water pressure. Within a month they were seeing each other several times a week. She was good for him, and a massive cat person, which sealed the deal. Dad started to finish work early, bought a new wardrobe and the balance shifted towards him focusing more on the future, rather than simply the day to day.

Thirty could be an exciting age for Elena. Clearly she was on a road of discovery. Perhaps she'd give up the office job and go travelling, having never been abroad before. Unlike his friends, who'd moaned about turning twenty-five, Rory had always embraced his big birthdays – sixteen, eighteen and twenty-one as well. Losing Mum had taught him at an early age that there were worse alternatives to growing old.

He clambered into bed and leant against the headboard. After pulling the duvet over his legs, Rory scrolled on his phone for a while before brandishing his pen.

Thursday 28th November

84 miles an hour, to be exact, on the moterway to work this morning... I mean motorway. My spelling might be off. Gotta admit I'm almost seeing double after trying to match Elena's number of wine glasses. Wouldn't normally comment on a bit of speeding, but this is Elena! Yo, to the new rule-breaker!

15 minutes treadmill, 4 sets of plate squats, 30 seconds of sit ups and then reverse lunges, bicycle crunches too. 1 smug look from experienced Gary, sailing through. Bastard!

5 coffees.

2 donuts that hit so many pleasure spots they, weirdly, made me realise I haven't had sex for a while. Like for a loooong time. Yet actually, if I'm honest, I don't want to play the dating game any more, unless it's with someone who's more than casual, who's the vinegar to my gherkin (told you I was a little wasted).

1 revelation from me, about my mum – i.e. telling Elena exactly where she is in Stockport. School taught me that hiding the truth was better. Once other people knew, they shot me piteous looks and asked me how I was doing every time they saw me. I just wanted to get on with my life. But excuse me, now, whilst I shed fucking tears – not because of the booze, but because tomorrow it's exactly 25 years since Mum passed. A whole 1/4 of a century. She would have been

53 this year. It always hits me the night before because Dad says that's when he finally accepted, for sure, Mum wouldn't survive, even though she'd been in the hospice for a while. It's when they said goodbye to each other, before she lost all strength and couldn't talk any longer. When I was in my teens, I asked him to tell me about the last moments. I wanted all the details. They didn't talk about the future and plans she'd dreamt of, to go backpacking around the world when I was old enough. She was something of an adventurer, and had loved the road trip movie Thelma and Louise that came out in her early 20s. Instead, their conversation was about me. He sang Mum's favourite song as she passed – 'Take A Bow' by Madonna. In her opinion, the most romantic song in the world. It had been played as their dance at their wedding. It was 1999, 3 years later, when their happy union was ripped apart. By a mere ripple in time, she missed seeing the new Millennium and everything it brought with it – me growing up, Dad's plumbing business really taking off, the introduction of mobile phones, Facebook, and AI. She didn't get to know cultural references, from the Twin Towers to Tiger King. When he got home from the hospice, Dad apparently told 2-year-old me that she'd gone to heaven, a place where the trees were made of chocolate and the rivers of honey. I'm still angry at the injustice, at the reason she died. The pain never lessens. I'm 28 next year, which is great, bring it on. But at the same time, fuck, that's shit, because this time next year I'll be older than she was when she left. *Sigh*. Sorry, Mum, if you're reading this. Booze brings out the youngest, most scared, most sweary part of me and that huge void that filled me at the school gates when other mums were hugging their kids hello or goodbye; the fear that I'd never, ever see you again – or go to heaven. Have to *admit, part of that concern was because I wanted to swim in honey.*

3 ferocious glares from a taxi driver that told me there'd be a huge price to pay if Elena redesigned his upholstery with the contents of her stomach.

10 minutes of Elena retching into the toilet bowl, which sounded like Uncle Tony singing his heroes' rock music.

1 long grin from me over a declaration Elena made tonight. Wonder if she'll remember it.

2 foxes and 3 fun facts, retrieved from my phone a few moments ago – they are the only breed of dog that retracts its claws like cats; they can hear a watch ticking 36 metres away; they run up to 30 miles an hour.

Time: 1:45am. Sleep now, with 1 eye open, in case Elena is ill again.

15

Elena stretched out in bed. Yesterday's clothes were still on. She ran a finger over her face. So was her make-up. She had – she'd done it again – stepped out of her comfort zone! Elena sat up and reached sideways for a glass of water Rory must have put there. After a glug, she hugged her knees, feeling younger and more carefree than she had since she was ten.

She hadn't gone to university like Mum and Dad, but had listened to their stories over the years from the eighties about them getting drunk on forty pence shots of vodka in a nightclub decked out like a tropical beach; of Dad throwing up on the dance floor after doing the 'Jitterbug'; of Mum peeing behind a dustbin with a group of uni friends on New Year's Eve. Dad apparently once went to a midday lecture still half-asleep and drunk. The two of them laughed about it now and rolled their eyes. Elena was ten years late in embracing the do-as-you-dare teenage life.

Now, sober but groggy, she yawned, mouth as dry as sandpaper. The last thing she felt like was a day in the office. Alcohol had stolen her passion for brainstorming. Having pulled open the curtains, she rubbed her eyes. It was still dark outside, despite a few remaining pops of stars. From across the landing came the sound of Rory's shaver. It stopped. Footsteps sounded. A knock on her door. He'd been a good friend last night. 'Come in.' The door opened.

'How you doin'?' he asked, mimicking Joey out of *Friends*.

The smell of lemony aftershave wafted in. He didn't wear it all the time, whereas Elena wore the same perfume every day. It felt reassuring. Rory leant casually against the door frame, his gentle nature at odds with his athletic look, the curve of his lip betraying his wicked humour, the floral shirt and bracelet shouting *You do you and I'll do me*. He looked as if he'd slept the full recommended eight hours, eaten his five a day and done everything else the government had ever recommended, despite his clothes and hobbies that held two rebellious fingers up to convention. It made for an intriguing combination.

'Fine,' she replied with a lively tone.

'Cup of tea?'

'That would be great. Thanks for... looking out for me last night. Sorry if I was a handful.' She grinned.

'Save your apologies for Tahoor. You did fall into his garden and flatten one of his shrubs, after all.'

'No!'

'You hadn't been out of the taxi one minute. It took a while for you to leave it. You felt so sleepy and cosy that you offered to pay the driver fifty quid to keep driving.'

Whoop! Now she had her own drunken story to tell. Who knew that, imprisoned deep inside Elena all these years, was such a happy-go-lucky person?

'And you certainly don't need to apologise to *me*,' he said, eyes twinkling brighter than the stars outside her window.

Her eyes narrowed.

'Three times last night, once in the taxi, you made me the happiest man in Cariswell. I'm so flattered. The driver didn't know where to look.'

No! She wouldn't have done that. Not with Rory. Not in public. A nervous laugh burst from her lips.

He pulled his phone out of his studded, white jeans pocket, went into an app, scrolled and then held the mobile in the air. 'I love you, Rory,' said a slurred voice. 'Love you more than... than... my Karen Millen trouser suit... Even more than cheese on toast.' She'd hiccoughed. 'With all my heart. F'rever and ever.'

Oh. Thank God. At least all she'd done was declare her undying love and... She'd *what*? Holy mother of Merlot! The L word had never passed her lips before, or not with anyone apart from Mum and Dad, not even casually. Certainly not to a work colleague, to someone so very different to her.

'Millie in accounts thought you'd be an amazing kisser,' the slurring continued. 'Why don't you show me? As mates? Wait! No! You keep that pickle tongue away from me.'

Rory caught her eye, stuck his tongue out and waggled it.

Elena covered her face with her hands and groaned. 'You are going to be unbearable now.'

'The heart wants what the heart wants, Swan.'

Indignation filled her face. 'You wish.'

'I wasn't sure whether to record it or not, but it was so funny,' he said and held out his phone, eyes crinkling. She duly deleted the recording.

'You can make me that tea now, to make up for it,' she said. 'Then I'm going back to sleep.'

Rory's brow knotted. 'But we've got to leave in thirty minutes. It's a big day ahead, what with Derek wanting us to refine his pitch to product development.'

'Not going in,' she announced grandly. 'I'm pulling a sickie.'

'You're joking, right? He needs you, Elena. Also, you're so proud of the fact you've never taken a sick day in over a decade, let alone been off with no good reason.'

'Exactly. Imagine the number of days off I'm owed,' she said. 'No one's indispensable. Derek's got you and the team. You've never taken a day off ill when you shouldn't?'

'No... I mean, there was one time, but I was only eighteen and—'

A satisfied look crossed her face. 'You're in no position to judge, then. I'll take two sugars, thanks.'

Rory tipped his head to one side and shot her a look, before heading off.

Didn't everyone act irresponsibly once in a while? That's what she'd witnessed over the years, not allowing herself that same freedom. Well, sod that! She curled up in bed but a niggle of guilt forced her to sit up. Should she go into work, after all?

No!

Just this once she wanted to break the rules. She deserved that. Her looming birthday was making Elena kinder to herself, in a way she hadn't been over the years. Instead of being her own jailer, she now wanted to be her own break-out buddy. Derek would manage and she'd work extra hard on her return to make up for her absence.

That phone recording. Those three little words she'd never said to a man... Her face fell. How sad was that? But... She propped herself up on one elbow. Elena still had time to say them, right? Even to a practical stranger. In fact, that would be better, because there'd be no deep emotional connection. No one would get hurt if the worst happened on her birthday. She couldn't say them to anyone she truly cared about. Elena just wanted to experience the moment. Her spirits lifted as she sat bolt upright, reached for her phone and googled dating apps.

There were still three and a half weeks till her birthday – plenty of time to make someone feel really special. A short-term fling would be perfect to achieve her goal. Yet a voice in her head nagged that it being a fling would be no excuse for playing with someone else's emotions.

But you took your chances with your emotions on a dating app, everyone knew that. And maybe she'd experience love at first sight and say those words for real. Anything was possible.

She'd never online dated before, unlike so many people of her age, but this new Elena would arrange a meet-up for tomorrow night, after her bungee jump. Oh my God! This was so exciting! She started singing 'Hit Me with Your Best Shot', one of Dad's favourites from years ago. It would be like in the movies! Like *Romeo and Juliet*, or Mum's favourite, *When Harry met Sally*, or *Breakfast at Tiffany's* which Gran always loved. It had to be. She *had* to be part of such a romantic scene, just once, that wasn't slurred and secretly taped on a phone.

Funny as last night was.

As if she'd drunk nothing but water last night, Elena jumped out of bed and air-guitared, leaping around whilst laughing out loud.

16

RORY

Friday 29th November

Hell, it was 1 strange day at Bingley Biscuits without Elena. Didn't blame her for taking a day off. Elena's a super hard worker and deserved it, and she seems so much happier since embarking on this journey of personal discovery. However, Derek, Caz and Gary were most worried knowing how serious her '24-hour bug' must be for her not to go to the office. Derek gave the back of his head 3 hand rubs, always a sign that the guy's stressed. However, 1 successful meeting with product development took place. 1 step further to reality for the Not-so-Broken Biscuits. Elena asked me about it as soon as I got in, and was thrilled when I told her. She texted Derek to say job well done.

1 big fat lie told by me – 'Elena's Boujee burger must have contained salmonella.'

30 minutes in the gym with Gary. Felt more confident. Seems like you can get a buzz from a sport that doesn't involve catapulting through the air or mounting mountains.

3 people asking me if I was okay, just because I was bit quiet.

3 more lies – 'Yes, I'm fine.'

1 squeeze of my shoulder from Gary.

1 Mum's Death Day, you see – see point above. Gary prised it out of me. I hadn't concealed my grief as well as usual, perhaps because I'd finally told someone – Elena – the truth about where my mother is. The padlock has been removed from the mental box I've stored that pain in all this time. Maybe that means... it's time to stop pretending my mum is still alive. 25 years today since she signed off. Last year I put a photo of her through a filter that made her look older. What a jerk. A sharp longing had overwhelmed me to meet the woman staring back from the screen.

2 phone calls with Dad. 1 first thing, 1 late at night – our yearly tradition. It's the 1 out of 365 days that his good-humoured voice reflects the hurt. He can't forget the images from that last year. When I was a teen, I overheard him talking to Granddad once. It had killed them both inside, how brave Mum had been, unafraid of what was to come but angry, devastated, about everything she was going to miss. That was the moment I found out the real reason for her death, and my life was never quite the same after that. Today is the one day of the year he chokes up when he says Mum's name, Linda, as if it's a favourite cough sweet that grows harder and jagged as time passes, instead of soothing and dissolving. Yet he's found Jenny, and she listens to him talk about Mum. She talks to him, too, about her late fiancé who had diabetes and died from complications with Covid. Life is pretty shit sometimes, but finding someone who understands is the best medicine. I've seen that.

1 visit to Mum's grave. I left 1 Snickers bar by the head-stone – she preferred its old name, Marathon.

0 piteous looks from Elena when she found out about the anniversary today and where I'd been after work. Instead she held me very tight and for the first time since waking up, I relaxed. Elena always smells the same. Floral, with a pinch of fresh spring mornings and sweet baked croissants. It's weirdly comforting. She fetched me a cold beer and a bowl of crisps, hugged me again and went upstairs. It was exactly what I needed.

1 magic trick again, from her – I went up to see if she wanted takeaway and couldn't find her anywhere. 45 minutes later, Elena came down saying she'd fallen asleep, but I'd checked her room and she hadn't been in there.

1,000 questions (or so it seemed) from Elena about the bungee jump tomorrow – not about safety but about how thrilling the rush must be. Her infectious enthusiasm cheered me up. She ordered the takeout and washed up afterwards, made hot chocolate and put my favourite biscuits out on a plate. Elena said she was there for me, if I wanted to talk about Mum, or we could just watch a movie, my choice. In the end, we sat with Brandy and Snap on our knees, chilling in front of some TV chat show, strategically planning how to nab the last biscuit. Pretty sure she let me win. Spending time with her like that had been... nice. An underrated word – we were told not to use it at school, were told it was a lazy adjective that didn't really mean anything. But this evening, with Elena, it meant everything.

1 smile on my face, at the end of the day, as Elena sings 'Ocean Eyes', through the wall. At first I wasn't in the mood, but I couldn't help joining in. When we'd finished, I shouted through, asking if she wanted a goodnight pickle kiss. Wonder if Tahoor heard the 2 emphatic swear words she hollered back in reply?

17

ELENA

'I'm not calling you Pickle.'

'But we could have cute housemate nicknames. I'd call you Houdini, given the way you keep disappearing,' Rory said and turned the steering wheel.

Elena had asked if he'd take his car so she could enjoy another rush of them driving with the roof down, her breathing in deeply, not caring about the exhaust fumes in the air. He left the motorway at the approaching junction and followed the signs to Horton Green Park, a thousand-acre, landscaped National Trust estate, forty miles northwest of Manchester. The bungee jump would take place from a bridge, over the Horton Mere, a large lake to the south of the estate. The weather was perfect – no rain, no wind, sun not too bright. Back at the house, Rory had asked her if nerves had set in. But no, she'd whistled louder than the kettle and waved cheerily to Tahoor as they drove past after breakfast. He was out the front in his dressing gown, examining a flattened shrub.

Voice hoarse from singing along to rock music on the car radio, Elena glugged some water as they parked up. Then she and Rory headed for the bottom of some steps at one end of the bridge. She gazed across at the mere, far into the distance. So much open space. Was that what the afterlife was like? One thing was certain: death couldn't be any more restrictive than her life up to this point.

'In the financial world, a bungee bet is an investment that appears to go wrong but then bounces back,' said Rory as they walked over to Tim, who must have been almost six and a half feet tall. 'Bungee jumping first started as part of a coming-of-age ceremony, on a Pacific Ocean island. Young men would jump from a tree with vines fixed around their ankles.'

Tim walked over and held out his hand. 'Great to meet you, Elena. I hope Rory hasn't talked you into this.' His shaved head was as tanned as his face.

'As if,' said Rory.

Tim studied Elena. 'There's nothing worse than peer pressure – especially when it's coming from a partner.'

'Dude, we're not dating!' said Rory and shook his head.

'We're just housemates,' Elena protested.

'Whatever,' said Tim and playfully punched Rory's arm. Elena and Rory rolled their eyes at each other.

She blew on her hands. A mix of excitement and fear, from the other jumpers, spiked the wintry air. Sure, Elena was nervous, but that was proof she was really *alive*. As advised, she'd dressed in comfortable long trousers and a top, and sports shoes that wouldn't interfere with the ankle harnesses. Tim explained the process and weighed her, his words not registering. Elena was too hyped about doing the most dare-devil thing in her life – apart from that dive off the top board of the local pool when she was nine, the last adventurous thing she'd done as a child. She hadn't even checked out Tim's credentials online. Normally an avid reader of disclaimers, Elena hardly read the paperwork he passed her, simply signing on the dotted line before he'd finished reading everything out.

Elena was the first person to jump. She climbed up onto the bridge with Tim and stared up at the baby blue sky.

'Are you sure Rory can't come up here, at the same time, to watch?' she asked.

Tim shook his head. 'I allowed a boyfriend up once and after I'd counted down to one, and the woman had committed to jumping, he shouted "No, wait!", messing around. She dislocated her shoulder by a panicked attempt to grab on to something at the last minute.'

But Rory wouldn't do that. What a spoilsport this Tim was.

The team asked Elena lots of questions as they fitted the harnesses and rope, no doubt used to having to distract people with last-minute nerves. They needn't have bothered.

'Do you want to touch the mere with your hands?' one of them asked.

'What?' asked Elena, who hadn't really been listening. 'No – I want my whole head dunked under the surface! Let's really go for it!'

She shuffled onto a wooden platform that stuck out from the bridge. Tim went on and on, explaining how to jump. Yadda, yadda.

He began to count, reminding her to focus on the horizon, and to launch herself outwards, not down. Five, four, three... Boring! Elena didn't wait for him to finish. Instead of holding them out, she pressed her arms against her sides and nose-dived straight down, like a bullet.

Sunlight sparkled on the water below like flashing cameras, as if paparazzi were capturing a newsworthy story. *Falling, falling, an unstable sensation, nothing like flying, no control over the direction, stomach lurching, whoa, the speed, hair flapping, water approaching, no time for jubilation, then smack! Down under the freezing cold water before... whoosh, being pulled back upwards, gulping for air, trying to focus. Blinking. Dripping. Swinging. Shrieking with euphoria.* She'd done it! Like an uncontrollable pendant, she swung in the air and an engine sounded beneath her. The bouncing slowed and she was lowered unceremoniously into the motorboat. A woman pulled her in and removed Elena's equipment.

By the time they arrived back at the bridge, Elena shook from head to toe, as if her body couldn't process the large amount of adrenaline that it had never experienced in nineteen years. Her body was high. High on life. High on a drug she'd avoided for so long, a free hit Mother Nature handed out. Who needed booze and weed?

'Oh my God, that was amazing!' she said to Tim, who stood, arms folded, next to Rory, who looked serious. 'Can I go again?'

'Sorry, but no way,' Tim said stiffly. 'The format of the jump is very important. Going outwards, with your arms stretched horizontally, makes the deceleration smooth and the bounce back kinder. You shouldn't just drop like a stone.'

'But I'm okay!'

Tim shook his head and Rory followed him up to the bridge, doing the jump exactly as Tim had advised. Elena whistled and shouted, punching the air when he got back to her.

'That was incredible!' she said.

'Let's just get back to the car,' he muttered.

'What's wrong?'

Rory ran a hand through his curly hair, the yellow of his hooded puffer jacket much brighter than his expression. 'Tim's not happy, Elena, and he was doing us a favour, fitting us in at such short notice. As well as ignoring his advice, you hardly listened to the disclaimer. Tim said he had to repeat it.'

It was like living in a parallel universe, where everyone else was more safety-conscious than her. 'I took on board the basics!'

Rory didn't reply, and Elena also went quiet as they walked back to the car. Why wasn't he being more supportive? The sky had clouded over by the time they got in and put their seat belts on, raindrops pelting down. Rory took out his keys.

'Any extreme sport has to be taken seriously,' he muttered. 'It would also be Tim in the shit if something went wrong. There aren't many deaths in the bungee jumping world, but they happen, like last year, in Scotland, a bit close to home. A man mistook a hand signal and jumped before the cord was attached properly. That's aside from the possible injuries, listed in that disclaimer and that I'd told you about, like eye problems, shoulder and spine issues, and...'

But she'd only gone a couple of seconds early, and obviously an aerodynamic shape was best, if you wanted to go fast. What a big fuss about nothing. Although she wouldn't have wanted to get Tim in trouble. Nor Rory.

Elena's ears felt hot.

'Sorry. Really sorry,' she said as they sat at traffic lights. 'It was selfish of me. I acted like a complete idiot. Please pass on my apologies to Tim.'

'It's only because Tim cares,' Rory said, the tension disappearing from his voice. 'What's more, who's going to create a bigger home for Brandy and Snap if you aren't around?'

'How did you know about that?'

'They told me. Put me right, in fact – said it hadn't taken a fellow female long to work out what they really needed.'

Her face broke into a smile.

'You were talking about it the other night,' he said. 'I came down for a glass of water and you'd just told them you'd finished that book you were binge-reading.'

One from the *Game of Thrones* series. The books were much better than the TV show. Arya Stark – now that was one fearless woman.

'Do you mind? About a bigger tank?'

'It's a great idea.' The lights changed and he pushed down the accelerator pedal. 'So... you'd jump again?'

'One hundred per cent. I loved every minute. Skydiving next. Can you arrange that?'

'You're sure?' They'd stopped at a junction and he gave her a surprised look. 'It's just lately... You are okay, aren't you, Elena?'

'Rory! Of course! Why wouldn't I be? Look, maybe I got a bit carried away at Horton Green Park. I'll stick, 1,000 per cent, to all the skydiving rules, however small. I'm honestly very sorry about today.'

They chatted about his skydiving experiences on the way back to Cariswell. Rory turned onto her drive and parked up. 'That all gives you an idea of what it's like. How about we cosy up over coffee and biscuits, and I tell you more about the local club I go to. Let's also research stick insect living spaces and—'

'Can't, I'm afraid.' She beamed. 'I've got to get ready for a date tonight.'

Rory stared at the garage door ahead. 'Cool. Going out for food?'

'He said he knew a good place and I'm just waiting for him to text. It's a bit of a rushed arrangement.'

Rory waved to Tahoor, who was at his window, and followed Elena inside as the rain became even heavier. 'I expect you've told Brandy and Snap all about him, before me.'

'Not much chance of that. I've never met him before. In fact, we've not even spoken. I only loaded my profile onto the dating app yesterday. We matched this morning.'

Rory stopped taking off his jacket, drips of rain falling onto the hallway's floor. 'You haven't got to know him a bit first?'

Elena threw down her keys on the kitchen unit. She flicked on the heating and filled the kettle with water. 'Rory. Next you'll be doing the moonwalk and telling me about the eighties.'

'Seriously though...' he said, walking into the kitchen. 'What does he do?'

She shrugged, having skipped his details in the spirit of being adventurous. 'Does it matter? He looks nice and gives good emoji.'

Rory put a hand on the backrest of one of the grey velvet breakfast bar chairs. 'Do you know anything about him at all?'

'He was prepared to meet me tonight. That's enough.'

'But—'

Don't question me. Not now that I've finally found my zest for tasting the life everyone else has been drinking all this time. 'I don't have to justify myself, Rory Bunker. It's a bit of fun, not an extreme sport with fixed procedures and disclaimers. Why are you making a big deal of it?'

He bit his lip. 'Taking on Brandy and Snap must be bringing out my paternal instincts.' He gave a small smile. 'Right. Might head over to Dad's early, better get changed. We're playing board games.'

'What do you usually play? I love Monopoly. Or there's Cluedo.'

'Risk,' he said and gave her a pointed look before pulling down his puffer jacket hood and climbing the stairs, two at a time.

Hot tears filled her eyes; she wasn't sure why. Fuck judgemental Rory. He hadn't lived the last nineteen years like a convict, punished for making a kind-hearted deal, imprisoned within walls that no one else could see. And if she was a man, he wouldn't have said a thing. Her phone beeped and she read the message, ignoring more than ten from her parents who were no doubt checking in with her after the bungee jump that they'd clearly been worried about.

> Hey Elena! I've managed to book a restaurant in the Northern Quarter, near where I live. The chef is a mate and has fitted us in. Details below. See you at 8! Carl

The words were followed by a row of emojis – the dancing man, dancing woman, flames, drinks, a knife and fork, a kissing face.

Elena stared at the message. Tomorrow was the last day of November, and then it was her birthday month. She pursed her lips and typed.

> See you then!

18

ELENA

Despite the frost that had already stuck to the pavement and the nip of chilly air, Elena had travelled into Manchester early, unable to resist the Christmas markets that always set up at the end of November. Mingling amongst the hubbub of bustling shoppers, she relished the aroma of mulled wine, of hot chocolate and German sausage. One stall sold nothing but pickles and she couldn't help taking a photo to show Rory later, even though she was still cross with him. For the first time this winter, festive excitement fizzed in her stomach, a buzz that used to be so much stronger when she was a child, caused by the prospect of presents and baubles, of turkey sandwiches and figgy pudding, as Gran called it. However, it was not caused by Santa. From ten onwards she no longer believed in Father Christmas, because life had shown her there was no such thing as miracles – things happened for a reason, whatever the incredulous medical staff had said about her mother's sudden and inexplicable recovery.

She ambled back up Market Street and turned left, heading into the Northern Quarter and Stevenson Square, passing the line of cosy, welcoming bars and coffee shops that the area was renowned for. She stopped outside a glass-fronted restaurant, R&B music shaking its ass outside, every time the door opened. Carl stood waiting, a grin on his face. He wore chinos and a navy huntsman jacket, looking as stereotypically handsome as in his profile, with snow-white teeth and hair tidily slicked back with gel.

'Great to see you, Helena.'

'Elena.'

He smacked his forehead. 'Sorry, it's ingrained, getting names wrong. My Aunt is called Amber but I got confused as a toddler and apparently, for several years, called her Auntie Hamburger.'

She laughed, unable to tell if he was joking or not. It didn't matter. 'Shall we?' she said, and they went in. Winding their way between singles drinking colourful cocktails to fuel their flirting, they followed the server to their table. She and Carl sat down opposite each other, under an old factory-style pendant ceiling lamp. They took off their coats, hats, scarves, and ordered a bottle of wine. Conversation covered the biting weather and the Christmas markets. No, he wasn't into football. Yes, she had lived in the northwest for her entire life. Elena was going to ask what his job was when a chef came over, twisting a tea towel, perspiration running down his cheeks. He flung the towel over his shoulder.

'Carl, mate, sorry but the oven's packed in. I'm about to announce that all food's off.'

'Oh man, that's too bad.' Carl stood up and clapped him on the back. 'Anything I can do to help? You sure there's nothing to be done about it?'

The chef shook his head and hurried away.

Elena took out her phone. 'What a shame. Let's see if we can book somewhere else.' Twenty minutes later, neither of them had succeeded. 'I can get a table in Spinningfields for ten thirty,' she said. 'But I'm not sure I'll last until then without carbs.'

'Never used to be this bad before Covid,' he said. 'Everyone's so used to booking now. It's become the norm, even midweek.' He put down his phone. 'Look... feel free to say no, but my flat's only around the corner. I can cook. You're more than welcome.'

Going to a guy's place on a first date? The old Elena would have balked. No point now. Life was for living, and she had got to know him a bit – he'd offered to help his mate and wasn't pressuring her to go to his. Carl seemed decent enough.

She picked up the half full wine bottle and her coat. 'Lead the way!'

Five minutes later, they stood in a dark alleyway, off Stevenson Square. It was a typical Northern Quarter building, made from red bricks, stained black over the years and covered in graffiti. Humming to herself, Elena waited as he opened the ground floor door, free from the usual over-thinking she suffered on a first date. She didn't fret about whether there'd be enough to talk about, if the kissing would be good, or if he'd turn out to own whips and handcuffs. Elena was too set on her mission to utter those three little words. Elena blew on her hands and blocked out the advice she'd ever read about personal safety. She hadn't told anyone where she was going and the building was a far cry from the cul-de-sac she lived in, in Cariswell. She tried to imagine what job Carl might have, determined to shake off Rory's concerns.

In any case... so what if tonight might be The End? People spent their lives worrying about when they were going to die, little realising a finite time on earth was what kept them happy. Immortality would mean never-ending anxiety about paying bills, losing loved ones, about climate change and wars, and it would still never be enough time to read all the books you wanted to. No, an end date in sight gave the present that piquant taste.

'Right. Let's go up and get warm.'

For one second, she paused. Fuck, was this mad? Elena curled her fists. Well, it was about time an element of foolishness entered her life. She'd spent the last couple of months being as careful as Rory choosing his brand of pickles. As for Rory, he took risks, whatever he said about taking safety measures seriously. Who was he to question her random first date when he'd jumped between roof tops with no net beneath? She followed Carl up a narrow staircase, with dingy wallpaper and a scratched wooden banister. He opened a door at the top and flicked on a light switch. She squinted at the brightness ahead. Deep breaths. Live a little, Elena Swan.

She strode in. He turned the heating and oven on.

'Wowww,' she said, passing him the wine that she'd brought from the restaurant. 'This place is gorgeous.' What a contrast to his conservative, dark clothes, with the cosy terracotta walls, mustard and green furnishings, a warm pine laminate floor and a Provencal print rug, its design depicting olives, sunflowers and bunches of lavender. Shelves contained cookery books, unusual glassware and ornamental plates. In the corner stood a lamp-stand in the shape of a tree, twinkling, welcoming. The room was open plan, with a small kitchen, much of the visible space tidily filled with bottles of spices and oils, herbs and condiments.

'I'm a chef. I've had a day off and spent the afternoon cooking ratatouille, perfecting my favourite recipe,' he said and signalled for her to sit down on the burnt-orange sofa whilst he opened the bottle.

'A day off on a Saturday, for a chef, must be a rare thing – and you've spent it cooking?'

He looked sheepish. 'I know. Call me sad.' He waved an arm

through the air. 'I've almost saved enough for a deposit on a bigger place – for a bigger kitchen. I only need one bedroom, and I'm not fussed about a bath, a small shower room will do. Don't even need a big living space – what I do need is enough work top and wall space to set out my pans and utensils.'

'I don't have this problem. The tools I use for my job are online, being in marketing. Any good at baking? Biscuits are my business.'

Carl took off his outdoor layers and draped them over the back of the sofa. Elena did the same and he passed her a glass of wine, before settling in a small armchair. The room smelt amazing... pesto, tomato and garlic.

'Haven't got much of a sweet tooth myself. Mediterranean food is my passion. It's my dream to own a little restaurant by the coast one day.' He talked about a holiday in the south of France that he'd gone on as a child, the vivid memories about the smells and tastes of Provence; how he'd once shared a flat with a trainee chef from Avignon and had learnt so much about the importance of fresh, seasonal ingredients. Carl put down his glass and rolled up his sleeves. 'Enough about my passion. What's your dream, Elena?'

This date was off to a pretty perfect start. Ambitious, funny and talented, Carl seemed almost too good to be true.

'Just to see it past my thirtieth birthday,' she said in a jokey tone.

'Good one, because your thirties are great. A few years in and a lot of the bullshit from my twenties has dropped away. I don't give a toss about people's opinion of me now' – he made a hand heart – 'as long as my heart and my conscience are happy. I speak my mind. I stand by my beliefs. I call people out if they're idiots. I've finally realised it's hard work that will get me where I want to be, not some fantasy about winning the lottery or a reality show.' He stood up. 'Right. Fougasse, with virgin olive oil on the side for dipping. It's flatbread containing cheese, olives and anchovies. I've got some in the freezer that I made last week.' He explained how Provencal food was heavily influenced by Italy.

Her mouth was watering, Elena got up and headed over to a small breakfast bar with two stools. 'I've never had a home-cooked meal on a first date before.'

Carl pulled the bread out of the freezer and put it in the oven. 'Any excuse. I'd cook for the postman if he could stay long enough.' He glanced over. 'Of course, it's much more fun cooking for a beautiful woman who has an impressive career. Tell me, what do you like so much about marketing?'

Inside, she glowed and the flattery made him look even more appealing.

'It's a job that's continually changing, alongside society and world events – and those global shifts, on so many levels, are what we're drawing from, to push our products. I love watching the news. Culture, politics and economics, those things have always fascinated me. I've been lucky enough to work with companies I respect, and that's part of it too, the satisfaction of persuading people to buy products I'm passionate about. Bingley Biscuits is ethical and transparent. The products are high quality. Nowadays, more than ever, people deserve an affordable treat.' She carried on talking, as he served the fougasse and they ate. After the last dip in oil, she gave a sheepish look. 'Sorry. Warning – I find it difficult to stop talking about my job.'

That was one good thing about her friendship with Rory – they were both equally passionate about marketing and never ran out of anything to say. In fact, it seemed now that there was so much more to their relationship, such as the lift each morning at the prospect of seeing him over a cuppa instead of sitting alone in her house; him waiting for her in the kitchen with a barbed, but affectionate, comment; his rendition of 'Ocean Eyes' providing a finale to each day. He used to sing it on the way to his car, after work, before he moved in. She glugged back a mouthful of wine. Why was she thinking of another man on her date with Carl, especially one with a penchant for silly dances and orphaned insects?

The ratatouille was outstanding, with its juicy, soft vegetables and deep, flavoursome herb and garlicky sauce.

'I bet you've travelled far and wide abroad?' she asked as Carl opened another bottle of wine and topped up their glasses with panache. 'You must find a lot of inspiration eating foreign street food.'

The delicious meal over, he got up and went over to the sofa. Elena joined him, enjoying the proximity. This date was going better than she could have ever expected. She stretched out her legs, picturing romantic scenes such as the two of them holding hands under a starry sky, bobble hats on, about to kiss under the moonlight, like in those cosy Hallmark movies her mum enjoyed watching.

'Not by plane,' he said. 'I was a child when I flew to France and had no say in the matter. I've seen parts of Europe thanks to the ferry or train, but you won't catch me up in the air knowing what I know now.'

'What do you mean?'

'About NASA pushing its conspiracy that the earth is a globe. Anyone with half a brain knows it's actually a round, flat disc under a dome. I wouldn't want to risk crashing into the side of that.'

Elena grinned. 'Yeah, right. What's the real reason? Not much of a jetsetter myself. I love a good English holiday. Cornwall's so quaint, with its olde worlde fishing villages and fifty different flavours of ice cream.'

He sat up and put his glass to one side, on the laminate floor. 'Come on, Elena, you're an intelligent woman who thinks for herself, right? You can't believe that we're sitting here, right this moment, on a giant sphere, without slipping off its sides.'

She waited for him to laugh. It didn't happen.

Uh oh.

'You're serious? About the earth being flat?'

'Take the sea.' He shrugged. 'You ever seen water hugging a curve?'

'But gravity—'

Carl held up the palm of his hand. 'Elena, Elena... you need to question everything you were taught at school. No one can prove gravity exists.'

What an arrogant tone.

'But when you throw a ball into the air, it comes back down,' she said and smiled sweetly.

'Of course. It's denser than its surroundings. Science isn't always right, you know. Take Einstein's theory of Static Universe that was later proved to be incorrect and—'

Elena fixed a glazed smile on her face. His good looks, his fantastic cooking, his attentive manner... It all slid away.

'How about the horizon?' she said. 'If a mountain comes into view, you'll only see the top of it first.'

He snorted and went into a long explanation of why that proved nothing. She glanced at his clock. Half past ten. This could carry on for hours.

'That's why the US government killed JFK,' he said in a confident tone. 'Kennedy knew man could never penetrate the dome over us, in order to fly to the moon. The powers-that-be realised he'd never lie to the public and support the fake moon landings. Therefore the Illuminati—'

Elena stood up and brushed down her jeans. 'This is fascinating, Carl, thanks for sharing. But I've got the most godawful headache. I'm prone to them and shouldn't have had all that wine. I'm afraid I'm going to have to leave.' She grabbed her coat from the back of the sofa and picked up her handbag.

Carl got to his feet. 'What? But... you can't go, I haven't even told you yet the reason why the truth isn't being told to us. It's because knowledge is power and NASA and the UN—'

Elena pulled open the flat's door. Thank God it wasn't locked. Her heart pumping, she raced down the stairs, almost tripping. She yanked open the door at the bottom and hurried outside, finding herself back in the dark, cold alleyway. Elena tightened her scarf and, walking at a speedy pace, turned right towards the lights of bars.

'That's not the best of it!' yelled a voice behind her. 'Covid proves, again, how we're being manipulated by those in power. No one *followed the science* when inflicting those lockdowns. The pandemic was just another example of—'

A group of stag night revellers passed her, singing, thankfully drowning out Carl's conspiracy theories. By the time she'd reached the train station and her heart had stopped racing, bubbles of laughter had replaced the adrenaline in her veins.

19

ELENA

Whilst Elena waited for thirty minutes on the train platform, her mirth morphed into something more sober. Physical goals like eating sushi and bungee jumping were do-able – emotional, romantic ones, less so. Perhaps... maybe... it had been a bit foolish, going to a stranger's house without even knowing his surname. Still, she was determined to remain positive. Whistling 'White Christmas', Elena came to Tahoor's house and, attracted by the light, spotted him sitting in his lounge, in front of the television, alone on a Saturday evening. It was almost midnight. A twinge of sadness for him, for herself, tugged inside her chest. He stood up and waved. He disappeared from view before the front door opened.

'Had a good night, lass?' Tahoor pulled at his beard, wearing his sandal-style slippers and striped dressing gown with a stain down the front, tied around the waist, creased Paisley pyjamas just visible underneath.

'Don't ask,' she said and pulled a comical face. She folded her arms, stepping from foot to foot, the air turning white as she spoke.

'You shouldn't be out on your own in the dark. Shall I accompany you to your front door?'

'It's okay, thanks. I've only come from the station, which isn't far away. I needed a brisk walk after the night I've had.'

'One reason Isha loved Christmas was that she said it put everyone in a better mood.' He gave a wry smile. 'I... I'm dreading this year's. My first without her. I don't want to get upset in front of the family.'

'I'm sure they'd want to be there for you,' Elena said, thinking back to when she was ten and worried that she might never have another Christmas with her mum, worried about Dad. She walked up to his front door. 'They'll be missing her too.'

'Still... I don't want to dampen the day. I need a practice run, to get the soppy stuff out of me in advance.' He forced another smile. 'Not just because I'd eat Christmas dinner every day if I could. Very traditionally English ours always was, apart from Isha's mushroom masala stuffing balls.'

Elena reached out and patted his arm. 'Right, I'd better get inside, run a bath and soak off my disastrous date.'

He raised his eyebrows. 'Oh. You really aren't interested in young Rory, then?'

'Tahoor! How many times? We are nothing but friends.'

'If you say so.' His eyes twinkled.

That man was impossible!

He bid her goodnight, retreating into his house. She went to walk away but then span around.

'Tomorrow's the first of December. We should celebrate, right? I'm going to put up my tree. Cook a roast turkey dinner with all the trimmings. We'll have crackers and cranberry sauce. Everything we need is already in the shops. It might be late-ish before we eat, but how about coming around at four in the afternoon?'

As if Christmas tree lights ran through his veins, Tahoor's whole demeanour lit up. 'You're serious?'

'Only if you dig out Isha's recipe and make those stuffing balls.'

'But... but what if I get... in front of you...' He cleared his throat. 'I have got a stiff upper lip about everything, apart from when it comes to my—'

'Don't worry. Rory will be bawling when he realises the soundtrack to the day is my Christmas jazz music CD on repeat.'

A wide smile crossed his face. 'You're a good lass.'

Whistling again, Elena strutted up her drive. She put her key in the lock and as soon as she entered, saw Rory to her left, in the lounge, frowning as he paced up and down. Elena took off her coat, hat and scarf and hung them on one of the hooks by the front door. 'Rory? Is your dad okay?' she said and joined him in the lounge. 'What's up? You look worried.'

'Elena? You're back? Good. I mean...' The lines disappeared from his brow and he exhaled. 'I didn't hear you come in.' He dropped onto the sofa and picked up her Kindle, studying it, even though it wasn't turned on. 'Oh... nothing. Just thinking about... about work.'

She sat down next to him and yawned. 'But...' A puzzled look crossed her face. 'The pressure is off for a while now. The board and product development both love the broken biscuit idea. A lot's riding on the campaign and there won't be as long a wait as usual for a new product to come to fruition, because the biscuits themselves aren't different to ones that we're already manufacturing... But certainly until Christmas, we'll go back to working on other campaigns until everything's been signed off and we get the official go-ahead on paper.' She smiled. 'We can ease off and refuel after our many late nights brainstorming. So how was your dad?'

'He thrashed me at Risk,' he replied in a monotone voice. 'I miss the days when he used to let me win.'

Something was off. But then it can't have been easy, facing a quarter of a century without one parent.

'How about a hot chocolate?' she suggested. 'I never even got dessert tonight and my taste buds are lobbying me for a sugar hit.'

'Not the best evening, then?'

'You'll laugh at the rubbish this guy spouted. It was going so well until Carl did his best to persuade me the earth was flat. He's a chef and had just served an amazing ratatouille at his place when—'

'Wait, what? *At his place?*' The frown lines came back.

'The oven broke down in the restaurant we booked and he happened to live around the corner from it,' she said, not giving him eye contact.

Rory tossed the Kindle to one side. 'But he was practically a stranger, Elena.'

She met his eyes again. 'He was entertaining company! Offered to help his friend, the chef in the restaurant.'

'It was a friend of his who said the oven wasn't working? Did all the other customers leave, then?'

'No idea, he didn't announce it to everyone whilst we were still there.'

'Convenient.' Rory stood up and shook his head.

'Don't be a dick... It wasn't like that. You weren't there.' Irritated, she got up. 'Don't you trust my judgement? You wouldn't be saying this stuff if I was a man.'

'Wow. I'm a dick *and* a misogynist?'

'Well, would you?'

'I'm wary of anyone who rushes things. Women are very vulnerable, but they're not actually the only ones. A mate of mine, Johnny, we used to work together – he went on a first date, and the woman said she'd love to cook him dinner. But when he got there it was clear she wanted a threesome. Her partner was there, twice the size of Johnny, and got threatening when he said no. Johnny managed to get out, but it really shook him up.' Rory threw his hands in the air. 'You could have ended up in a risky situation.'

'But Carl turned up early, was super polite, asked me about me. Honestly, leave it, Rory. I knew what I was doing. Let's not argue, especially as tomorrow is Christmas.'

'What?'

She grinned. 'It's the first of December. Tahoor is coming around. I'm putting up the tree, cooking a roast, I'll buy crackers and—'

'Wait, stop... Last year you groaned when the tree went up in the office, right at the beginning of December. You never put yours up until the week before the big day. What's the rush this year?'

'Because...' His directness had caught her off-guard. 'Tahoor was saying he'd like a practice run before the big day, to get the upset out about Isha not being there. He doesn't want to break down in front of his family and ruin their Christmas, and... anything could happen before the twenty-fifth.' Her voice wavered. 'Celebrating Christmas now means... means no one misses out.'

'What are you talking about?'

He wouldn't understand. He'd really doubt her judgement if she told him the truth. Why couldn't he just see the fun in her idea? 'If you don't want to take part then go out,' she found herself snapping. 'Tahoor will be around at four.'

She strode out of the lounge and headed straight upstairs, tears running down her cheeks, as if determined to wash away her good humour. She'd had a great night out, one that had provided her with another entertaining, dramatic story that proved she lived life on the edge, and to the full. Damn Rory and his hypocritical reservations. She changed for bed, didn't bother cleaning her teeth, half-heartedly took off her make-up and turned off her phone.

By the time Rory came up, thirty minutes later, and knocked on her door, she didn't reply.

Because Elena wasn't there.

RORY

Damn. Rory hated going to bed on an argument. It was one thing Mum never allowed, according to Dad. Rory shouldn't have fussed over Elena; she had her own life – they were colleagues, friends. He wasn't her lover or parent. Now she wasn't even in her bedroom so they couldn't clear the air. Elena had done her disappearing act again. Wherever she'd vanished to, it wasn't his business. Rory cleaned his teeth, pulled on his pyjama bottoms and T-shirt-style top, before crawling under the covers.

Celebrating Christmas, tomorrow? It was too much after a day of putting on a brave face with his dad, after feeling he should have moved on so much further when it came to his mum. Something was holding him back from carving out a full life. It was as if he'd moored himself to her death, with no chance of an Anchor Aweigh! Rory pressed the balls of his hands into his eyes and lay still for a moment.

Sorry Mum. Bit of a pity party here. It's you who took your last breath, not me. He clenched his fists. He needed to get a grip – especially as a big concern loomed, in the current day.

What *was* going on with Elena?

At first, having the roof down on the car, the sushi, drinking the four-year-old Dom Perignon on a whim and getting drunk on a night out in Cariswell had made Rory chuckle. He'd found Elena's new, carefree behaviour refreshing. But slowly that had changed, from the moment she took a sickie. It was so out of character, followed by her dismissive attitude over Tim's bungee jump safety advice, and now going into a complete stranger's house on a first date.

Worse than all that, what really made him shiver, even though he was snuggled under the covers, was her comment tonight, about not knowing what could happen before the real Christmas Day arrived, almost as if she didn't expect to be here.

Rory sat bolt upright. The day before they'd gone to the pool for that swim, she'd left work early for a doctor's appointment. It was a Friday. It had been from that weekend on that her behaviour changed, with the sushi at her parents' place on the Monday.

He wrapped his arms around his knees and sat in that position for the longest time, until cold ran through his body, like a shard of ice. A deep, dark empty pit formed in his stomach, and Rory reached for his journal.

Saturday 30th November

1 realisation. Elena must be really ill. That's the only explanation for her behaviour this last week, acting as if she'd got nothing to lose. She doesn't care what happens any more because her behaviour isn't carefree... it's actually careless.

Elena is dying.

Elena pulled up the car boot and heaved out two shopping bags, glad for her scarf and gloves yet hoping snow would soon fall. She'd like to see it one last time. Elena took a moment, indulging in memories of whizzing down a hill with Mum, on a sledge, the two of them laughing every time it bumped over a clump of grass. Even more excited than Elena, at the first sign of snow, Dad would be insisting they needed to build a snowman. As those warm thoughts dissipated, a crisp winter breeze brushed over her again. She was about to dump the shopping on the ground, to look for her keys, when the front door opened. Tinsel draped around his neck, like a cabaret performer's boa, Rory stood there.

'You found the Christmas decorations, then?' She'd got them down from the loft this morning before heading out to the supermarket.

As if doing a striptease, he held each end of the tinsel and tugged it from side to side. Then he gave a little bow, reached forwards and took the bags. He carried them into the kitchen. Elena locked up and followed him.

She stopped in the hallway and stared through the lounge's glass door. 'How did you guess that's the exact spot where I like to set up the tree?' A naked, plastic pine tree stood to the left of the television. Her chest hitched. It hit home. Christmas was coming and she really might not see it. Might not laugh at Dad, tipsy, doing 'The Electric Slide' line dance after his post-dinner Bailey's. Nor Mum insisting they sit through *It's a Wonderful Life* for the umpteenth time because of her crush on James Stewart.

'I didn't dare dress it, though. People can be very possessive of their baubles,' he said. Rory handed her a mug of coffee. 'Sorry. You were right. I *was* a dick last night.'

She turned to him. 'Oh... I'm sorry too. We... were both idiots.'

'Makes me realise how set in my ways I've become – not with my sports, but with the day-to-day. I haven't shared digs with anyone since uni and back then it was the norm to go out spontaneously, to be more impulsive. Now I even check on Brandy and Snap each night, even though there's no way they can get out.'

'I think that's called love,' she said.

'Are you saying I love you?'

'The heart wants what the heart wants, Bunker.'

As if. Rory and Elena? That would be like bringing together chalk and cheese, night and day, salt and pepper, black and white, oil and water.

Although, lately she had thought of him as more than a colleague. Rory had become a... friend. She'd not held onto many of those, over the years, keeping the past to herself, not wanting to get really close, aware that she might not always be around. Elena held out her free hand. 'Thanks for caring,' she mumbled. 'I do appreciate it.'

He slipped his hand into hers and she squeezed, both of them giving each other an understanding nod. She respected her colleague for several reasons, and one was that he never hesitated to apologise if he knew he was wrong.

'I've got used to living on my own too,' she said. 'Not sure I could go back to an interrogation from my parents every time I got in.'

They unpacked the bags and Rory listened, mouth agape, whilst Elena talked about Carl's J F Kennedy theory and how NASA was supposedly the bad guy. She also showed him the photo she'd taken last night of the pickle stall, and groaned dramatically when he insisted they must find time to visit and buy a selection. When they'd both stopped laughing, she lifted up the chicken.

'They only had frozen turkeys, not fresh ones, so chicken it is. But I've got everything else required for a perfect festive dinner – cranberry sauce, Christmas pudding, crackers, a holly and mistletoe paper tablecloth. How about we decorate the tree and then prepare the vegetables together?'

Rory led the way into the lounge. He took out his phone, scrolled for a moment, tapped and then placed it on the coffee table, volume on full.

It was playing Christmas jazz that he must have known Elena would love.

She opened a cardboard box on the floor and sorted through baubles. Together they hung them on the tree's branches, some from her childhood, like the little pink unicorn covered in glitter and the yellow rubber duck wearing a Christmas hat. A large, rainbow metal star went on top. Dad used to put her on his shoulders when she was little so that she could place it. Her parents insisted Elena have it when she moved out.

'I was expecting the decorations to be as coordinated as the rest of the house,' he said as Frank Sinatra serenaded them.

'It's not Christmas without everything clashing – cranberry and turkey, cheese with grapes, raw eggs with nutmeg, relatives that hate each other... A Christmas tree should reflect the chaos that everyone pines for as soon as Halloween is over.'

'Santa Claus is Coming to Town' came on the phone and she grabbed Rory's hands, her, for once, instigating the Good Times Dance. Elena needed to relish every moment of today. Once the tree was done, they peeled carrots and parsnips and Brussels sprouts. After cheese on toast for a late lunch, they both went to get changed. The dining room table was set and Rory brought a packet of cards from the spare room. Elena stood waiting by the tree.

Rory entered the lounge and looked as if he'd seen Santa. He gave a drawn-out whistle. 'You look great, Elena. Red really suits you.'

She wore a full-length halter neck dress that clung to her curves. She'd bought it, carried away after a champagne lunch to celebrate her mother's birthday a couple of years ago, but had never worn it. Now was the time. Elena would get Rory to take a photo and send it to her parents. It had seemed too extravagant before, but now she wondered how could *anything* be too much for life on earth that shouted beauty from every corner of the natural world. From the unnatural one, as well. Elena loved her round terrazzo coffee table, the swing seats in that Polish café in Manchester, the retro drinks trolley at Mum and Dad's and the fake fish tank in Gary's flat, and especially the pod swivel chair in Rory's apartment that had made her feel like Captain Kirk from Star Trek that time she saw it when he invited the whole department round for drinks. Yet she'd tip-toed through life, in her twenties, wearing sensible trouser suits and flatties.

Rory wore a plaid kilt and matching blazer.

'Nice,' she said and waved her hand up and down.

'This outfit might do for the office Christmas night out. What have you got planned? I promise not to tell Gary.'

Elena gasped. 'Oh crap! I haven't planned it yet, what with... with the broken biscuit idea taking over. What the hell am I going to do?'

He raised his eyebrows.

'Got any ideas?' she asked. Everyone would be so disappointed that she'd let them down.

'Hmm... I saw an event advertised for the twenty-second. A little late, granted, and it's a Sunday, so people might have family stuff on, but it looks amazing. A GPS-enabled festive treasure hunt around Manchester. It takes you to bars and ends in a restaurant for a buffet, with a mystery prize for the winning team, handed over by a local celebrity. It takes you from the Northern Quarter to the Village, to Deansgate and Spinning-fields. Didn't look too pricey, either. People could bring a plus one if they wanted to pay for them, seeing as it's so near to Christmas and their partners might be off work.'

'The twenty-second? That's the day after my birthday.' Her smile faltered. 'No... it's got to be before then. Leave it with me. I'll sort something out.'

'Why is the date so important? Have your mum and dad got something planned?'

She stared at the carpet.

He took her hand and led her to the sofa. 'Everything okay? You haven't seemed yourself lately. You can tell me, in confidence. What's going on?'

Earnest chestnut eyes stared her way, as if they were reading her mind. If only that were true, then she wouldn't have to say out loud what sounded like a ridiculous story. But then Rory had never been one for laughing at her, not even when she came up with a totally absurd marketing concept. Like the time they were running ideas past each other for a festive biscuit. Elena suggested a Christmas pudding-flavoured one, said Bingley Biscuits could hold a competition to find a random biscuit containing a golden sixpence. He'd tactfully pointed out they might receive dental work claims.

He took her hand again and rubbed his thumb across the top of it. Tingles went up her arm and she shivered. Must have been because her red dress wasn't the warmest.

Elena took a deep breath. 'Nearly twenty years ago,' she said, 'when I was ten, one night, I went on the common near our house, an open piece of land that had wooded areas. It was my birthday. I'd often sneak out to play with next door's cat. That night I... I didn't feel well, you see, and Mum was in hospital, because she'd been in a terrible accident. Dad was with her. A neighbour, Gayle, was looking after me.'

Rory nodded encouragingly.

'I... I walked through the wooded area, needing fresh air. I was so warm wearing my Disney pyjamas, even though it was December, when suddenly—'

The doorbell rang. Elena swallowed. Relief filled her chest. Had she lost her mind? Why would she tell anyone about that night? She pulled her hand away from Rory. If she told him everything, and in the unlikely event that he believed her, he'd only try to stop the inevitable outcome and might risk himself in the process. She went to the door, him following her.

Tahoor came in, rubbing his arms, and he raised an eyebrow at Rory's legs. He took off his coat and Elena kissed his cheek. Tahoor had made an effort too, wearing a waistcoat over a shirt that had actually been ironed. He patted his head.

'I went out and got a haircut this morning. I've brought...' He passed Elena a Tupperware box. 'My Isha's masala stuffing balls – made by her. I found them in the freezer.' He stared at the box. 'I thought it would be difficult, eating her food, but it'll be like having her with us.'

'You don't want to keep them for another time?' asked Elena, gently.

'She'd want you to try them. I'll dig out the recipe if you like, and you can add it to your collection. A woman's recipe box is one of the most important things she'll bring to a marriage. Office skills are all very well, but they won't be much good once you settle down and have babies.'

Rory shot Tahoor a helpless look as Elena reached into one of the deep red pockets that had attracted her to the dress in the first place. She waved a yellow card in the air.

'You made them!' said Tahoor in a delighted tone. 'It's as if I've got my family living next door. Right, Rory lad, you and I need to discuss Wednesday's match. It's against Newcastle United. Those magpies are a canny lot and...'

Tahoor kept in high spirits and, throughout the meal, didn't suggest Elena watch how much she ate when she went for seconds of roast potatoes, like he had once when she'd gone around to check on him and he'd asked her to stay for tea and biscuits. He also turned a blind eye when she knocked back a second glass of Bailey's, after dessert. Elena had seen his signs of grief this last year – the stained, un-ironed clothes, the shadows under his eyes, the lonely glances out of his lounge window – but she'd been so wrapped up in herself that she'd let the friendship slip, telling herself he'd, no doubt, rather be on his own. She was about to draw out the second yellow card when the meal was over as he suggested to Rory that they watch television until

Elena had finished clearing up. But she didn't. Couldn't. Elena had pretended not to notice, but she'd seen Tahoor dab his eyes with his reindeer paper napkin as soon as one of Isha's stuffing balls went in his mouth.

'Stuff the washing. We'll tidy up later,' she announced. 'Let's chill for half an hour before playing cards.' Fingers crossed he didn't suggest playing Old Maid. She and Rory sat on the sofa, Tahoor in a nearby armchair. With the help of black coffee, they eventually found enough energy to play, then took another break. Elena passed around a box of chocolates. She told Tahoor about the bungee jump and Rory reminisced about one he'd done in France, from a cable car in a ski resort.

'Ah, la belle France,' mumbled Tahoor. 'I surprised Isha once with a weekend in Paris. I chose a family run hotel in Saint-Germain-des-Prés, a beautiful area where famous artists and bookish types used to meet and live. I've never forgotten its name – Hôtel Madame Chic – or our room's old-style French furniture, highly carved, with upholstered chairs. Isha loved the floral designs and cosy colours – said she felt like royalty staying there. Paris is a clichéd romantic destination, but she'd always wanted to go. And it turns out, you really haven't lived unless you've climbed up the steps to the Sacré Coeur and looked down at the Parisian skyline.'

'Never been,' said Rory.

'Me neither,' said Elena.

Tahoor clapped his hands. 'You should go together! It's safer for a woman to go with a man. The underground there is...'

Elena's fingers itched to slide into her pocket for the yellow card as he carried on talking.

'It must be wonderful at Christmas,' he continued, 'the City of Lights especially sparkly, so full of life.'

Full of life. Elena needed to cram as much as she could into the next three weeks, in case...

Paris? Why not?

'Let's do it, Rory!' Her eyes were sparkly now. 'How about next weekend? A city break to do Christmas shopping.'

He laughed. 'Nice one. Imagine the scramble to get flights and hotels at this late notice, at this time of year. As for you, flying... Have you thought this through?'

'Yes! It's about time I did it. I'm not joking about this trip!'

'Have you even got a passport?'

'I had to get one for my last job, but never needed to use it.' Or rather she'd avoided trips to the head office in Seattle. A little white lie about an ear infection got her out of the last one.

'Go on, lad! You won't regret it,' said Tahoor, and he stood up, went next door, and came back out of breath and shivering from the cold, grasping a small photo album. Elena turned the pages, filled with photos of roadside portrait painters, beautiful Haussmann-style buildings, passersby wearing cool sunglasses, plates of mussels and crêpes. Elena hummed 'April in Paris'.

'Please, Rory. I need to do this,' she murmured. More than he could ever imagine.

Tahoor couldn't have looked happier as he left to let them get on with searching for flights and hotel rooms. He gave Elena a hug by the front door, whilst Rory set up his laptop.

'Thanks for a lovely evening,' he said. 'It wasn't as bad as I expected.' But with those words, he looked down at the album he was holding and his face crumpled. A sob escaped his lips. His arms curled around his body as he went to leave.

'Tahoor! Come back in,' she said.

Vehemently, Tahoor shook his head. 'Mustn't let another man – shouldn't let anyone – see me crying.' He gulped.

Elena paused, delved into her pocket and passed him a red card. He sniffed and with a puzzled look on his face, took it.

'You get the cards for sexist comments, right? Well, that comment is sexist towards men. There's nothing wrong with you crying, Tahoor, and don't you forget it.'

'I miss her so very much,' he croaked. 'I dream about her too. The pain when I wake up and find she's not there...' He gave another muffled sob. 'It's more than I can bear, and I'm worried this sense of helplessness will never go away.' The shudders that ripped through his body eventually slowed. Elena held his hand tightly. 'Sorry, lass – making a show of myself.'

'Don't you apologise. It will get better, I promise,' she whispered. 'The death of a loved one is traumatic. As a child, I suffered a trauma. Time doesn't make you forget but it gives you coping mechanisms.'

Tahoor wiped his eyes with the sleeve of his coat. 'You must think me a right... What's that word my granddaughter, Sharnaz, uses...? Wuss.'

Elena leant forwards and gave him a hug. She stepped back and placed a hand on one of his shoulders. 'Quite the opposite. It takes an incredibly brave person to share their tears... to share their inner fears,' she said. 'Come round again this week.'

'For the football on Wednesday?' he said, and his face lit up. 'Snacks on me.'

'It's a date,' she said. 'But Tahoor, I'm also always here if you need to chat. I've always got time.'

'I know. You lasses aren't as busy as us men, with our heads constantly rolling with important thoughts and responsibilities...'

Her mouth dropped open but he winked, smiling through the tears, and he turned to go, clutching the red card.

'Everything all right?' asked Rory as he came into the hallway.

Elena closed the door. 'I hope so.'

'That thing you were telling me... about your tenth birthday night... Fancy carrying on over another cup of coffee before we book our weekend away?'

Elena rolled her lips together. She wasn't as brave as Tahoor. 'No,' she said and forced a grin. 'It was nothing, really, and we've no time to waste if we're flying to Paris in six days!'

22

RORY

Friday 6th December

This week has been the first time in 19 years that I've failed to write in you, journal, apart from when I was younger and got blind drunk on a night out. There was that time, when I was 16, when I threw you across the room because I'd messed up my English mock exam. Sorry about that. Plus when I was 10 and caught glandular fever. I've never known exhaustion like it, not even when I did that desert half-marathon in Jordan.

I haven't put pen to your paper since last Saturday, when I worked out Elena must be ill – and then realised the way she's been lately could be down to something even worse, if that's possible. What was worse than a terminal illness? Elena was going to tell me something. Her tenth birthday... Out in woods... Her mother's accident... Whilst she was talking, her voice sounded afraid and uncertain; nothing like the Elena I work with.

Midweek I prodded her again, but she shut me down.

She's gone so quiet and is clearly stressed, as if her problem, whatever it is, has reached some crisis point.

I've not been able to face writing this down because seeing the words, in front of me, would make me feel even more useless about my friend going through something so terrible that she's become reckless over her personal safety; about me being unable to do anything to help, being unable to stop Elena making dangerous choices.

I'll attempt to briefly recap the week.

Sunday 1st December – 3 plays too many of 'White Christmas' by Bing Crosby. 8 Brussels sprouts, I regretted those later. 6 card games with Tahoor. He's the fastest Go Fisher in the West. 3 coffees with Elena whilst we looked for hotel rooms and flights to Paris. We leave at 9am on Saturday the 7th and fly back on Sunday the 8th at 7pm. Tahoor is over the moon we succeeded in booking the boutique hotel that he and Isha stayed in all those years ago, a sentimental touch I wouldn't have thought of. It was Elena's idea, and she'd been thrilled to find out it was still there, still run by the founding family. She'd texted Tahoor with the news and he'd texted back 4 clapping hands – plus 2 hearts followed by 2 winking faces. Elena instantly regretted her decision, Tahoor clearly assuming that her booking the same hotel meant that romance was on the cards.

Monday 2nd December – A 50-minute meeting with Derek. He wants us to put together an initial plan of how we foresee the packaging for the broken biscuits. Product development hopes to have a prototype ready early next year, when the paperwork is signed off and a product name has been confirmed. 30 minutes in the gym with Gary. 2 pickles accompanied by 2 frowns from Elena. 1 hour in the evening where

Elena insisted we attempt to speak nothing but French. Given the only French I've got comes from a travel handbook I briefly looked at a few years ago, when I did the bungee jump in the ski resort, all I had was 'The bill, please,' and 'Have you got medication for diarrhoea?'

Tuesday 3rd December – 30 minutes Elena spends on the phone in the evening, convincing her parents we are not going to Paris for a surprise proposal, mainly because we are strictly mates and haven't even kissed, let alone... Her dad ended the call at that point. Elena and Rory dating? How the office would chuckle at that idea. Gary joked about it once and concluded we were as well matched as Princess Anne, with her smart but no-nonsense style, and Timothée Chalamet in his backless blouse.

Wednesday 4th December – 2 hours in Tahoor's company as he came over to watch City play Newcastle. 90 minutes of being... well, fairly invested in the game, I have to admit. What a goal!

Thursday 5th December – 100 per cent less chat from Elena than usual. A very quiet day. 1 bottle of wine consumed by her in front of the telly that night. I wasn't in the mood. Elena's not usually a lone drinker.

Friday 6th December today – Elena did what she never does when we all finish early at 4 p.m. and go to the pub – she was fully intent on getting stone drunk on chasers and cocktails. She made another cryptic comment about perhaps not being around for Christmas. When we got back, she just about managed to pack her bag for tomorrow. I treated us to takeout, hoping it would soak up the alcohol, but she left half of her pizza and most of the garlic dough balls. I sang 'Ocean Eyes' as usual, a minute ago. 0 joining in by Elena. Could have sworn 1 sob came through the wall.

I DON'T UNDERSTAND WHAT'S GOING ON AND HAVE HARDLY SLEPT ALL WEEK.

CAN I FIGURE IT OUT BEFORE SHE TAKES A RISK TOO FAR?

23

ELENA

Dawn's lilac hues hadn't yet lit up the morning sky as Elena stood in the kitchen, head thumping. They needed to leave in thirty minutes. For the first time in her life, she was benefiting from living near Manchester Airport. Wearing pink cords, white trainers, and a grey hoodie, Rory appeared. She handed him a mug of coffee and yawned.

'I didn't change to mocktails early enough last night, proved by the last thing I did, before leaving – spinning round in circles, with Gary, to "Cotton Eye Joe".'

Rory gave a flicker of a smile in response. Dark circles hung under his eyes too. 'I've researched some numbers for you,' he said, 'to make you more confident of our journey. Each day there are around a hundred thousand flights worldwide. In 2023 there were only two loss-of-life incidents. Compared to driving a car...'

Rory went on. Elena appreciated it, but hardly listened. Everyone knew flying was one of the safest forms of travel. However, despite this, in the last few days, she couldn't fight off the anxiety. Bungee jumping, going on a date, eating raw fish, those things had given her a modicum of control, but flying in an aeroplane? In that situation she'd have zero means of averting a disaster, rare as such an occurrence might be. Therefore, Elena did what she'd done so many times over the years, and put on a front. She joked with the taxi driver, ate a full English breakfast at the airport, playfully battled with Rory for the window seat.

Elena did up her safety belt and took a deep breath, eyes closed as the aeroplane's engine started. Slowly at first, they moved down the runway, then full throttle, everything shaking. Her blood rushed and thumped in her ears; the knots in her stomach were tighter than any monthly cramps; perspiration dripped under her arms, and nausea came. Oh God, what if she threw up? Forcing her eyes open, she peered out of the window, onto nothing, wishing she could join in with a baby in the row behind that was screaming. There were no fluffy white marshmallow clouds, nor Pearly Gates sparkling above, just emptiness; a desert made up of light and water vapour that wouldn't protect her from cascading to earth should something happen. She wouldn't cry, wouldn't have a meltdown; she had Rory to consider and the other passengers. Elena *would* enjoy this trip to Paris.

When the sign came up to remove their safety belts, Elena gagged and covered her mouth with her hand. The cabin span for a moment before her breathing calmed. 'Those facts you gave me really helped,' she muttered to Rory in a weak tone, not wanting him to know how she really felt.

Fists clenched, ear buds in, she listened to coffee shop jazz. For the first time in her life, she didn't reach for a book to save the day, even though her Kindle was in her rucksack. She wouldn't be able to concentrate. The minutes ticked by. One by one. Her fears magnified. What if a terrorist was on the plane? The pilot might suffer a heart attack. A door might blow off. Finally, finally the engine started revving again.

A beeping warned Elena to put her belt back on. She removed her earbuds. Rory put down the in-flight magazine and took her hand. She held on tightly. Her relief that the journey was almost over proved to be short-lived. Elena had done her own research. The descent was the most dangerous part of the flight.

Please don't let me die. I'm not ready. Not yet. These last weeks have shown me I've got so much life to live – I'm doing this travel, I've had wild times out, but there's still that one thing left. That love thing. There could still be time for that, right? And I'll miss Mum and Dad. My friend Rory. Gary, too. Brandy and Snap are relying on me to set up that bigger tank I've ordered, and Tahoor, next door, needs a shoulder to lean on.

Elena began to hyperventilate. Why, oh why, had she suggested this trip? Who cared about a stupid Sacred Heart basilica and iconic iron lattice tower and all that fancy food? Blackpool had a tower too, and Asda sold ready-made crêpes and French wine.

Her chest tightened as the smell of a baby's filled nappy invaded her nostrils, and she swallowed. Voices caught her attention and she opened her eyes to see a flight attendant crouched by Rory's side. He'd called her over. Elena listened as the woman instructed her on how to breathe. A colleague then brought over a glass of water and Elena took several sips. They took the glass away and returned to their seats, having told her to carry on with the breathing exercises as the plane headed down to Charles de Gaulle airport.

Rory. His voice counting numbers for me to breathe to. My eyes screw up tightly as we land. Bounce. Bounce. The plane is bound to explode! At top speed we career down the runway. We're going to crash! There's Rory's voice again, soft and sympathetic. And breathe. Breathe again. It is, the aeroplane's slowing...

The attendants saw everyone else off the plane first. They dismissed Elena's apologies and said they'd seen it all before.

'I felt like a right fool on that flight,' she said to Rory as they got out of the taxi in Saint-Germain-des-Prés, outside their hotel.

He put down his bags and gave her a big hug. Elena lost herself in it for a second. It reminded her of how her parents' cuddles used to fix her problems when she was little – until the promise. She learnt, at that tender young age, that adulting was hard.

'How about a second breakfast?' he said cheerily. 'We can drop our bags off first. Didn't the hotel manager email to say we could check them in early?' He went inside.

Yet Elena stopped for a second, mesmerised by her surroundings. The beauty, the quaintness of Paris had struck her in the car, but seeing it through the window had been like watching a TV show. Whereas now it was undeniable. Elena Swan had flown to Paris. She had! Her spirits lifted. What an achievement! A smart woman in large sunglasses strolled past, speaking expressive French into her phone. The smell of *good* coffee came out of a café next door to Hôtel Madame Chic. Not far away, water splashed. Elena squinted and spotted one of the many fountains she'd read about in books set in the French capital. Oh, the classic clothes, elegant, simple, and yes, she saw a beret; the ornate architecture, an iconic Métro sign; the pastry and garlic smells, the Edith Piaf song playing from a passing car; friends kissing each other on both cheeks and people-watchers sitting outside cafés; the pampered dogs in prams, their owners breaking rules like crossing at red lights... One by one the knots unravelled in her stomach and when an elderly man in a sharp suit, with a cigarette hanging out of his mouth, tipped his trilby in her direction, she beamed back.

Keen to drop off her rucksack and explore, not wanting to

waste a second of this weekend, she hurried inside the hotel, which did not disappoint. In the reception area were two charming, upholstered chairs, with buttons and carved legs, styled like furniture from the seventeenth and eighteenth centuries. The colours were all reds, purples, yellows, with floral designs across walls that had dark wood coving and skirting boards. Yet it wasn't glitzy and had a worn, homely feel. French patio doors opened onto a small courtyard. The man at reception, in a black jumper with the sleeves rolled up, had short wavy grey hair and introduced himself as Jacques, the owner. He handed them a tourist leaflet and waved them off, saying to return whenever they wanted as there was a night porter. They stood outside the hotel's honey-coloured front and took all of ten seconds to head into the café next door. Rory ordered a croissant, Elena a pain au raisin. He told her how it was also called an escargot – a snail – because of its shape.

After the first mouthful, she gave an appreciative sigh. 'Oh my. That pastry is so very light.'

Rory slathered jam onto his croissant and offered her the first bite.

Look at me. On holiday abroad. I flew here. Now I'm eating snails – well, almost.

Elena opened the leaflet. 'What first? Christmas shopping? Sight-seeing? A trip down the Seine in a Bateau Mouche? I want to do everything!'

Rory chuckled. 'How about—'

'Actually, I've got it all planned.'

'Of course you have,' he said and rolled his eyes in a comical manner.

They caught an underground train to the Arc de Triomphe, ambled down the Champs Elysées, then continued to the Tuileries Garden, passing clusters of green chairs and military lines of trees losing their leaves. When it was dark, they would follow Tahoor's instructions and make for the Sacré Coeur. That's how Elena summarised the day in a text for her parents.

However, their actual time in Paris, so far, had been so much more than that. The Arc de Triomphe looked utterly majestic, lauding over the chaos below of circling cars, honking and speeding, and over the wealthy Parisians and tourists who were shopping down the Champs Elysées boulevard. Rory rubbed his hands as he relayed facts – the Arc de Triomphe had taken thirty years to build, was fifty metres tall, and a giant, three-tiered elephant was almost built on the spot instead. The two of them ambled, Parisian style, down the Champs Elysées – 1.9 kilometres long and seventy metres wide – past Dior, Guerlain, Louis Vuitton, Lacoste too, and Apple.

They had an incredible French onion soup in a fancy bistro, with melted Gruyere on top of pieces of baguette, floating on top, served by a waiter in a burgundy waistcoat and black bow tie. Christmas lights hung in the elm trees lining the boulevard. They must have looked amazing at night. Decorated fir trees stood in the shops' glass fronts, their lights already twinkling. The two of them chattered excitedly as they walked on from the Champs Elysées down to the Tuileries Garden, a stunningly pretty Paris park, named for the tile factories that used to be there. Normally Elena would stick rigidly to her plan that, originally, had included a trip to the Eiffel Tower, straight after the Champs Elysées. However, feeling more... carefree – that was it – she allowed a diversion. They'd visit the Eiffel Tower tomorrow and instead would spend the next couple of hours enjoying the Tuileries Garden and the Christmas markets there.

She linked arms with Rory as they toured the little wooden chalets, marvelling at the North African food items, the house ornaments and jewellery, the candles, handbags and wine, breathing in spices and the smell of waffles. Elena's parents loved experimenting with foreign cooking, and she bought them some harissa paste, spiced olives and dates. Rory found a Dashika print T-shirt for his dad, and Elena couldn't resist a City of Lights tote bag for her mum. For Tahoor, they found a box of cardamom-flavoured chocolates. They'd also planned to take photos of the hotel and a video of the Parisian sights for him. She bought a second-hand book, which was in French, so she couldn't read it but the embossed cover was so beautiful, so solid. It gave her comfort to think that inside, on its pages, a happier world might exist, without complications.

As the late afternoon chill set in, they sat on a park bench sipping mulled wine, or *vin chaud* as Elena insisted on calling it. Gratefully, she wrapped her cold fingers around the warm mug. They'd just finished eating waffles out of polystyrene containers, slathered with cream, fruit, and a coulis that was as pink as Rory's trousers.

'I've spent the last two hours speaking French to actual French people. I've said *Merci. S'il vous plaît. Au Revoir.* They actually understood me!'

Rory clinked her glass. 'Same here. *Va te faire foutre* got rid of that guy who bumped into us and jabbed his finger in my face, as if it were my fault. I've picked up more than I realised, from watching the occasional subtitled French series on Netflix.'

'Now for the best bit, according to Tahoor – the view of Paris, at night, from the steps of the Sacré Coeur. It's about thirty minutes away on the Métro.'

Rory pulled a face.

'I know, the underground system's stuffy, stinky, and everyone looks so miserable, but that busker was amazing. This is what I came for – the real Paris, not just a picture-postcard view. I've never understood people who travel abroad but then hunt out the nearest English pub. What's the point?'

'You'd know if you've ever been stuck in a Greek bar that serves nothing but Retsina. It's infused with pine tree resin and tastes like paint remover.'

'What were you doing over there?'

'Cliff diving.'

'How on earth have you fitted in so many holidays into your life?'

'Many trips were just weekends away and I used to take a few weeks off in between jobs, when I did contract work. Might have to slow down since I've only got twenty-eight days off a year, now.'

Despite the cold, she blushed and waved her hand in the air. 'This... simply shopping and walking... must seem so lame to you. All the memories you have, your experiences... I... I wish I'd done more. Maybe even taken a sabbatical.'

His brow furrowed. 'You speak as if it's too late.'

A muscle in her cheek twitched.

He stretched out his legs. 'Want to know something? The many countries, the countless adrenaline rushes, the competitive banter, it's kinda meaningless now. It's as if I've been on a quest my whole life, without really realising what it is. Whereas today, we've strolled and taken the time to soak up Parisian life. We've even bought matching berets. Tahoor will love that...' He tilted his head and shot her a sultry look. Elena couldn't suppress a laugh. His face turned more serious. 'I've also spoken to locals...' He gave a wry smile. 'Even if it was only to swear. We've shared an experience that hasn't just been about getting off on our individual adrenaline kicks.' He stared at the Christmas market chalets. 'In some ways today has meant more than any other trip I've taken.'

Elena wasn't sure what to say. Still wasn't when they sat on the underground train.

The more Rory opened up, the less she felt she knew about him.

They exited the station and stepped into the mystery of Parisian night. Elena shivered and pulled down her beret, as the faraway sound of a Peruvian flute band eerily floated through the December frostiness. A sign pointed to the Sacré Coeur and they were about to walk that way when someone tapped Elena's shoulder.

She turned round.

Gulped.

In front of her stood a woman in a bright purple shawl, clutching a pack of tarot cards.

Elena dropped her rucksack.

'You are English?' said a heavily accented voice. The woman pointed to a nearby cabin. 'Come inside. Perhaps I can tell you your fortune. I have a strong sense that you'll want to hear what I have to say.'

The world span. The hubbub of Paris disappeared. This wasn't happening. It wasn't. Noooo. No! She closed her eyes, counted to five, opened them again, but the woman was still there. With terror etched across her face, Elena backed away.

'Don't be shy,' said the woman in an ominous tone. 'The spirits have a message for you.'

An animal-like howl shot up into the night sky. It took her a few seconds to realise that sound was coming from her own mouth.

'*Va te faire foutre!*' Elena screamed, and without her rucksack, without Rory, she ran, ran away, in the direction of the white basilica high up in the distance.

Thirty minutes later, Elena sat out of breath, on the steps

directly approaching the Sacré Coeur, body jerking, as if she were sobbing. She wasn't – Elena was too much in shock even for tears. Her legs ached. She should have taken the funicular instead of climbing the slope to reach this point. She'd had to stop on the steps, halfway.

'Mademoiselle?'

She turned to her right. A rough sleeper, with a straggly beard and a dog lying by his side, held out his bottle of wine. In his other hand he held a half-chewed baguette. Elena hesitated. Why not? She reached out her hand and took the wine as Rory appeared, panting. He took the bottle from her.

'That won't help,' he said quietly, and handed it back to the man. '*Merci beaucoup*,' Rory said. The rough sleeper shrugged and took a swig. Rory sat down next to Elena, his face pale, eyes widened. He put her rucksack on the ground, next to her. 'That woman with the cards kept me a while. She was very persistent. In the end I just walked off. What's going on? Come on. Tell me. These last few weeks have been so out of character. At first I reckoned you might be ill but... I sense it's not that. You can trust me, Elena, whatever it is.' His voice sounded urgent.

'You wouldn't understand.' No one would. Not even Mum and Dad. How could they?

'Why were you so scared of that fortune teller? Let me help. Please.'

Elena focused on the horizon beneath them. It was so very pretty, like in Tahoor's photos, a busy stretch of glittering lights that contrasted the solemn, calm grandeur of the basilica behind them. Further up the steps, behind her, a jazz musician, busking, added a touch of magic. Elena Swan didn't do scared. She'd gone against the whole team at work when she'd reckoned they were wrong. She'd advocated change where necessary, such as suggesting mental health sessions during the pandemic. Elena Swan was *strong*. She'd always had to trust in that.

'Okay, let's do a risk assessment of the situation,' said Rory, 'like I do before every extreme sport event.' He took both her hands. 'What's the worst thing that can happen if you confide in me?'

'You won't believe me – or you will. Both are terrible outcomes.'

'Then it makes no difference as to whether I know or not. You can't go on like this, Elena. I mean, what's next when we get back to England? Eating one of my pickles? It can't get more dangerous than that.'

'Idiot,' she muttered, and relief filled his face as she smiled.

He'd think her an idiot if he told him about what had happened years ago.

Swaying slightly, the rough sleeper stood up, having finished the baguette. His dog trotted over and licked Elena's hand, before its owner said *bonsoir* and went to go. She pulled out her purse and held out a five euro note. The man raised his eyebrows, his deeply lined face softened, and he muttered something in French, ending with the word *merci*.

'Is it something to do with your thirtieth birthday?'

The man and his dog went down the steps. She opened her mouth. Closed it again. Then said, 'Yes, it's two weeks today and... I'm probably not going to reach it.'

The colour drained from his face. '*Are* you sick?'

She shook her head.

'Then it's to do with what you almost told me last week – about when you were ten?'

Elena exhaled as a young couple walked past, laughing and smoking weed by the smell of it. Further down, a group of students drank and took photos.

'I'll tell you a secret, from when I was ten,' said Rory. 'I used to creep out at night, too, and nick Dad's ciggies to smoke in the backyard, as if smoking would make me more grown up, make me more like a mate for him – a mate I felt he needed. But he found out one night, went mad and quit on the spot. So... where did you creep out to?'

Elena bit her lip.

'Onto that common, near your house?' he nudged.

A longing to share her story that had lived deep inside for so many years, seeped out of the cracks in her hard exterior. Elena could no longer ignore it.

A broken biscuit still mattered, still had a purpose, could reinvent itself with a future away from the dustbin. This new product at work may only have been confectionary but its message spoke to Elena in the way she hoped it would to customers. Breaks and scars, over time, hurt so much; they changed lives, but they also made people brave and resilient.

That resilience was more important than ever now. Elena had to finally face her past – before she lost her present and future.

Voice shaking slightly, Elena started talking.

24

ELENA

21 December 2004

Elena lay in bed, face down, sobbing, body covered in sweat, hair stuck to her cheeks. Gayle, the next-door neighbour, had gone downstairs to fetch a glass of water. Daddy wasn't there because of Mummy... Body jerking with emotion, Elena sat up. She reached for her teddy bear. Leah at school said cuddly toys were babyish. She also called her parents by their first names, said it was more grown up. Elena didn't care. She hugged Teddy oh so tightly. Gayle gave really good cuddles, but only Teddy heard Elena's deepest secrets.

'I feel sick again,' she said to her bear 'Auntie Gayle says I've got a temperature. I want to go to the hospital to see Mummy but Daddy said no, because I'm not well and because...' She sobbed again. 'He said I should concentrate on the fun times I've had with her instead, as if memories are all I'm going to have.'

A knock at the door sounded. Gayle came in and put the water on the bedside cabinet, next to a ramshackle pile of books. She sat on the bed and held Elena's hand. Big beaded necklaces hung around her neck, so different to Mummy's delicate gold chain, and Gayle smelt of strong perfume that made your nose wrinkle, whereas Mummy smelt of yummy baking.

'I'm sorry you're going through this, love,' she said. Her eyeliner had smeared down her face. 'Your mum is one of the strongest people I know. Don't forget that.'

'Thanks for the drink,' Elena said and sniffed loudly. 'I... I want to be on my own, now.' She had to be a big girl, if Mummy was ill. Daddy had sounded so upset... A sob rose in Elena's chest.

'Are you sure? I could sit on your bean bag, if you wanted, keep you company until you fall asleep. Or how about I read from one of our favourite stories, say Alice in Wonderland?' Gayle reached forward and gently straightened the bow around Teddy's neck.

'I'm okay... thanks, Auntie Gayle.' She wasn't her auntie but Elena had always liked calling her that. She lay down and turned her face away, not wanting to show her tears, feeling so hot as if it were July and not December. She wasn't going to fall asleep. Not whilst Mummy was alive.

A kind sigh. 'Okay, my love. I'll be in the lounge. Come down or shout if you want anything, anything at all. Another top-up of water. A hug. Call down if you feel sick again. I've put a bowl by your bed. Try to sleep, it's already so late.'

A pat on Elena's shoulder and the door closed. The television came on downstairs. For what felt like hours, she tossed and turned. If only she could get some fresh air, and go for a wander on the nearby common, like she did on summer nights. Mummy and Daddy never knew, but she'd creep out and give their other next-door neighbour's cat a Dairylea Triangle of cheese. The liquorice black cat was called Bumper because he'd bump his nose against people's legs. Bumper would understand what she was going through.

Breath sounding raspy, Elena got out of bed and put on her trainers, half-heartedly tying the laces. Mummy had taught her to do that, and how to braid her hair, how to plant flowers and do maths equations. Elena crept downstairs and past the lounge, like she had so many times before. Not bothering with her coat, she snuck out the back door. The cold air took her breath away and with it, the horrible, suffocating feeling she'd been suffering. She pushed against a loose slat in the fence, at the bottom of the garden, breathing in mossy, soily smells. The gap gave her just enough room to squeeze through. A shiver ran down her back as she faced the common, an open stretch of land with mist across it, always empty at night. Hoot, hoot. A familiar sound. She'd actually seen an owl once. Bats, too. Children played cricket and football on the common, and sometimes grown-ups held events like the little touring Christmas fair that had been running for a week. Today, Tuesday, had been its last day, the end of its tour, before Christmas Eve on Friday.

Elena's bottom lip trembled... Mummy had taken her there last weekend. The stalls were mainly food and gifts, although there was a hook-a-duck one, and a small carousel for children. Mummy let Elena go on twice. They'd both eaten mince pies and drunk hot chocolate. Elena had spent her pocket money on gifts for her parents. Mummy had let her go off with her friend from school, Lucy, for half an hour, whilst Lucy's gran went to a fortune teller's stall. Later, Lucy's gran had said how the fortune teller knew so much about her – that she had painful arthritis, that her sister was ill, and that she saw a lot of money in her future. Elena had bought a Christmas spiced bottle of hand cream for Mummy and a silly drinks coaster with a picture of a snowman melting, standing by a cosy fire, for Daddy. She also bought them each a packet of fancy Christmas biscuits.

Would Mummy get to eat hers?

A meow sounded at her feet. Bump, bump. Elena knelt down and touched the wet nose with her finger, before falling to the frosty ground and burying her face in Bumper's fur. But still images of her mum filled her head, in hospital, covered in blood. She got to her feet, patted the cat's head and then gave in to an urge to run across the open space *of land, away from the sadness. Except it followed her into the woods. She almost tripped, even though she was actually running much more slowly than usual, in a wobbly line. She stopped in a small clearing and bent over, throwing up onto a patch of icy leaves.*

'Mummy, I want Mummy.' The words came out in big gulps. Now the cold air pierced her lungs. She looked up. Her eyes widened. A small tent had been pitched, straight ahead. By its side stood a woman wearing a purple shawl, her black hair scooped up high on her head and under a colourful beanie hat. Around her neck was a thick woolly scarf. Elena squinted. In one hand was a crystal ball. Of course. The fortune teller from the Christmas fair. Bumper ran over and bumped the woman's legs. She put down her crystal ball for a second, picked Bumper up and gave him a hug. Elena stood transfixed at the image of the fortune teller, holding the black cat in her arms.

'Child, what are you doing out here? It's the middle of winter. And why the upset?' She put Bumper down and delved into her trouser pocket, then went over and handed Elena a tissue.

The woman had an unusual accent. Elena shouldn't talk to strangers, but Bumper liked the fortune teller, and Lucy's mum had sat down at her table, at the fair.

She put her arm around Elena's shoulder. 'Tell me. What is troubling you?'

'My mummy. She's going to die. Her car was hit. She's in hospital, and...' Rambling, Elena told the woman what had happened – how her mum was supposed to have been at home, helping her celebrate her tenth birthday. 'I'd do anything to save her, like...' The words 'a life for a life' came into her head... 'Like swap my life for hers. Mummy's thirty. I could die at thirty instead of her. We'd have twenty more years together, then.'

The woman didn't tell her off for suggesting such a thing and simply stood back and held out her crystal ball. 'What is your name, child?'

'Elena. Elena Swan,' she said in a small voice, scared now. 'How will I live without Mummy? How will Daddy? We're like Blossom, Bubbles and Buttercup, the three of us against the world. Daddy says so when he reads me Powerpuff Girls books, although he doesn't think he'd look good in a skirt. He's always making Mummy laugh.' She let out a sob.

'You can't take a promise back once it's made, child. A life for a life – that's a serious business. Do you understand?' the woman said. 'It might have unforeseen consequences for both of you – dealing with dark, unknown forces. By making this promise you'd be taking a big risk.'

'I understand.' Elena's voice quivered, the air turning white as she spoke. 'A promise is a promise. Mummy and Daddy have taught me that. Please, please just help me save her.' Surely the consequences for Mummy couldn't be worse than no longer being around? Was it self-ish, to want to not let go of a parent, at all costs? Elena's fingers curled, the nails digging into her palms No. It wasn't. And... and even if it was, she couldn't live without her mummy. She couldn't! Elena turning thirty was such a very long time away. Surely any dark forces would have forgotten about Elena and her mummy by then.

The woman shot her a piercing look, hesitated. 'You should go home. Go to bed. Things might end well.'

'They won't! The doctors said.'

Everything went blurry as the woman gave a big sigh. 'Okay. A life for a life it is.' She picked up the crystal ball and ran a hand over the glass. 'Elena Swan, your mother will be saved, this very day, at midnight. In exchange for her life, on your thirtieth birthday, YOU will pass onto the next stage of our world.'

After what seemed like only seconds later, Elena stood at her front door, the purple shawl around her shoulders, Bumper at her feet. The fortune teller held her hand. Elena avoided Gayle's face and muttered something to her about having wanted to see the cat. A worried Gayle *felt Elena's forehead with her hand. She sent her straight upstairs with a kiss, and told her to get into bed, concerned the night chill would make her bug even worse.*

Elena woke up next morning and beside her, on the pillow, lay a playing card with a fancy back. The king of hearts? She had no idea where it came from. She yawned and sat up. A jolt went through her body as memories flooded back from the night before. The door creaked and it opened slowly. Gayle came in.

'I've let you sleep in, sweetheart, but you should know that... you see... this morning the hospital rang and... it's incredible...' Gayle's face broke into a wide smile. 'She's going to be okay.'

Tears sprang into Elena's eyes. She hugged Gayle, who had rushed over. The two of them held each other tightly, rocking from side to side. Mummy wasn't going to die! Daddy wasn't going to be alone. Everything would be all right for Blossom, Bubbles and Buttercup.

Bumper. The crystal ball. The fortune teller. She remembered it all now.

'Miracles do happen!' continued Gayle. 'I told you she was strong. The doctors could hardly believe it!'

'When exactly did she wake up?' asked Elena in a small voice.

'Funny you should ask that – exactly on the stroke of midnight.'

Slowly, Elena nodded, accepting the truth. The deal she made had done its work.

Elena had saved her mummy! Pure joy filled her heart. Yet it lay in an icy pool of terror that would bide its time until Elena turned thirty. Although, that was years and years into the future. She could hardly imagine being that old. Gayle shuffled uncomfortably on the bed. 'Do... do you remember much about last night, love?'

Elena kept quiet. No one must ever find out about the promise. Mummy would blame herself for Elena's shortened life. Her parents would be so upset. As for the warning the fortune teller had issued, about making a pact with dark forces... Elena wouldn't think about that. She wouldn't.

'*That lady was very kind to bring you back,*' said Gayle. '*An odd sort, though. She passed me that playing card after you went upstairs and told me to give it to you. Then she said I should visit my dentist.*' *Gayle broke eye contact.* '*But you slipping out alone, to go onto the common, isn't something we need to worry your parents about, not right now...*'

Gayle left to make Elena's favourite chocolate spread on toast. Her last words were about Lucy, Elena's best school friend who had rung earlier. Her gran had just found out she'd won big on the lottery.

25

ELENA

Elena stared at the ground, between her legs, shaking as she zoned back into the present, sitting on the steps leading to the Sacré Coeur, with Rory's hand, warm and reassuring, in hers. It must have slid in whilst she was talking about her childhood.

'You're not ill, then,' said Rory, his voice scratchy as if the words had left a mark.

Elena tilted her head. 'Why would I be?'

'Your attitude seemed to change... You becoming less careful... after that doctor's appointment you had the day before we went to the pool. You didn't mention what it was about – and why should you?' he added.

'Rory, it was for a cervical screening. I didn't think you'd want to hear of its ins and out – literally.' Through the dim light, they both managed a smile and Rory held her hand even more tightly. But Elena's face soon became as dark as the Parisian sky again. 'I never told anyone the truth about that night on the common. My parents would have been furious about me creeping out like that and talking to a stranger. Gayle would have got into trouble and... Mum and Dad would have also been so sad at the idea of their little girl making such a pact, whether... whether they believed it was true or not, because I did.' She side-eyed Rory. Did he think her foolish, delusional? His face was impossible to read, like a plain book cover with no fancy font or illustration.

'I found out more details in the following weeks that only confirmed everything that had happened,' she said quickly. 'Mum's condition had deteriorated badly. And then, five minutes before midnight, she went into cardiac arrest and needed CPR. As the clock's hand turned to twelve, the doctors were about to call an end to their efforts when Mum took a deep breath and came back – on her own, the staff said. Medical staff, Dad, Gayle, they talked about what happened as some miracle. Then Lucy's gran winning the lottery and coming into big money, in accordance with what the fortune teller had mentioned, enforced my belief that the deal I'd made was real. As did Gayle going to the dentist – it turned out she had the early stages of oral cancer. It sounds stupid all these years later, but if you'd been there, Rory... People always told me I was a sensible girl. Down-to-earth. I kept my room tidy, almost too much so, my parents said – and I saved my pocket money apart from buying books. I didn't just make up what happened and—'

'Whoa!' Rory held up his free hand. 'You don't have to justify your story, Elena, not to me.'

'I don't?' she croaked.

He shrugged as if it was obvious. 'Of course not. Never. Nothing's proved wrong until there is evidence against it.'

'You don't think I'm as crazy as Carl with his flat earth theory?' she said in a barely audible voice.

'No way. This is completely different and based on personal experience. I doubt Carl's ever chartered a spaceship and seen the proof against his theory for himself. Whereas you were there that night, it's not hearsay. This doesn't mean I believe the outcome of what you said happened is set in stone.'

'That... I'll die?'

Rory hugged himself. It was cold. That must have been why he couldn't reply straight off. 'Yeah. I find it hard to accept that some stranger... some mystical power... would perform the good act of saving your mum, only to take a different life instead and take you onto – what did the fortune teller call it? *The next stage of our world* – as some punishment. And dark forces involved? I don't know... There are lots of good, natural forces out there too, counteracting any bad.'

Elena leaned forwards.

'If you nurture a plant, say – feed it, give it water – your kind act will be paid back with beautiful flowers. And Pilot fish keep sharks clean of parasites and in return, the shark wards off predators. I learnt that once, when I went snorkelling. All I mean is... I hear what you're saying, I'd be bricking it too, but... Perhaps going onto "the next stage of our world" doesn't mean death. Maybe the outcome of this deal isn't what you've always thought. This fortune teller did make sure you got home safely, after all. If it was a life for a life, why not just take yours then and there? Why let you live until thirty?'

Elena had never thought about that.

'All kinds of beneficial deals are made in nature. Like bacteria living in our guts. They help us digest food and we effectively feed them. It's called mutualism and it helps our planet thrive.' He looked sheepish. 'Sorry. Going off on a tangent here...'

'Is it like me letting you live in my home? You repay that by bringing in stick insects, eating my biscuits and relegating me to the kitchen when your elderly football buddy comes around?'

'Exactly.'

Tentatively, they smiled at each other once more.

'Am I being a dick again?' he said. 'I totally get why you're so fucking worried. I'm just trying to give a different perspective. Not saying I'm right.'

Her body relaxed further as he pushed her arm playfully. Rory jerked his head towards the bottom of the steps. 'All of this is why the fortune teller, at the underground station, freaked you out?'

'She was wearing purple, like the woman I made a deal with.'

'This promise you made also explains why, a few months ago, you started to take more care, putting bolts on your door and taping down the rug by the office entrance?'

Elena simply stared back.

'Then what made you change and become so careless very recently? Like not listening to every bit of bungee jump guidance, or that date with—'

'Several reasons – one being you. The adventurous life you lead inspired me. Then there's Brandy and Snap, who shed their skins... I felt tired of the Elena who'd been living her life in the shadows. I long for a sense of renewal. To be honest, Rory, what have I got to lose? You want proof of my looming death day? I've been sent clear signs that my promise is going to be called in: that firework nearly exploding in my chest, almost slipping on Gary's coffee and cracking open my head, and that man diving on top of me in the pool... Three near misses in such a short space of time.'

'Near misses or coincidences?' he asked.

'But three, Rory? That firework could have instantly killed me.'

Rory stood up and paced up and down as a mime artist started his act several steps away.

Elena got to her feet too. 'You think I've lost it, right? It doesn't bother me. I know what I know.'

He stopped in front of her. 'I get that there are things in this life that we can't always explain. I still leave Mum's favourite chocolate bar at her grave and I swear she's there, laughing in the way Dad says she used to when he showed his disgust at her liking peanuts in nougat.' His shoulders bobbed up and down. 'We need to look at the facts. Find out more about them. I like my statistics, my figures. I deep dive with research. Let's do that. Track down evidence. Go right back to that night in... 2004, right? Let's speak to your old neighbour first. I for one would also like to track down this fortune teller. If she did make that deal with you, I'd let her know how deeply she's affected your life.' He coloured up.

'Visit Gayle? Try to find out more?' A fizz, ever so small, ever so tiny, built in Elena's chest in reaction to his practical attitude, him taking her seriously. Was that fizz... hope?

'Does she still live next door to your parents?'

'Yes, Gayle's in her seventies now. Widowed.'

'Let's go over and see her, Monday after we leave the office.'

That would work. Her parents would be in Manchester city centre. For months they'd been looking forward to a musical set in the eighties and had booked the matinee, to be followed by dinner. She didn't want them asking questions.

'In the meantime, let's research fortune tellers,' continued Rory. 'In fact, I've come up with a good first step.' He took out his phone and tapped away. Scrolled for several moments, reading, then showed Elena the screen. 'Apparently purple is a common colour worn by psychics and fortune tellers. It's supposed to represent calm and spiritual awareness. It might mean nothing that the woman we just saw wore purple too. It doesn't necessarily have to be a sign linking the present with twenty years ago.'

Elena exhaled and handed back his phone. 'You're really up

for doing this? We've not got long left, what with my birthday being two weeks today. December is such a busy time of year. You'll want to shop for your dad and—'

'Hey, that's plenty of time. You and I, we're used to working late, to thinking out of the box and surfing the internet for relevant data.'

Elena looked up towards the Sacré Coeur, lost for a moment in its serenity, its understated grandeur. For over a hundred years it had stayed steadfast, despite the riots and wars; it had remained on this hill, peacefully overlooking the chaos.

Elena could do this.

They both sat down again. 'Okay. Let's enjoy tomorrow and then, Monday, get on with it. I trust in my heart that what ten-year-old me experienced was true, but that doesn't mean I can't fight for my future. I... I wouldn't change a thing, though, you know? My life for twenty more years with Mum? I'd do it again in a heartbeat.'

They sat in silence for a while.

'Sooo, I inspired you to be more careless – or perhaps adventurous is a better word,' he said and gave her a smug look.

Elena groaned. 'God, I'm never going to hear the end of this.' The mime artist acted out being a marionette with broken strings, and she moved closer to Rory and bumped her arm against his. 'I may be a broken biscuit, and I've fallen apart lately, but that's okay. I'll find my inner strength again by facing my fears and the past head on. Thanks for helping me do this.'

Rory got to his feet and went off to find a couple of takeaway coffees. Elena stared at the horizon before her, the man-made view, with its lit-up buildings, as beautiful as any sunset. She'd done it. Shared her secret. A weight lifted from her, like dense fog evaporating, water drop by water drop, taking with it the chill, leaving her bones and her heart to warm.

She turned round to watch Rory leave, coat collar up like an eighties band member. Elena smiled, but then she sat very still.

Huh?

Noooo...

Mum's words came back to her, from the last Moussaka Monday evening. *You'll meet someone special and open up, and I think you'll find that means you're in love.*

No, that would be ridiculous. Elena and Rory? They were like two completely mismatched biscuit ingredients, like chocolate and chilli. She'd never understood the appeal of that combination. Just because Elena had spoken her truth to Rory didn't mean he was special to her – even though he'd brought a sense of stability into her home these last few weeks, with his cooking, his singing, simply with his presence. Elena had seen him through different eyes. His love for sharing facts represented a passion for knowledge; it actually wasn't boasting or mansplaining, and he'd shown a vulnerability around losing a parent... When she was with him, Elena enjoyed a sense of calm and trust she'd not experienced with anyone since leaving home; not really enjoyed since she was ten. But she wasn't in love with him. Imagine living the rest of your life with someone who wore your fancy dressing gown better than you; who treated condiments as if they – not the food – were the main attraction; who made you do a silly dance in the office, and sang the same song night after night, on repeat. And who liked pickles. Elena gave a giggle.

Christ.

She sounded about sixteen. Elena didn't do giggles. Not unless she was drunk and listening to Gary sing karaoke. She sucked in her cheeks, trying to stop herself creating fantasies... of her fingers running through Rory's wavy hair, then undoing one of his stylish belts, whilst looking into that caring face of his, that stared back with equal desire; of sensing that protective instinct he had that had made him take in Brandy and Snap – and that had saved Elena's life three times.

The horizon became blurry. Her throat ached.

Mum *was* right.

Elena had left it until two weeks before her death day to realise that the most precious gem of a man had been sitting in her office day in, day out.

Oh Rory.

Rory Bunker.

Her absolute nemesis at times!

The love thing that she really, really wanted had been in her life all along.

Yet it had been invisible to her, despite the brightly coloured clothes and extroverted dance.

A lump rose in her throat.

Elena sat, digesting the revelation.

She couldn't say anything. He'd only cringe, especially now he knew her deepest secret. Privately he must think her a joke, and who would blame him? Their friendship was too precious to ruin. Telling him would tear their easy camaraderie apart. What if they didn't make up in time, before her birthday? Elena wiped her eyes. It was enough that she'd finally recognised and felt true love. Utter gratitude filled her for that. This true love had been skulking in the shadows this last year, waiting, watching for the moment it could boldly walk into the sunlight. Rory moving in, Elena's three accidents, her changing attitude to safety and confiding in him about the fortune teller... it had taken these huge events to make her face how she felt.

Yet, deep down, she'd *known*, Elena could see that now. She'd been the one to suggest Rory have the desk opposite hers, and there was that time she'd made a paper plane and aimed it at his head. They couldn't agree over the pitch for a product and were both doing more research. A playful gesture she'd never made to anyone before. And Rory had lost a dear relative at the beginning of the summer. The upset he tried to hide in the office had completely affected her focus and... it had hurt. Then there was the karaoke. Gary had been on at her for ages to arrange it, but she'd balked at getting up on stage. However, once he'd paired her and Rory together, for some reason those nerves lessened.

A cough behind her. Rory sat down. He passed her a takeout cup.

'You talked about being a broken biscuit,' he said. 'Tell me, are you one of our employer's vanilla sandwich fingers, or a chocolate-covered oatie one?' The corner of his mouth twitched and a deep yearning rose inside her, wild and unharnessed, to kiss those lips.

Instead, with an innocent air, she flipped the finger at him as her answer and privately adored his soft laugh whilst she sipped her coffee.

26

RORY

Rory sat perched on the edge of the bed. He and Elena had adjoining rooms, and they'd left the door open so that they could shout through and talk. However, they'd hardly said a word on the way back to the hotel and Elena had gone straight to bed, wanting to read a book. Rory understood. After the distressing confrontation with that fortune teller, after reliving the past, she must have been exhausted.

A grunt came through the adjoining door – Elena was clearly asleep. He felt wide awake and hadn't even got undressed yet. Rory studied his surroundings, focusing on the details, hoping it would stop his mind racing. The bedcover was decadent, velvet and burgundy, and it matched the heavy curtains. The oak furniture had carved legs and on the opposite side of the room was a drop-front desk with a floral, ceramic plaque on the front. On top of it was a bowl of pot pourri, spicing up the room with its heavy floral scent. A large mirror dominated the wall above the desk, its gilt frame glinting in the dim light. Next to the entrance door to his room, on the left, hung an oil painting of Montmartre, with artists sitting in front of easels and people nearby, outside bars, drinking red wine. The phone to call down to reception was an antique black candlestick one.

He stood up. It was no good. Rory couldn't get Elena's childhood story out of his head. It erased the beautiful images that should have been there, like the magical skyline of Paris or the latte art in the café they'd visited tonight. Each of their drinks had a chocolate sprinkling of a balloon on top, in the shape of a heart. Despite their fervent denial, the server thought they were a couple, as did the tired-looking woman who came in off the street, intent on selling Rory a red rose to give to Elena. Elena had blushed and, on impulse, he'd bought the flower. No, instead of all that, Rory only saw, in his head, a little girl in Disney pyjamas, out in the woods, scared, on her own, promising away her life, in exchange for her mum's.

A ball of fire sparked in his stomach. How *could* the fortune teller have let a child make such a deal? How cruel to let young Elena – older Elena, too – believe she only had two more decades to live? Yet then see that child home safely? It didn't add up.

He picked up his journal and phone and headed down the winding staircase to the reception. The owner, Jacques, was handing over to the night porter. It was one in the morning.

'*Bonsoir*,' said Rory, and he attempted a smile. 'Any chance the bar is still open?'

The night porter shook his head, but Jacques studied his guest. '*Oui*. I was just heading that way myself. One last glass before bed?'

Rory followed him to the left of reception and into the dining area, next to the glassed-off courtyard. Rory tapped into his phone. Let the research begin. So… Fortune tellers were different from psychics in that they might tell you what could happen in the future, or if luck was heading your way, whereas psychics might also tell you why. Mediums were not the same either, as they used a person's spiritual energy to predict events. Some so-called fortune tellers simply used their skills to help you reflect on your life and understand it, not proclaiming to know what was coming your way. Rory scrolled further... Crystal balls, palms, dreams, tea leaves, cards... He rubbed his head. Elena was one of the most grounded people he knew, so if she genuinely still believed her life was under threat, twenty years on from her mum's accident, then there was no way he'd dismiss her story outright. However, sometimes there was what looked like concrete evidence for the wildest theories. Like the supposed Illuminati existing and being linked to government organisations. If you spelled illuminati backwards and put it into a search engine, the result was quite, well, illuminating.

Rory rubbed his head again as Jacques brought over two small glasses, a spirit bottle and a carafe of water.

'May I, monsieur?' he asked and pointed to the seat opposite.

'Please. Call me Rory.' He tossed down his phone.

'You can't come to France and not have Pastis.' He poured the spirit into the two glasses and when he topped them up with water, the liquid turned white.

Rory raised a glass in the air. 'Cheers.'

'*Santé*,' said Jacques and took a mouthful.

Aniseed? Rory hadn't tasted that since he was a child. He coughed. 'Um, very nice.'

Jacques bellowed with laughter. 'It grows on you.' He yawned. 'You can't sleep? Is there anything else your room needs? An extra blanket perhaps?'

'Got any tranquilisers?' He took another glug. Jacques topped up both their glasses.

'You are in marvellous Paris with... may I say it... a beautiful woman. What is the matter, my friend? You are on holiday, *non*?'

Rory nodded.

'Affairs of the heart? I see you've booked two rooms. Perhaps you wish for more than friendship? Are you secretly *amoureux de...*'

Rory looked confused.

'I mean... in love with her?' Jacques said.

'No!' he said. This Jacques was worse than Tahoor.

The man gave a chuckle. 'You have to excuse me. My wife is always telling me off for being too outspoken.'

'How long have you been married?'

'Twenty-nine years. We met at the student protests, in the mid-eighties, never imagining we would one day be upstanding hotel owners, with responsibilities and a reputation to keep. We were going to change the world back then.' He shook his head in an affectionate manner, as if sitting opposite himself and his wife all that time ago. 'Are you in love, *mon gars*? Someone else back home has attracted your attention?'

'Not at all. I don't think I ever have been.'

Jacques' eyes bulged and he put down his glass, loosened his shirt and rolled up his sleeves further. He leant forwards. 'Impossible.'

'Of course you'd say that. You're French,' said Rory, a twinkle in his eye. Jacques hesitated and then burst out laughing again, a friendly roll of humour that filled the room.

'*Bon*, of course, and you English eat cucumber sandwiches with the King,' he said, a mischievous glint in his eye. 'Never in love? Are you sure?'

'Well, how do you know?'

'That is like asking how do I know how to breathe? It's not something you consciously think about, and that's the point. You simply wake up one day and realise how much this person has become part of your life, that they are in your mind every day,

every hour; their problems, their successes, their amazing qualities, flaws, the mysterious parts of them... You accept it all, as you
accept yourself. The person you are in love with is like... home.
They are your secure place. Your happy refuge. Your escape from
the world.' He raised his hands in the air. 'For me, home is not a
building, it's not a town... it's a person who makes you feel you
are exactly where you should be, when you are together.' He
raised his eyebrows hopefully, but Rory shrugged. 'It hit me, one
day, when we went to the Eiffel Tower. We stood underneath,
eating ice cream, and Michelle was so keen to go up to its top.
Neither of us ever had before and I'm afraid of heights. But then
and there, looking at her excited face, the mouth that kissed me
so gently, but was equally forceful shouting at rallies, the fiery,
intelligent eyes... I'd do anything to make her happy, to keep her
safe. I knew her happiness and safety came before mine. I'd
never felt like that about anyone before.'

'You went up the tower?' asked Rory, sitting up straighter
now.

'Scariest day of my life.' He lowered his voice. 'Not that she
ever knew that.'

'But what about hearts and flowers, a fanfare of music,
candlelit moments, fireworks and Cupid with his bow...?'

'Mere frivolous decorations to what really matters. Although
there was a song I found myself singing, ever since I met her.
"Venus" by an English group, Banana... Bananarama. It was
released by them in the mid-eighties and the lyrics resonated.
We were in a bar, after the demo where I first met her, with a
crowd of people, and it came on and we all sang along. Ever
since that night, now and then, I've sung it when alone. Michelle
is my Venus – was from that first moment. My goddess of love.'
Jacques knocked back his drink and got to his feet. 'Bon, I am
rambling. Pastis always loosens my tongue. I would be no match

as a spy for your British James Bond.' He pushed over the bottle. 'On the house. Sleep well, *mon ami.*' Jacques held out his hand and Rory shook it, hardly able to move, acting as if on automatic. Eventually, he reached for another Pastis. Then another.

Sunday 8th December

With the help of 4 glasses of Pastis – Jacques is wrong: it does not grow on you and now my mouth tastes of moth balls – and after 1 hour of examining the evidence, until 2.30 a.m., I crawl into bed and for the 100th time, mull over everything Jacques said.

Elena has... let me see... at least 6 outstanding qualities! She is hardworking, funny, kind, generous, intelligent, and has incredible taste in silk dressing gowns.

3 outstanding flaws – she doesn't reach out for help enough, plays 'gentle jazz' (aka KILL ME NOW music) and doesn't like pickles.

Also, she carries 1 big mystery – where does she disappear to, upstairs in the house?

1st epiphany – I would do anything to make her happy. Even eat pineapple on pizza.

2nd epiphany – I would do anything to keep her safe. Like finding an answer to what happened that night, in the woods, in 2004.

3rd epiphany. Oh God. I even have a song. 'Ocean Eyes'. I've sung it every night since working at Bingley Biscuits. On the very first day of my first contract, Elena's eyes struck me as being so very much like the ocean, clear and blue... and yet, when I peered in, when she was earnestly talking, I saw trouble and sadness – as if a shipwreck were hidden in the depths, hiding a tragic story; a shipwreck that also held the most precious treasure.

4th epiphany. A sense of home. I've felt that ever since we've worked together. I didn't know that's what it was, but now I recognise it. With Elena, wherever we are, I feel enveloped in a warm, safe feeling that I won't be made fun of – unless I deserve it! – or hurt; that... yes, Jacques is right... that I'm where I should be. I look forward to seeing her every morning. It makes me feel as if the day will be okay, or that if it isn't, no matter, I've got Elena to laugh or cry or talk things over with. I don't think I appreciated this before the last few weeks. Like the time I found out, whilst at work, that Dad's cousin, Tasha, had passed. It was at the beginning of the summer. She was close to him and Uncle Tony, being an only child and living near them when she was little. Tasha loved Mum too and was thrilled to have a woman near her own age in the family, and they became the best of friends. I knew Tasha was ill but she'd always been so tough over the years, telling me other children were saps for teasing me for having no mum; pushing Dad into dating several years after Mum had gone, saying Linda wouldn't want to see him on his own. The tears ran down my face at my desk in the office and I wiped them away as discreetly as I could. Tasha had told me stories about my mum when it was too raw for Dad, like how Mum had asked for a swimming with sharks experience for her twenty-fifth birthday and my dad bought her a session at the local aquarium. My grandparents went to watch and she said it was her happiest day ever, third to getting married and having me. Tasha had teased her, saying anyone with any sense would have just asked for a spa weekend. Elena came over to my desk – the only person who had spotted my upset. She put a hand on my shoulder. She didn't do any of that stuff like starting sentences with at least, or going on about how Tasha was no longer suffering. Elena simply said she was there if I needed to talk and then fetched us coffees, and the world began to feel okay again.

And breathe... But I can't; my chest's bursting with the 1 big conclusion from all of this. HOLY CRAP, JACQUES, HOLY PASTIS! Is Rory Bunker in love, for the 1st time ever, and with the most unlikely person?

No. No way. It doesn't add up, on paper. Gather the statistics and there would be too many differences... right? Yet you only have to look at science to see how opposite charges attract...

Rory tossed down his journal and held his head in his hands, worried that if he didn't physically hold his skull together, it would explode. There was no denying it. Rory was in charming Paris, with its cobbled streets and twinkling lights, with its buskers and mime artists, and he *was*... Rory Bunker was *amoureux d'Elena Swan*.

The way her nose twitched before she laughed, those exquisite ocean eyes that rippled with every emotion; that intense look on her face, at work, when she was putting together a pitch, full of know-how; the way her blonde hair bounced up and down when she talked excitedly about her ideas for marketing the latest product; how Elena chatted when she thought no one was listening to Brandy and Snap, gently, respectfully, acknowledging the sentience in them; her eyebrows that said more than a million words if she was upset, excited, or thought him to be an idiot. Rory grinned to himself. Like every time he made her do the Good Times Dance. As for those lips that stood for no nonsense, that could be so sympathetic, lips he longed to kiss, and that laugh that lifted the day, like the catchiest Top Ten hit, and the curvy waist, those long legs and... The thoughts and emotions that he'd harboured for so long, without understanding them for what they were, overwhelmed him. Now it made sense why such primeval pain had cut through his body at the sight of the firework in her chest, and why he'd not hesitated about pulling her to safety in the pool, even though the diver could have hit him with full force. It explained why this job at Bingley Biscuits had felt like no other – like sun on a cold day, summer holidays, like Friday afternoons, and freshly baked cookies, and not just because the company made biscuits! His sport-loving friends hadn't been able understand why he'd given up the freedom of contracting to sign permanently with one company. Rory hadn't been able to give them a good reason.

But now he understood. It was because of her.

He punched the duvet. However right this felt, it was wrong. Elena must never know. He couldn't risk ruining their friendship. Right now, above everything else, Elena needed a good mate. Opening up would make her embarrassed. There was no way his feelings would be reciprocated. She'd laugh at the idea of them being a couple, just as much as Gary or any of their colleagues would.

Rory lay on his front and put his pillow over his head. Elena was like no person he'd ever met. Independent, strong, determined... and yet troubled by a secret in a way that went against the everyday logic and reason that had always flowed, in such large volumes, through her veins. He'd taken her at face value this last year, until her behaviour changed, and he moved in, and until she'd told him about her past.

He'd loved her before, when he'd only seen her surface.

Now he loved her even more.

Oh, the irony. Oh, the bad timing. Elena was a woman he'd waited his whole life for – a woman who believed, with every fibre of her being, that she'd be dead by Christmas.

27

ELENA

Giving off a buttery aroma, the croissant melted in her mouth, like no pastry she'd eaten in England. The coffee was smooth and rich, comforting. With her bobbed hair scraped back in a short ponytail, Elena sat opposite Rory in the hotel's restaurant. He seemed quite chummy with the owner, Jacques, who'd insisted they were welcome to leave their bags there all day and pick them up before going to the airport.

'Bit of a bromance going on there,' she said and reached for more jam.

'Far safer falling in love with someone you aren't attracted to,' Rory replied.

For some reason his smile didn't seem as if it came from the heart. Perhaps he really wanted a relationship with Izzy, his mountain-biking friend, the one he had casual dates with. Although he hadn't talked about her for a while now. Discomfort rose within Elena's chest at the idea of the two of them getting close, however unlikely that might be.

'I've planned out today but is there anything you'd especially like to see?' she asked and wiped crumbs from around her mouth.

'I wanted to say, first... do you want to talk any more about last night? Or would you rather I didn't mention the fortune teller, or any of that, until we're back in England? What I mean is... I'm here... as a mate...' His cheeks flushed.

He really had become the best friend ever. All the more reason to keep her emotions – and desires – to herself. How she'd love to spend the day ambling through the sparkling, Christmassy boulevards, her arm snugly around his waist, leaning in every now and again for a kiss underneath the striking architecture and gaze of approving Parisians, the tension building as they held hands on the plane, then the rush for the bedroom as soon as they put the key in her front door, back in Cariswell...

Cut! No point playing that movie, even if it was make-believe. 'No. I'm okay. Thanks. Let's just have fun today.'

He put down his cup. 'I did have something planned – for you – but it doesn't seem appropriate now. You organise things so well, it's better we follow your schedule.'

He had? A sizzling sensation shot across her chest. Previous boyfriends bought her flowers and chocolates, but rarely surprised her with holidays or days out. Yet who could blame them? She'd always kept partners at a distance, not physically but when it came to sharing desires for a future together because a voice, at the back of her mind, would tell Elena not to promise boyfriends something she might never be able to deliver.

Rory was different from the first day he walked into the office. He'd picked up a rose gold pearl bracelet from her desk tidy, half-hidden amongst a pile of safety pins. Elena had bought it on a whim at the local market, but it didn't feel like her. He'd slipped it on his wrist and said it was cool. Jokingly, she'd told him to keep it. He gave the thumbs up and wore it for the rest of the day. Quickly she'd worked out that Rory was truly authentic and didn't care what other people thought of him – a rare beast in a profession where the focus was on image and projection. Working on products had always made Elena conscious of the look she projected. A sensible, down-to-earth one, she hoped. Meeting the fortune teller, and making that promise, had been a real event. However, she'd experienced a sense of shame, over the years, at what others might think if they knew she believed such a preposterous-sounding thing. This had made her determined not to be considered remotely frivolous or flighty.

'What was your idea?' she asked.

He broke eye contact. 'Nothing. Honestly. I'm sure yours are far better.'

'Rory Bunker! Don't make me lob this croissant at your ear.'

'It's boomerang shaped, would only come back.' He gave one of those lopsided smiles of his, and like the butter on the dish in front of her, Elena's heart melted, just a little. 'Okay. To visit the famous Père Lachaise cemetery. It's iconic.' His speech sped up. 'It's one hundred and ten acres big and it has three and a half million visitors a year, with eight hundred bodies buried there. I thought you'd like it because we'd visit the graves of some fantastic writers, like Oscar Wilde, Proust, and Molière.'

She loved the slant of his mouth, the flame in his eyes when he teased, the lanky build on which clothes hung so well, the strong hands that suited fancy rings. But most of all, she loved Rory's *way* – his thoughtfulness, that kind nature, like choosing a place to visit specifically to do with her interest in reading, when he could have chosen a fashion museum, to suit him. He'd missed a much-awaited concert once to go out for a drink with Gary, who'd had a bad argument with his husband.

'The cemetery has monuments, a chapel, and an ossuary... If

burial plots are not renewed then the remains are bagged up and
stored there whilst the plot is leased out to someone else.' Rory
cleared his throat. 'Sorry... is this too much, in the light of your
looming birthday and—'

'No!' Her eyes shone. 'Oscar Wilde? I love his novel *De
Profundis*. He was banned from writing stories during his spell in
jail but was allowed to write letters – so he wrote this fifty thou-
sand-word one!' It was addressed to his former lover and reading
it always gave Elena equal pain and pleasure, never having experienced such a romantic attachment herself... Not until now – if
that's what this thing with Rory was, this compulsion to be with
him, desire to touch him.

They left their bags at the hotel. Jacques winked at Rory
before waving them off. A wintry bite still nipped the air by the
time they reached Père Lachaise. No matter; they both wore their
berets and thick scarves. Rory wore bell bottom jeans and his
blue and pink, tie dye padded anorak. Maps in hands, they
walked up and down the cobblestone lanes, with towering trees
either side, in awe of the well-tended tombs and busts and carv-
ings. Rory had done his research and said broken columns
commemorated people who'd died before twenty or suffered a
violent death. They got lost twice and followed a crowd to find
Oscar Wilde's tomb, outstanding with its Egyptian vibe. Elena
linked her arm with Rory's, only to keep warm, she reassured
him, as they came to Marcel Marceau's grave. Apparently he'd
taught Michael Jackson to moonwalk. She had to take a photo
for her dad.

The cemetery smelled of woody oils emanating from the
trees, of dewy grass and lattes carried by tourists in takeaway
cups. Elena took sideways glances at Rory as they headed for
Proust's memorial, and he reeled off more facts. What a zest for

life her colleague had. Gary jokingly called him a fun fact nerd once, knowing Rory wouldn't care. That banter fuelled their friendship and there was no denying, anyway, that Gary found Rory's revelations fascinating, such as how, before rubbers were invented, stale bread was used as erasers.

Proust's black marble tombstone was more understated than Wilde's, apart from the red heart-shaped bauble topped with fake snow that someone had laid on it. Rory looked up from his phone. 'Proust wrote a novel called *Remembrance of Things Past* – the longest novel in the world, with a word count of almost 1.3 million. One of its sentences contains nine hundred and fifty-eight words. Would you like me to buy it for your birthday?' he joked. 'I mean...' His face dropped.

'It's okay,' she said quietly.

They carried on walking and came to a bench. She tugged his sleeve and they sat down. 'I mean it. It is okay... Somehow, finally saying out loud, to another person, what happened all those years ago has made me... less afraid. So you can mention my birthday.' Elena couldn't help leaning forwards and kissing him on the cheek. A swift recovery followed and she pushed his shoulder. 'Thanks matey, for being there for me.'

A glint in his eyes died with her words. He must have come up with another joke and decided against it.

'In that case, I've got a proposition for you,' he said. 'Neither of us can predict what is going to happen on your birthday. Therefore, why don't we make plans to celebrate it, regardless? Throw a party at your house? Invite Tahoor, your parents, Gary and Diego and...'

'Are you mad? What if something bad were to happen? I don't want to traumatise the people I care about most.'

Rory kicked a small stone with the heel of his cowboy boot.

'What I admire most about you, Elena, is that you never give up. At work you sink your teeth into a pitch and won't let go until you've got your point across. The Elena I know isn't just going to sit and wait for her birthday, kowtowing to the prophecy that's lurked in her life for so long. We've got just under two weeks to find answers – and to plan you the best party ever. To hell with the *what ifs*, to hell with the *a deal is a deal*. The worst thing that can happen is that you give up. Your mum wouldn't want that. Nor would the ten-year-old girl who did everything she could to save her. Despite fearing what might lay ahead, that girl made the most of every day, every year, every opportunity, and got you to this point. You owe it to her to fight this, Elena. You and I, we're going to find that fortune teller and get some answers.'

Elena sat up rigid, straight, solid, as if her bones were made of iron instead of calcium.

She lifted her chin. He was right.

'Okay. You're on,' she beamed. 'Why don't we get something to eat and plan the food for my birthday meal? I'll draw up a list of guests. Perhaps we'll play party games.' Weirdly, she was more excited for this potentially last birthday than any from previous years, those having always felt like a countdown. 'We also need to discuss Brandy and Snap. That bigger tank is arriving this week. Could you message Julian and ask about the best accessories and...'

Suddenly the world seemed full of possibilities.

The cemetery was so peaceful, with birdsong providing the soundtrack to the excited noise of tourists and cameras clicking. In Père Lachaise, death was something to be celebrated, in terms of the lives of people buried there. She stared at a small opal ring on her middle finger. It had belonged to her gran. Elena also needed to write a plan for how she wanted to be buried. She'd want a non-religious funeral and someone to read a wonderful poem she'd once read about the dead person being a ship disappearing on a horizon, with mourners waving goodbye, whilst people, out of sight, far away, on the other side, excitedly waved hello. As for the music... 'Somewhere Over the Rainbow' by Eva Cassidy. *The Wonderful Wizard of Oz* had been a favourite read as a child. Dad used to do a brilliant impression of the scarecrow.

A sense of calm filled her. A sense of taking control. Tears streamed down her cheeks.

'Elena, what's wrong?' asked Rory, face crumpled with concern.

'Nothing, they're happy tears. It's so good to plan as if I'm mistress of my own destiny – for the very first time.' She wiped her eyes. They both leaned close. Closer still. Ba boom, ba boom, her heart thumped and she became hyper-focused on his lips. Hers parted slightly as their eyes met and—

'*Monsieur?*'

Elena pulled away. They both looked up at a sylphlike young woman with bright red lipstick. Her raven hair was styled in a chic pixie cut and she wore a black trench coat, with a Chanel scarf and a patent crossbody bag. She smelt of expensive perfume and dropped her cigarette, stubbing it out with her heel.

'*Bonjour monsieur,*' the woman said, ignoring Elena. '*Je m'appelle—*'

'Um... *désolé*... sorry... but I am *Anglais*,' he said and stood up.

'English?' She looked him up and down. 'I am surprised. You are so stylish. But of course. That is why you have a... different vibe about you. Love your look. Fantastic jacket. Great cheekbones.'

'Pardon?' He looked puzzled.

'But I am being rude.' She smiled and held out her hand. 'Nicole Moreau. You live here?'

'No. Gets a bit busy at nights – you know, all those wandering souls. Although Jim Morrison is wild to hang out with.'

She hesitated and then laughter pealed across the cemetery. The woman took him by the elbow and guided him a couple of metres away and talked in an animated fashion. Rory shot Elena a look and then became more animated too. He touched this Nicole's arm, cackling really loudly at something she said. It didn't sound natural. Yet they'd really seemed to hit it off. And why wouldn't they? Both were gorgeous. Both had their whole lives stretching ahead of them. Thank goodness that woman had come along and saved Elena from the embarrassment of having kissed Rory. He would have been horrified. Perhaps she was an artist and wanted to paint him. The woman had been impressed with Rory's appearance.

Understandable.

Elena busied herself, studying the map. When she looked up, they seemed to be saying goodbye. The woman pressed what appeared to be a business card into his hand and kissed him on both cheeks.

Rory walked over to Elena in a daze. She felt sick. Nicole must have really made an impression.

'What was that about?' she asked in as disinterested a voice as possible.

'Don't laugh.'

She forgot Nicole for one moment and immediately wanted to chuckle. Elena reached out her hand and pulled him onto the bench.

'She's a model scout. Says I've got a really fresh look. Her agency has a client with a big show coming up. A designer who puts a bold twist on classic pieces. She says I'd be perfect and such exposure would quickly lead to me getting other assignments. Nicole wants me to email her some photos. Says my frame, my face, both are perfect.'

Elena took the card. Dubois Agency. She googled it and checked out the contact email address. The logo matched. It looked like this woman was kosher.

'You aren't laughing?' he said, and a bemused grin spread across his face. 'Wait until Gary finds out. He'll never be able to call me a nerd again.'

'But this is great, Rory. Doesn't surprise me. True style is about uniqueness, right? I've always seen that in you. Of course you were going to be spotted in Paris.'

'It's bonkers! I'm Rory Bunker, the solid statistics guy, the common sense Mancunian through and through.'

'Exactly. These models can earn thousands. What could be more common sense than enjoying the ride for a few years and building up savings? Aren't you in the least bit tempted?'

'I have a career.'

'One you could always come back to.'

'No. It's ridiculous. I wouldn't even know how to walk.' He stood up and strutted up and down, as if the cobblestone path was a runway and the tombs the audience. He had no idea how natural, how sexy he looked, oozing pure confidence. 'In any event, the show is on the twenty-first of December and I have a prior, very important, engagement.'

'It's only a birthday party.'

'It's much more than that,' he said, and those chestnut eyes looked firmly at her. 'And I don't know if modelling would make me feel as valued and inspired as my job in marketing.'

'Nicole was nice. You should keep in touch with her, at least. You two looked good together.'

Rory stared at her with an unfathomable expression that disappeared quickly. 'She was pretty cool. Smart too, she spoke brilliant English. I suppose it's not that far, to hop over the Channel, if I want to take her out for dinner. I did scoot over to Calais for kitesurfing once.'

Elena forced a smile. Thank God she hadn't made a move on Rory. He had clearly been immediately taken with the stylish French woman.

28

Rory lay on his bed in Elena's spare room and yawned. They'd got back a couple of hours ago, after an uneventful flight from Paris – unless you counted a baby in a Santa Claus baby grow projectile vomiting onto the flight attendant. Elena had stared intently at her lap during the take-off and landing, but no one else would have noticed the nervousness. How different from the flight yesterday. She'd hurried into the lounge to check on Brandy and Snap as soon as they walked through the front door. She couldn't stop laughing as Rory gently pushed her away, to get their full attention himself, as he talked about being scouted by a modelling agency. The stick insects remained suitably unimpressed. She bolted the front door after locking it, something she hadn't done in a while, then said goodnight to Rory, giving him a kiss on the cheek and thanking him for going to Paris with her.

Having just cleaned his teeth, Rory leant against the bed's headboard and swigged back a mouthful of water. He hadn't sung 'Ocean Eyes' tonight. His heart wasn't in it. Not after Elena had encouraged him to text Nicole as soon as they sat down in the lounge. They'd put the heating on high. Over the weekend, the temperatures had plummeted in Manchester, and the road outside was already icy. In front of the Christmas tree lights, they'd enjoyed mugs of gingerbread hot chocolate, with festive jazz playing in the background – a cosy, romantic scene for sure, if Elena hadn't been matchmaking him with someone else. A futile mission because the black of Nicole's eyes, whilst striking, was empty and lifeless compared to the enigmatic, vibrant blue of Elena's. Yet he'd played along and promised to contact the French woman. He was partly to blame for Elena thinking the two of them well-suited. He'd put on an act when talking to Nicole in the cemetery, pretending he was super happy and interested, because he didn't want Elena to guess his true feelings, not after he'd leaned in and almost kissed her. How lucky that Nicole had interrupted right at that moment, otherwise he'd have made a right fool of himself.

He stared at the ceiling and ran his hand over his cheek, where Elena had kissed it. The trip to Paris had been fun. He'd eaten great food, seen fabulous sights and been enormously flattered by Nicole's attention. More importantly, he'd admitted his true feelings for Elena, to himself at least, and respected the fact that she didn't feel the same. All in all, it had been a successful trip. He gave a deep sigh. Then why did his insides burn and twist, as if they'd somehow simultaneously been stirred with a hot rod and screwed into a tight ball?

Love.

Dad spoke once about how he'd never regretted meeting Mum, never regretted how losing her made the following years difficult to get through, especially Christmases, because the love he'd had when they were together made the suffering worth it. Rory saw now that he'd shied away from deep and meaningful relationships because he was afraid of going through the suffering Dad had endured. It was years before his dad had dated again and only recently that he'd formed a close, long-lasting, satisfying bond with another woman. But now Rory understood. That hurt was the price you paid for experiencing feelings and longings that would create the biggest drug cartel in the world, if they could just be bottled and marketed.

When Elena had kissed him on the cheek and called him matey, sitting on that bench in the cemetery, that 'm' word had sliced through his heart, leaving a raw, painful gash behind. How alive he'd felt at the touch of her lips on his skin, a rush that no future skydive could ever replicate. A wry smile crossed his face. Jacques had known the truth and collared Rory before he left, when they'd picked up their bags. Elena had gone to use the bathroom and Jacques patted Rory on the shoulder.

'Love is everything, *mon ami*. No one lies on their deathbed wishing they'd spent more hours at their computer. The most important thing is to be true to yourself and that means opening your eyes to the *people* you want to spend your life with. A great job, fancy clothes, a sports car, exotic holidays... None of it really matters. All that's on the surface.' Jacques had thumped his chest. 'What matters is what's inside this body that we discard on death, because that spirit, that emotion, is who we really are; it's what lasts forever.'

Under any other circumstances, Rory would have then and there declared his love for Elena and risked rejection. But he couldn't burden her with anything that might distract from their investigations. She'd lightened up since telling him about the fortune teller and seemed more relaxed than she ever had in the year he'd known her. It was wonderful to see. Rory mustn't jeopardise that.

He reached for his journal.

Sunday 8th December

I've sat here for 10 minutes, doodling sprigs of holly, but the numbers and facts won't come about the weekend in Paris. I've always found it strange, over the years, when people talk about diaries as if they were friends. However, now I get it. You are my confidante and my only option for sharing my truth.

I've never fallen in love before. Izzy is fun, clever, good company, but I don't feel anything deeper and it's obvious she only sees me as a good-time pal. It's an arrangement that's worked well and I've always thought a connection like that would be enough. The closest I've got to one of those relationships that I see amongst friends, or in movies, was with Antonia, three years ago. I met her family. She met Dad. We talked tentatively about the next steps... Moving in together, saving for a mortgage deposit. However, I always changed the subject when marriage came up. Antonia wasn't one for waiting around, so one night, in a restaurant, a big grin on her face, she knelt down, in front of the staff and customers, and asked me to marry her. She'd even bought a ring studded with emeralds, my favourite stone.

The humiliated expression on her face when I said no... I'll never forget it, along with her embarrassment as diners hastily turned away. Outside, in the street, she shouted, called me a classic male commitment-phobe and accused me of wasting her time. She wasn't wrong, but not for the reasons she believed. I wasn't afraid of marriage and kids, of signing a certificate to promise myself to one woman for the rest of my life, to look after her and let her look after me, to be part of a forever team... No, I was afraid of having all of that taken away from me, by an illness or accident, knowing the pain my dad had suffered. Guess I was a coward. Yet saying no was the right thing to do. The way I love Elena has proved that and gives me a strength I've never felt before. Antonia had so many attractive qualities but I didn't miss her on my sports trips abroad, didn't rush home from the office to be with her. Not in the way, before moving in with Elena, I'd jump out of bed and hurry into work, keen to see Elena roll those blue eyes at my pickle jar; to see her admire my latest outfit, or fire off marketing ideas; to chat to her about breaking news items.

It's a cruel blow that, now I've finally found true, compelling love and am ready to risk what Dad suffered, I can't say anything.

29

ELENA

Elena and Rory stood in the frosty staff car park and Rory went to take out his keys. It was dark now, unlike earlier when a few flakes of snow had fallen. Watching through the window, this afternoon, the office staff had been almost as excited about the festive weather as they'd been when Derek had brought in Christmas pudding-flavoured donuts last week. The board had eased off complaining about a lack of strategy to rebuild profits, and he was celebrating. Elena had been mesmerised by the snow that cheerfully tumbled down. Her wish had been granted! She'd actually got to see it again before her... Elena tightened her scarf, trying to block out the words *death day*. Following the weekend of travelling, she'd be glad to get back home and chill out – after she and Rory had visited Gayle. Mum had texted to say that the eighties musical had been fab and she and Dad were currently drinking cocktails in the Northern Quarter. Her mum had signed off with a string of emojis – a heart, microphone, music notes, cocktail glass and thumbs up. Emojis were small, fun, frivolous things, but if Mum had died back in 2004, the possibility of even one emoji from her mother now would have meant everything. Before putting away her phone, Elena ran her finger over the text.

Gary came out of the building and joined them, rubbing his goatee beard. 'I still can't take it in. Rory. You, scouted? Asked to model in Paris? It ain't right.'

'Is it so unbelievable?' Rory feigned indignation.

'Yeah,' replied Gary, deadpan, as he turned up his coat's collar. 'Although Diego won't be surprised. He's always said you dress with the flair of the fashionistas in Madrid. I could get jealous if you were real competition for him,' he added airily. 'But you're no match for my wit and knowledge of craft beers.'

'Then there's that small matter of me not being gay...'

Gary playfully swiped the air near Rory's chin and the two of them pretended to box.

'Ninety per cent of men called Gary who get into fights, lose,' said Rory, light on his feet but still nearly slipping over due to the ice.

Panting, Gary stopped. 'You made that statistic up!'

Rory's mouth twitched and he boxed the air again as Derek came out of the building. He adjusted his glasses and stood, anorak buttoned up, tight at the front, eyeing the other two men. 'Just because our department is going to be working on broken biscuits, doesn't mean I want staff with broken teeth and noses.'

Gary saluted him and stopped playfighting, along with Rory.

'Good work today, guys,' said Derek, waving goodbye in the air, above his head, as he passed them and walked into the distance. 'I'm really optimistic about this campaign,' he called.

Gary shivered and took out his car keys. 'Right. Got to go. Diego's not home for a couple of hours and I want to research cooking a traditional Spanish Christmas dinner to surprise him this Sunday, as we can't get to Toledo this year due to his work shifts.' He looked Rory up and down, shook his head again and sashayed off in an exaggerated catwalk style, with none of the natural panache Rory had.

The car fell silent as Rory drove Elena to Bridgwich to see Gayle. Elena hadn't slept well and was relieved, this morning, to see him out on the drive, unlocking his car. She stared out of the window, planning what she would say to her parents' neighbour. Far too quickly they arrived. Oh. How lovely! Snow was falling again! She zoned out, entranced by it. Then, heads ducked, they hurried up to Gayle's front drive. Elena nipped back to the car, briefly, to double-check she'd shut the passenger door properly, and then stood next to him.

'Ready?' asked Rory.

Elena exhaled. 'She's going to be completely baffled as to why I want to bring up an event that happened so long ago.'

'Does it matter what she thinks?'

Elena hesitated. No. This was a life and death matter. She pressed her thumb firmly on the bell. The door opened. Elena hadn't seen Gayle for a while. The beaded necklaces were still there, along with the pungent perfume and eyeliner, not as straight as years ago. The dyed brown hair was streaked with grey. Gayle's eyes lit up behind gold-rimmed glasses.

'Elena, dear. What a lovely surprise.'

'This is Rory. A work colleague and... friend,' said Elena and leant forwards. The two women hugged. Gayle felt so much more fragile than in years before. 'Sorry to just drop by like this. I hope we aren't disturbing you, but... could I have a chat? It won't take long.'

'My Elena can come in for as long as she likes!'

Elena blushed.

'Her friend as well, of course.' She smiled at Rory. 'No need to hurry away. I love a bit of company these days. It's been four years since Alf passed but I still miss him all the time. I didn't realise how noisy he was, until he went – always humming and whistling, or tapping out tunes with his fingers on furniture.'

'He used to sing whilst mowing the lawn,' said Elena. 'That song... "One Man Went to Mow".'

'I'd forgotten that!' said Gayle. She stared into the distance for a few seconds, and then refocused. 'Come on in, you two, and get warmed up.' She pointed to a coat stand and Elena and Rory slipped off their shoes. 'Coffee and cake?' she asked hopefully. 'I bought some Kipling slices yesterday – comfort food is the best antidote to this wintry weather.'

'Sounds perfect,' said Rory.

Gayle went to go into the kitchen, on the right, and then stopped and turned around, concern etched on her face. 'Don and Melanie are okay, aren't they?'

'Yes, fine,' said Elena. 'It's nothing to do with them. Not really.'

That collection of pottery owls still stood on the kitchen windowsill. Elena had loved them as a child. The walls had been repainted in a fashionable oat shade and a coffee machine had replaced the juicer. Elena peered outside. She hadn't been in Gayle's house for years, only seeing her, in recent times, in her front garden or around at Mum and Dad's. The familiar garden ornaments still sat outside, like the glowing mushroom, the happy snail and two ceramic bunnies. The fence at the bottom of the garden, whilst new, still blocked out the view of the common. After that traumatic night, Gayle had continued to babysit, but the two of them never mentioned what had happened, as if what happened with the fortune teller had driven a wedge between them.

Gayle filled up the coffee machine's water tank and insisted the two of them went into the lounge to sit by the electric fire, while she made the drinks. Photos of Gayle and Alf filled the shelves there. The couple hadn't had children. Gayle used to work in a boutique and loved every minute of it – the clothes, the accessories, acting as a personal shopper to customers who'd lost their way with fashion. Whereas Alf dressed in overalls, being a warehouse manager. As a little girl, Elena would rummage through Gayle's wardrobe, trying to walk in the high heels and wearing her colourful hats at a jaunty angle.

Elena sat on the crimson sofa, with Rory, leaning back on an embroidered cushion. Just like Gayle's carefully put together outfits, the colours in the lounge gelled well, with reds and creams against an oak laminated floor. Paintings of flowers adorned the walls and shelves of DVDs. Movies were to Gayle what books were to Elena and babysitting nights often involved the two of them talking about their favourites. Sometimes that overlapped as Gayle loved all genres of film, including children's movies and Disney cartoons. They both loved the Willy Wonka story and Gayle would read it to Elena when she was tucked up under the covers. *Alice in Wonderland* was another joint favourite that they'd watched together a few times. Gayle would bake jam tarts in advance, or make toast in the shape of butterflies.

Gayle came in, carrying a tray. Rory jumped up and placed it on the red and cream marble-effect coffee table, and Gayle made herself comfortable in one of the armchairs. After insisting they help themselves to the lemon slices, Gayle sipped her drink and gave a contented sigh. 'Tell me about work. Are Bingley Biscuits bringing out any new lines? I do love their chocolate-covered oatie ones.'

They told her about the broken biscuits pitch, before Elena asked, 'How are you doing, Gayle?' She looked around. 'Aren't you putting up your Christmas tree? You and Alf always used to decorate your lounge at the end of November.' Elena would have grimaced, but not this year.

'It's too much bother. I can't get it down from the loft, on my own, any more. In any case, Christmas isn't the same without Alf. My sister's very good. I'm going to hers again in a couple of days.'

'How about I get it down?' asked Rory. 'Elena and I could help you decorate it before we go, right?'

He glanced at Elena. A wave of warmth broke inside her chest. What a kind suggestion. Gayle didn't want to take up their time, but they both insisted.

'That would be lovely,' she said, eyes shining. 'Thank you. Have to admit, I do miss seeing Alf's favourite baubles. I bought him a gingerbread man one years ago and had his name painted on. Alf laughed at it every Christmas, complaining how the ornament kept its waistline but he didn't. He used to call it Skinny Gingy.' She smiled at Elena. 'But first... why have you come around, love? How can I help?'

Elena put down her mug and plate. Took a deep breath. How to start?

'That evening, twenty years ago, you were babysitting, Mum had been rushed into hospital, and... It must seem weird, me bringing this up all these years later but—'

Gayle held up her hand. 'I wondered how long it would take. I'll tell you everything I know.'

30

ELENA

Gayle gave a small laugh. 'Don't look at me like that, love. It was only matter of time...' They sat in silence for a moment and her face became more serious. 'You... you changed, subtly, after that night. You were subdued and started checking that things were safe, more closely than ever.'

Rory frowned. 'What do you mean?'

Gayle talked about how Don and Mel were very proud of the fact that Elena was such a sensible child. Even before that night, she'd check her windows at bedtime and never once let a bath or sink overflow. Her alarm was always set to the right time. Her parents never had to wake her up for school. 'If we baked together, it was Elena who checked that the hob was turned off. That's why I'd been so surprised to discover a careful child like that had snuck out at night. In the weeks following the accident, your parents and I became concerned about the checking. Sometimes you were late for school, because you'd nip back home to check you'd turned off the taps in the bathroom, and you'd check the hob more than once when you were around at mine.'

'I snuck out to the common often, in the summer,' Elena said, and a sheepish look crossed her face. 'I loved reading adventure stories and thought I'd have one too – as well as lots of fun with Bumper. Although that night it was because I could hardly breathe, what with Mum. I'd hoped the chilly air would help.'

'You stopped playing with Bumper after what happened though. I asked you about it once. You said black cats were bad luck. Then around at mine, one time, you were playing with my make-up and dropped my hand mirror. You were inconsolable when it cracked and said that meant seven years bad luck. It was as if spending time with that fortune teller had made you very superstitious. You told your parents it was bad luck that your house number was thirteen and tried to persuade them to move.'

Rory listened intently.

Elena's ears burned. 'A silly childhood phase.'

'And...' Gayle swallowed. 'Things were never quite the same between us.'

'You felt it too?' Elena raised her eyebrows. 'I... I think I wanted to simply forget everything about that night.'

'I always wondered, as you got older, you' – her voice became unsteady – 'you must have lost respect for me, not telling your mum and dad that you'd slipped out whilst I was supposed to be looking after you.'

'Elena told me what happened,' said Rory in a gentle voice. 'Sounds as if you did what you could to protect Elena's parents from even more upset at the time.'

'That's what I've always thought,' said Elena. She reached forwards and squeezed Gayle's arm.

'I did mention you slipping out for a wander a couple of months later on, you know. It did worry me. Once your mum's health scare settled right down, I told your parents that I'd seen you, out the back, near the common one night. I kept it vague. Your mum's health was still a little fragile.'

That explained why, six months or so after making the promise, Mum and Dad had adopted a new policy of setting the burglar alarm after dinner, so that if an outside door was opened it would go off. Elena hadn't realised that was to do with her.

'What happened that night, love?'

Elena glanced at Rory and he gave her an encouraging smile. 'The woman who brought me to the door, the fortune teller... I met her on the common. She was sleeping there, in a tent, after the last night of the fair, and... and...'

'Go on,' murmured Gayle, gently.

'She had her crystal ball and... we...' Elena clenched her hands together. 'I made a pact so that Mum would live. Then that night Mum made a miracle recovery, at midnight too,' she continued. 'I remember that particular time on the clock as being important. No idea why.'

Elena hardly dared meet Gayle's eyes, aware of how ludicrous it must have sounded. The guilt flooded back around how Elena had been selfish, risking dark forces causing consequences. As a little girl, she'd fret that meant her mum would go to some hellish place when she eventually passed, penance for going against the laws of nature and not dying when she should have – simply because Elena had been too weak to let her go. A hell with devils and demons, with fire and thunder, with torture and screaming... On a good day, she dismissed this theory, telling herself she'd done the right thing; that the only sacrifice would be Elena dying at thirty; that her mum was safe.

'You avoided oral cancer because of what that woman said,' she continued. 'Lucy's gran won on the lottery – the fortune teller had talked to her about seeing big money in her life. All of these things confirmed what I already knew – that the promise

I'd made on the common, that night, would also come true. But the... the agreement I made with her has haunted me ever since and, once and for all, I want to get to face it head on. I want to meet this woman again.'

Rory lay his hand over Elena's.

'That night must have been very frightening,' said Gayle. Red blotches appeared on her cheeks. 'I wish you'd told me at the time, love. What person makes some deal with a ten-year-old child?'

'Exactly what I thought,' muttered Rory.

'You don't think I imagined it?'

'You were never giddy or scatter-brained, even when you were little. This pact... was it something bad?'

A life for a life? Yes and no. Elena didn't want to worry Gayle. 'It's just something I need closure on... Probably to do with the fact I'm coming up to thirty, the same age Mum was when she almost died.'

'Understandable.'

'What was the woman like?' asked Rory. His voice had a hard edge to it.

'She seemed kind,' said Gayle. 'But now I'm questioning that...'

'The card, the king of hearts... Any idea why she gave that to me?' asked Elena.

Gayle shook her head. 'No. She just said it would be important to you one day. But the card makes sense – whereas one part of your story doesn't. The fortune teller at that fair definitely didn't have a crystal ball. I remember distinctly that her talent was reading cards. That's playing cards, not tarot. It's called cartomancy.'

Elena knew what she'd seen. There definitely had been a crystal ball.

'After I shut the front door that night,' continued Gayle, 'after you'd gone to bed, memories came back. I'd see her at the fair every year, laying the cards out on a table. She always struck me as a down-to-earth sort.'

'Any idea of this woman's name or how I find her?' asked Elena. 'I've searched online under the words "touring Christmas Fair" and "touring fortune teller", but nothing concrete came up. There are so many fairs, across the UK, at that time of year. I've never felt able to talk to Mum and Dad about it. When I was younger I was too scared to go to the fair again, in case I saw her and she called in the promise early that I'd made to do with our pact. Then the common was sold to property developers and the fair didn't come back.'

'No idea what she's called, sorry, love. Her accent was Scottish; perhaps she comes from the Highlands.'

Scottish? Of course. That explained why, over the years, Scottish TV shows made her uncomfortable. The hint of a Scottish accent spooked her out. It wasn't an accent thing – she loved listening to voices that were different to hers, like Diego's. It was because the sound made her afraid for no apparent reason.

'I do know the fair's owner was called Jimmy. When you were a toddler, there'd been a big hoo-ha because a child went missing at the Christmas fair. The police were involved. Turned out the boy had been hiding under his bed all along. The story might be on the internet still. If it helps, it was a fair that toured the northwest only. Alf got talking to Jimmy once. We'd gone to look for Christmas gifts. The fair kicked off in the middle of November. Six weeks, six towns. Jimmy would pick them from near the cities – Manchester, Liverpool, Newcastle... It went as far north as Edinburgh, I think. If you get his surname, you might be able to track him down. He could know what happened to the fortune teller, because of course it's possible that she isn't still...'

'This is really useful,' said Rory, swiftly.

'Thanks so much,' said Elena. 'You've given me a lot to think about, Auntie Gayle.' The two women looked at each other and Elena went over and gave her a hug. 'You really helped Mum and Dad out all those years, babysitting,' she said quietly. 'I loved coming round here. It was like a second home, like a safe haven during those years I had a difficult time at primary school.'

'You were – still are – like the daughter I'd never had. I wanted to go into your class myself, to sort out those bullies.'

'You were bullied?' asked Rory in astonishment.

Gayle blushed. 'Sorry, Elena. Hope I haven't said too much.'

'No, it's fine.' Elena turned to Rory. 'I was bullied because I had a slight speech impediment. Eventually we got a new head-teacher and she took my ordeal seriously in a way the other head hadn't. And I grew out of the lisp.'

'Your mum and dad were so worried at how withdrawn you'd become, some days,' said Gayle. 'You'd come round to do drawing and I'd stick your pictures on the fridge. I've still got one somewhere, of Alf in his overalls.' Gayle delved into her pocket and pulled out her phone. 'Why don't the three of us get onto this straightaway? I'm going to search for "Missing child found, Christmas fair, Bridgwich"... I'm not sure of the exact year.'

Rory and Elena did the same.

'Bingo!' said Gayle as she clicked on a tabloid article. 'That was easy.'

The other two agreed. Elena scoured the article she'd found in a local paper. The other two read articles from the nationals.

'It was 1997,' said Rory. 'No mention of Jimmy in the article I'm reading, though.'

'Nor in mine,' said Gayle.

'Nothing here either, in the *Manchester Evening News*,' said Elena. 'Only a mention of the police having interviewed the stall holders and the fair's owner.'

'But that local piece does mention the fair's name, in small italics, under that photo of the stalls,' said Rory. 'Fletcher's Fair.'

'Fletcher must be his surname then!' said Gayle.

Elena's hand shook as she googled Fletcher's Fair. A website came up! A photo of Jimmy! Oh, but it hadn't been updated for years. 'There is a contact email address,' she said. 'It's worth a shot. Looks like a personal one. He might still use it, even if he's closed or sold the business.' She beamed at Gayle. 'This is a great start. You're a superstar. I'm one step nearer to getting answers.'

Gayle's cheeks glowed as the three of them explored the website and spotted a couple of photos on the gallery page of Bridgwich Common. She made another coffee and insisted on putting together a plate of sandwiches. They trawled the internet once more, looking for Jimmy on social media, but didn't come across any profiles that fitted.

Rory wiped his mouth and stood up. 'Right. Loft ahoy! Let's get that Christmas tree down.'

'I'm having a birthday party next week,' said Elena, looking at Rory. He winked. 'I'd love it if you came, Gayle.'

She pushed herself up from the armchair and her eyes shone. 'Fantastic! I don't get much opportunity to wear my party dresses these days. Count me in. I'll get my hair done. Right. Enough of the detective work, then. Let's go find my Alf's pal, Skinny Gingy.'

31

RORY

Rory pulled up on the drive. It was ten days to Elena's birthday. She still hadn't received a response to the email she'd sent Jimmy Fletcher as soon as they'd got home from Gayle's on Monday, a couple of nights ago. Rory yawned. Last night had been a late one too. He'd gone to his apartment to check on the building work, found a few minor issues and had to list them in an email to his builder. The renovation work end date had run over by a week but was now on target to be reached by the weekend after next, very close to Christmas. Then tonight he'd just got back from an after-work, midweek kayaking trip. He'd been to the artificial whitewater centre several times in the last year and it was good catching up with the people he'd kayaked with before. But this time his heart hadn't been in the actual sport. He didn't understand why.

He got out of the car and spotted Tahoor at his downstairs front window. Rory waved. Tahoor nodded back. He wasn't smiling. It was late. Perhaps he was tired. Rory went to Elena's front door and put his key in the lock. The evening coldness smelt almost smoky. The lights were off downstairs, but then it had gone midnight. He and the others had gone for a pizza after the kayaking. Rory went to turn his key.

Tahoor. Something wasn't right. He left his holdall behind a bush and went to Tahoor's. He rang the doorbell.

The door opened. 'Evening lad. Everything all right?' Tahoor's eyes had deep circles under them. Looked a little red. Although his dressing gown was spotless and it looked as if his pyjamas had been ironed.

'I'm good, just... checking in. Everything okay?'

'Fine thanks. You been out with friends?'

'Yes, to a whitewater centre. Boy, it was cold tonight.'

Tahoor's face brightened. 'Can I tempt you with a hot chocolate then? I've been meaning to come around to see if you want to watch the match with me Monday night. No need for us to take over Elena's place. I've bought in drinks, and snacks.' An embarrassed look crossed his face. 'No pressure though. As tonight proves, I imagine you've got far more interesting things to do than stay in with an old codger like me.'

'More interesting than extend my range of swearwords in Urdu? In fact I could do with one right now, to express my annoyance that you've so easily seen my true motive for coming over. A hot chocolate is exactly what I need after capsizing, in icy water, in December.'

Tahoor chuckled, and for a moment the shadows under his eyes didn't look quite so severe. Glad for the warmth, Rory headed inside. Whilst Tahoor put on a pan of milk, Rory settled in the lounge. The room looked... tidier than last time he'd visited and the air smelt fresh and clinical, as if Tahoor had been cleaning. The rug on the floor, printed with colourful patterns, was newly vacuumed, and there wasn't a speck of dust on the collection of vibrant wall plates depicting snakes, birds and tigers. Also, as he'd walked along the hallway, Rory had passed three black dustbin bags of clothes, a colourful sari sticking out of the top of one. Tahoor came in and passed him a mug before sitting down in the mustard, studded wingback armchair opposite.

A look of ecstasy crossed Rory's face as he sipped. 'I need this. My kayak upturned and...' He stared at Tahoor's mantelpiece and his face broke into a grin. 'Did Elena give you that red card?'

Tahoor focused on his mug.

'You kept it?'

Tahoor set down his drink on the round, wooden coffee table between them. Underneath was a neat pile of puzzle books and football magazines. 'I did, lad. It's a good reminder of why Elena gave it to me. I... I got upset, in the doorway, when leaving after that Christmas dinner the Sunday before last. You see... I miss Isha so very much and I started crying, but then I felt ashamed and said I shouldn't cry in front of anyone – especially you, another man. Elena said that comment was sexist towards men and gave me the card. She said' – his voice wavered – 'that it's fine for us men to cry. I... I needed to hear that.'

Oh, mate... Poor Tahoor.

'I've been holding it in. The upset. So I've given it a go, given myself permission to let it out. I've... I've cried a lot over the last week. The first couple of days it left me in bits. I hardly ate, hardly got out of bed. But then...'

Rory nodded for him to go on.

'It's difficult to explain, but the tears do make me feel better. The crying fits are less frequent now and don't last so long. I even cried on the phone to Yalina. She did too. I told her I loved her so very much. We're going to visit Isha's grave when she picks me up for Christmas.' His eyes glistened. 'I see now that I've been hanging onto Isha's death, using it as an excuse not to move forwards with my life. I've stopped seeing my friends so often. I used to go bowling and walking but couldn't face the jokey camaraderie. Secretly I was pleased this cul-de-sac's residents are now mostly women. It's felt easier to hide away. But then you moved in...'

The men smiled at each other.

'This crying malarkey...' Tahoor continued. 'It's helped me finally sort out Isha's clothes.'

'Well done,' said Rory. He got up. Crouched by Tahoor's side. Took his hand. 'You must feel lonely. That's how my dad felt after we lost Mum, even though I was around. Things will improve, I promise.'

Tahoor wiped his eyes. 'Elena said the same. Thanks, lad. You two youngsters have given me the push I needed. Now I've got a sense of... hope, for the future. I think I was waiting for some magical moment when I'd suddenly get over her death. But it doesn't work like that.'

They chatted a while longer and then Rory left, after giving Tahoor a hug. Not wanting to wake up Elena, he tip-toed up to the spare room after bolting the front door. She'd never left a note out before asking him to do that. After getting changed and cleaning his teeth, Rory sank into the bedclothes and an uncomfortable sensation rose in his chest.

He picked up his journal.

Wednesday 11th December

I realised in Paris that I've been holding back from committing to a relationship, because I didn't want to get hurt like Dad did, when Mum died. Tonight with Tahoor has confirmed that. Like him, I've also been waiting for some magical moment when I'd get over Mum's death. Perhaps grief is like that for everyone, a song you sing that never ends;

there's always a different verse to add. When death first happens, you assume the song is already written. It's not. The lyrics, the music, for my song about Mum, started off soft, when I was a toddler. They became angry and wild during the teen years, when I felt sorry for Dad and envied friends with mothers at parents' evenings; when I found out exactly why she died and blamed myself. During my twenties, the tune has settled into a routine, me visiting Mum's grave, me avoiding emotional intimacy with partners; a tune that's become back- ground music – weak, in a way, without direction. It just goes on and on and on. Whereas I can see Dad's song has grown in recent years, in strength, in vibrancy, as he's trusted romance again and now found his long-term girlfriend, Jenny. It's reached an end point of acceptance and harmony, the baseline of which is everlasting love for his Linda. She's there, always there, but not in a way that holds him back. His song is solid, everlasting, but the volume's turned down.

Chatting to Gayle told me more about Elena... How safety-conscious she was as a child, a child who liked routine, a child like an adult in so many ways... Perhaps she'd grown up quickly, what with being bullied. My neighbour, Julian, had a difficult childhood and had to grow up quickly too. He loved his mum but she was domineered by his dad, who teased Julian about his gap teeth and said working with animals was a cop out, and who was generous with his fists when Julian tried to protect his mum. I never knew mine, but Dad always did his best to support me like two parents would have.

Okay. In case I'm losing your attention with my musical metaphors and reflection on my childhood, I'll share some figures.

1 tank arrived for the stick insects – it's huge! 45 x 45 x 60 cm. But as Elena pointed out, it's nowhere near as big as a

rainforest. She'd also ordered a special substrate for the floor and a little rope bridge, along with a guide on how best to look after stick insects. Her excitement was contagious and I wanted to wrap her in my arms as she chatted about Brandy and Snap's new home, to feel her breath on my neck, to run my fingers along the curve of her hip and... I need to keep those dreams in check.

30 minutes is how long Elena disappeared for last night. One moment she was in her bedroom, the next she was gone. I'd knocked on her door when I got back from surveying the building work at my apartment to see if she wanted a drink, as I'd put the kettle on. She'd been on the landing, heading for her room, when I'd got in and took off my coat. But there was no response, even after I knocked harder. 30 minutes later, the landing floorboards creaked and I opened my bedroom door. Elena stood stock still, as if she shouldn't have been there, and mumbled some excuse about having been downstairs to fetch a drink of water. But if that had been the case, surely she'd have brought a glass back up?

32

ELENA

Elena sat at her desk, lost in the romance of Jane Austen's *Persuasion*. She couldn't help picturing Rory in a cravat and tailored Regency jacket and trousers, floral of course, further enhanced by his unique charisma. Gary and Rory stood opposite her, arguing over which was more impressive – to have been scouted to model in Paris or have a Spanish boyfriend who'd once cooked for Taylor Swift.

She sipped coffee and her phone beeped. An email from Jimmy Fletcher! It'd been several days, and she'd almost given up on getting a reply to her short message saying she was trying to track down a fortune teller from 2004. There was no reason why he should help. As Gary and Rory continued to argue their cases, Elena put down her book and read it.

> Hello Elena. The fortune teller was called Morag. I remember
> her well! She was Scottish. But I gave up the fair when my
> arthritis got bad about seven years ago, and didn't keep in
> touch with everyone. I never did like computers – my wife
> makes me have this email and, back in the day, I hired a

company to set up my old, basic website. I didn't have the enthusiasm to edit it myself, therefore details showcasing the stallholders, for example, were never put online. I used to work out the figures for my tax return manually and send them to my accountant. I have kept the paperwork. You're welcome to drop by and look through the boxes yourself – there's a stack of them in the outhouse. Sorry, I'm not up to it. There should be copies of the invoices I sent the stallholders, for their pitches. Your email sounded as if it's important. I live a few miles outside Liverpool. Best, Jimmy

Singing 'Shake It Off' out of tune, Gary went back to his desk. Elena held up her phone. Rory read it and gave the thumbs up. He insisted on going with her. She wholeheartedly thanked him. If only Elena could show her gratitude with a long, lingering kiss that wouldn't be out of place in any Regency romance. With a little over a week to her birthday, she'd emailed back and asked Jimmy if there was any way she could make the journey from Manchester today.

Relieved he'd said yes, she drove whilst Rory told her he'd called in on Tahoor last night and that he seemed to be doing better and had even started sorting through Isha's clothes. Rory didn't seem as fired up as normal though while talking about his latest sport activity. Yes, the whitewater kayaking was tiring. No, he'd hadn't swallowed too much water when his kayak upturned. The last time he'd been, Rory had come into the office, full of excited bluster, explaining how the river rapids were graded like ski runs and that he was still on a high from the exhilaration. Instead he talked about their visit to Gayle.

'So, as a child you were super-sensible? Like you are now? Checking windows and the hob... They were the last things on my mind as a little boy. In fact, I haven't changed much. I left the heating on once, twenty-four seven, when I was away on a week's trip. It cost a small fortune.'

'It's just the way I am. Gran was very particular about things. She'd say, "It costs you nothing to double-check." She'd been burgled twice and suffered a chip pan fire once. Perhaps that was why.'

Rory stared at her intently. In so many ways the two of them really were so different.

They pulled up outside a small bungalow and Elena got out, a very fine layer of snow crisp under her feet. It had only fallen lightly again today, and hadn't settled until the temperature went below freezing, when the sun disappeared. Having double-checked she'd locked the car. Elena surveyed Jimmy's lawn that was perfectly square with neat borders, filled with lines of shrubs. A lit-up reindeer stood in the middle of the lawn. The full moon revealed that the tiled roof was free from moss and the plastic, white front door was spotless, with a Christmas wreath tied to the knocker. Across the front of the bungalow hung twinkling fairy lights. Elena couldn't help feeling disappointed. She'd imagined that the owner of a touring fair lived a ramshackle, bohemian life that every person, trapped in suburbia, secretly envied. She knocked and waited several minutes before the door finally opened. A man smiled at them, bald with a face deep with wrinkles and tanned, giving away the number of years he'd spent outside. His body leaned to the right and his misshapen fingers displayed the damage done by his arthritis.

'Jimmy? Thanks so much for seeing me so quickly,' said Elena. 'I do hope my visit isn't too much of an inconvenience.'

He smiled to reveal pearly dentures. 'Not at all. My Val is out, she goes to the Bingo on a Thursday, but she made a flask of tea for us before she went, and has left out three mince pies. My hands aren't so good in this weather and the kettle's heavy.'

'This is my friend, Rory,' said Elena. 'I hope you don't mind if he helps.'

'Good to meet you, lad. Come on in, it's Baltic out there.' Jimmy beckoned for them to enter and Rory shut the front door behind him. Limping, he led the way to the back of the house and the small kitchen, as tidy as the front garden. The only indication of Jimmy's past was a framed photo of him in the hallway with his arms around two men in front of the carousel.

Jimmy rubbed his hip and then pointed out of the window. 'See the outhouse at the bottom of the garden? Val unlocked it before she left. When you go in, there's a light switch on the left. The cardboard boxes you need to sift through are in there. I accidentally threw one out a couple of years ago. I was sorting through, only keeping the records from the last five years of the fair running. Morag didn't attend every one, so what with that and losing some of the paperwork, I can't promise you'll find what you want.' He passed them the flask. 'I'd suggest we have a drink together first, but you'd better crack on, as it could take a while. I always did like setting up shop on Bridgwich Common. It was a shame when property developers bought it. Morag had something to say about that.' He grinned.

'You said you remember her well?' said Elena.

'Quite a character but sound as a pound. Very no nonsense. She used to camp out at some of the locations, instead of booking a B&B if it was far from her home. Even in the middle of winter, can you believe?'

Yes, more than he'd ever imagine.

'Morag didn't rate technology – hadn't got a mobile phone, let alone a laptop. It was nothing to do with saving money. She used to get cross when people accused her of being that money-pinching Scottish stereotype. It was more a case of believing in simple living. Apparently she grew her own fruit and vegetables and bought her clobber from charity shops.' He leant against a kitchen unit. 'One year, towards the end, I had to cancel the first week of the fair at a location on the outskirts of Sheffield, at the last minute, as one of the worst storms the area had ever seen was due to hit. The ground would have been too muddy even if the storm passed quickly. Morag was the most difficult to contact. There had been bad weather in Scotland too and her landline was down. She'd given me the email address of a neighbour who kindly agreed to Morag giving it out to a few people for emergencies, but I didn't hear back until it was too late and Morag had already left.'

'She must have been fuming,' said Rory.

Jimmy beamed. 'Not at all. She had reluctantly booked a B&B ahead that time, due to the wet conditions. It didn't cross her mind I would actually cancel, having never done so before the times she'd taken part. She mentioned the place to her neighbour and I found the B&B's number in the phone book. I saw her in Liverpool the following week. Her motto for life was very much that everything happened for a reason. Morag always struck me as a very content person. She'd stayed in Sheffield for the week as the owner wanted her to read her cards for guests. He'd booked evening entertainment for the whole of December, as part of a special bookings deal, but the magician had fallen ill.' He gave Elena a curious look. 'You must have been a child when you knew her?'

'That's why I want to see her again, to... clarify a... a prediction she made. Kind of.' Elena blushed. 'Now that I'm an adult.'

He patted Elena's arm. 'Her card reading was always on the mark.'

Jimmy probably thought he was being reassuring.

'Did she have a crystal ball?' asked Rory.

'No. As I said, Morag was a common-sense person and I

always assumed there had to be a kind of logic to reading playing cards, whereas a crystal ball? That's a bit airy fairy if you ask me.'

'Did she strike you as a cold-hearted type, out to fleece customers, not really caring about the outcome of her readings?' Rory continued.

'No, lad! Why would you ask that?'

Rory pursed his lips.

'Morag was a lovely lady. Caring in her own way. One of the younger stallholders got blind drunk one night, caused a scene in the pub he was staying in, near where her tent was pitched. He got thrown out for being rude towards the landlord. Morag had a word and got him his room back. Then she sat up with him all night, worried he'd choke in his sleep, he'd drunk that much thanks to some idiot lacing his drinks.' He limped to the back door and opened it. 'In fact, she told me, the last time she worked for my fair, that I should retire before my arthritis really started complaining about winter bookings. I never thought it would get this bad. Morag had a real kind of sixth sense about her. Anyway, that's enough of me rambling on. Val put the heater on in the outhouse, to take the pinch off. You'll still need your coats. Good luck.'

Elena poured Jimmy a mug of tea out of the flask first and carried it, with a mince pie, into the lounge for him.

Shyly, she reached into a bag she was carrying and brought out a box of chocolates. 'A small thank you.'

'But you haven't found anything yet,' he said, nevertheless keenly reaching for the box as his face lit up.

They smiled at each other and Elena and Rory made their way outside. She shivered as she headed along the narrow path, across the back lawn to the outhouse. The grass looked white due to its gossamer carpet of snowflakes. She opened the outhouse's door and ran her hand along the wall, for the light. It wasn't so tidy as the garden and house, with boxes stacked in a higgledy-piggledy fashion. The air smelt musty and the room was chilly, despite the plug-in electric radiator ahead.

Elena bit her lip and caught Rory's eye. 'She did have a crystal ball – whatever Gayle and Jimmy say. *They* weren't there that night. I *was* and didn't make it up.'

Rory put his hands on her shoulders. 'There will be a rational explanation for any discrepancies. Come on, let's get looking. An Indian takeaway, my shout, is calling. Nice and warming when we get back.'

Elena put down her bag. They pulled down the top cardboard boxes. There were four to look through, all in all. Other boxes filled with random objects, no doubt cast-offs from stalls over the years, made perfect seats. Almost an hour later they'd each gone through one box of paperwork, with no luck. They'd sifted through invoices and receipts for owners of craft ale stalls, ones selling Christmas baubles, homemade water bottle covers, chocolate tea cakes and organic toiletries, but didn't find a single one for Morag. Other paperwork too, from local councils, granting permission for Fletcher's Fair to take place at the various sites. Bills, too, for repairs to the carousel. The cold had almost numbed Elena's feet. Yet, despite the circumstances, this was... nice, the two of them quietly getting on, comfortable with the silence, exchanging smiles now and again. Even though she'd rather have pulled him to his feet, torn off his clothes and created their own heat. God he was handsome. They drank the tea and ate the mince pies, then each moved on to their second box. She picked up a bundle of invoices. One fell onto the floor and Rory picked it up. She flicked through the sheaf in her hand but stopped when Rory punched the air.

'Here we go. Morag Macbay. An address, email details and landline number.'

Elena's eyes widened and she took the piece of paper whilst Rory tapped into his phone.

'She lives in a place called Leith which is a northern district of Edinburgh,' he said. 'Are you going to email her?'

Elena stared at the sheet. 'No. I've not got much time. I need to see her face to face. I'll ring.'

'No time like the present. Go for it.'

The prospect of speaking to Morag, after twenty years of worry, took her breath away. Feeling like a little girl again, unsure and scared, yet determined too, she took out her phone, punched in the number and pressed dial. It rang. And rang. No one picked up. No problem. She'd email instead.

Elena typed as Rory tidied up. It was difficult to know what to say, so she kept it to a minimum. This message would be going to the inbox of a neighbour of hers, after all, according to Jimmy. After fifteen minutes, the room was tidy again – or as tidy as it had been, when they walked in – and the two of them were headed to the door when her phone beeped, but a jubilant grin soon slipped from her face. The email had bounced back. It said 'non-existent email address'. Oh no. Morag's neighbour must have changed email provider. There was only one solution left, then. Elena slipped her phone back into her bag.

'I'll ring again,' she said, 'but either way this weekend would be my only opportunity to see her. I'll take my chances as to whether she is there. Fancy a road trip to Scotland the day after tomorrow?'

33

RORY

Friday 13th December

Oh boy. Not a good day. I'm glad to get into bed. As her birthday nears, Elena's becoming more careful again. It seemed as if she'd found a balance, but what with bolting the door and checking the hob again now, and regimentally checking the windows... She jumped up quicker than a frog on speed to clear up a coffee spillage in work this morning. Someone jokingly mentioned today's jinxed date and she turned whiter than the snow we saw in Scotland. What's more, it turned out, what with everything going on, she still hadn't organised the staff's Christmas activity night out. She disappeared to the toilets for a while when she realised and came back with red eyes.

Over 1 pint, Gary and I put together a night out next Tuesday. We were drinking in the Three Horseshoes and the sign was still up for the Christmas quiz night next week. Our marketing team is made up of 15 people. The landlord said he had two tables left, but would squeeze in another to accommodate us, seeing as we were regular customers. Each quiz team needed 5 people. To be honest – and it galls me to compliment that lad – Gary smashed it as on the way back to work, he stopped at the small bookshop opposite and asked for the latest novel that people were most talking about. He didn't even read the blurb, but Elena was almost in tears when he handed it over. It had been on her wish list. Gary said he still had the receipt and would take it back if she talked any more nonsense from having let the staff down.

I'm worried about her, having seen what my neighbour, Julian, went through when he got stressed. How his illness grew and grew way out of control, affecting his whole life. Was Elena suffering that badly? Has she got the same, specific problem as him?

No. Surely not. Not Elena. For sure the fortune teller will give her all the answers she needs, and explain away the promise, ending the sense of dread once and for all.

At least, I hope so.

I don't want Elena to lose her life.

I don't want to lose Elena.

3 calls to Morag Macbay's landline number, but it kept ringing out.

240 miles from Cariswell to Leith, just over 4 hours driving; we're setting off at ten o'clock tomorrow morning. Elena insisted we take her car.

2 rooms booked at a B&B.

2 1/2 hours Elena vanished for tonight. She went upstairs as soon as we got home, but wasn't in her room when I called her for dinner, and I had to go up. I didn't ask questions when she came down and simply reheated her risotto. She looked much happier and that's what counts.

For 20 minutes we stared at the new stick insect tank, after Elena had eaten, willing Brandy and Snap to go on the new rope bridge. But I guess they aren't that sort of pet. Brandy moved a little, from leaf to leaf, but Snap was so still we had to poke her, gently, to check she was okay. We'd set the tank up last night, after getting back from Jimmy's. It was late but Elena hadn't been sleeping well and a hot chocolate was enough incentive to help her. On the way home tonight we stopped to cut more bramble leaves. The large tank doesn't fit with the well-planned-out lounge, but Elena doesn't care. I... I had to turn away and gather myself when she said that. If anything happened to her next week, I had to promise to keep them in the big tank. Her voice was quite matter of fact.

1 Post-it note left out on the breakfast bar, in the kitchen. Elena had written herself a reminder to check her will was in order. I wanted to screw it up into a tiny ball and throw it away. It was another example of how full of common sense she is. A wave of nausea takes me by surprise every time I think about her birthday, next weekend. My insides are knotted. I'm not sleeping either but I didn't tell Elena that – this is about her, not me. Even though losing her would tear my heart into 1,000 pieces.

34

ELENA

Elena reached for her water bottle. 'Last Christmas' by Wham! had spooked her. Rory had insisted they play festive songs on the way up to Scotland. Three hours in and they'd jingled bells with Frank Sinatra and wished Slade a Merry Christmas. Thirty minutes had been added on to their journey due to a Christmas tree falling off the roof of a van. She turned off at the services for a quick lunch. Rory had rung Morag's number again, but still no one picked up.

Her parents had invited them round for Sunday lunch tomorrow. She hadn't told them they were going to Scotland. Instead, Elena texted first thing today and said she and Rory had a work emergency this weekend. She hated lying, but what was the alternative? *Sorry Mum and Dad, going up to Scotland to find a fortune teller I promised my life away to when I was ten.* Elena said she'd see them next Saturday for her birthday party.

The wind blew more strongly the further north they went from Manchester, and grateful to be inside, she and Rory ordered burgers. Elena forgot to ask for no pickles and Rory gladly took her slice before he'd even taken off his beanie hat, scarf and tie-dye coat.

'How are you feeling?' he said as they sat at a table by a window, watching cars park up.

'Dunno. Morag might not even be there.' *But at least I'm with you. Precious time.* 'Thanks for coming. I appreciate the support.'

'No problem. I've only been to Edinburgh once and that was years ago.' He twisted the beaded bracelet around his wrist.

'For an extreme sport?'

'No. With school. We toured historic buildings and went to the theatre. Our teacher made us taste haggis. I was the only one who liked it. But I hated the trip.'

'Why?'

'It was the tenth anniversary of Mum's death whilst I was away. All the other mums were there to wave off their children, or so it seemed, when the coach left. I was twelve, almost a teen, and it hit me harder than it ever had before. I'd only recently found out the reason Mum got ill and...'

'Was it cancer?' she asked gently.

His head jerked up and down.

Elena put down her burger and leaned forwards, but Rory clammed up.

'We had a trip to Swanage,' she said. 'Some hills were so steep we climbed them on our hands and knees. Even back then I was more bookish than sporty and was happiest sitting on the coach with a bag of crisps, re-reading *The Hobbit.*'

Rory smiled. 'I... I sat on the coach to Edinburgh cheered by how excited Mum would have been, on my behalf. Her favourite film was *Thelma and Louise.* Dad said she loved travel and had always dreamt of backpacking; that she was something of an adventurer and, to please her, he'd do these activities on their holidays, before they had me... like zip-wiring and rock-climbing.'

'Really? Could that be where your passion for adventure comes from?'

He shrugged. 'S'pose. That's what Dad's always said.'

'I feel a *but*,' she said.

'I've thought a lot about her lately – how her death has affected my life. Guess I've wanted to be like her, but lately it's not given me the same satisfaction. Other things have given me the buzz I used to crave... Like football. I actually like watching it. A lot. Also, since moving in with you, I...' His neck flushed red. 'A change in circumstances has given me a fresh perspective on life.'

'How?'

He opened his mouth. Closed it again. Eventually he spoke. 'It's made me look at what really makes me happy – what gives me that natural high.'

Elena sucked on her straw, the coke fizzing in her mouth. He didn't need to say it – that it was her impeding death that had made him reassess his life.

She tilted her head. 'I could be wrong but... I've got another take on your sporting hobbies. When Mum... When I believed she was going to die, I sat, in shock, alone in my room, having just spoken to Dad on the phone and hearing him cry, understanding that her condition couldn't have been more serious. My parents had been saving for a full-on week in London. They wanted us to go and see all the sights, catch a West End show, visit the Crown Jewels. Then there was the voluntary work Mum talked about. She said when I was all grown-up, she might take a sabbatical and teach children in Africa for a few months. I swore, then and there, that if she died, I'd do those things on her behalf, imagining that, somehow, she'd be looking down, still living her life, through me.' Elena raised an eyebrow. 'Have *you* been doing these adventurous sports on behalf of *your* mother, rather than simply having inherited her enthusiasm for them?'

Rory hadn't taken a bite of burger or sipped his drink; he'd continued to fiddle with his bracelet, listening intently. It snapped at her words and beads crashed down to the ground. They collected as many of them up as they could and sat opposite each other once more.

'Christ. You might be right,' he said. 'I've never thought of it like that. On that coach to Edinburgh, when her death hit me hard, it all being new to me that there was someone to blame for her cancer...'

He broke eye contact for a second.

What did he mean? What wasn't he telling her? 'Want to talk about it?' she asked gently.

Rory shook his head and swiftly continued with his story. 'As soon as I got back to Manchester, I asked Dad if he could book zip-wiring. Guess it began from then. At the time, I wanted to do it, simply to feel closer to Mum. But then, doing activities like that somehow became *my thing*. Maybe they've not been my thing after all. Perhaps they've been hers all along.'

'And I get it. But Rory... you don't have to do those things any more. You are your own person. She'd want you to honour *that*.'

He reached into his pocket and pulled out a Snickers bar. 'I still eat her favourite chocolate bar. Never have really liked it.'

Elena reached forwards and took it from him. 'Good thing I do. What do you really like?'

'Brittle honeycomb chocolate. Nice and crunchy.'

Despite his protests, Elena got up and went into the services' newspaper shop. Swiftly, she returned, bearing a giant honeycomb bar. She placed it in front of him.

'It's time that you did you, Rory Bunker. Like with that fashion sense that got you noticed in Paris.'

He gave a wry smile. 'Yes, my way of dressing is certainly nothing to do with Mum. Dad said she lived in sweatpants and hoodies.' His eyes shone. 'I miss her. Is that weird as I haven't any concrete memories?'

'You have,' said Elena softly, and she placed a hand over his chest. 'In there. Memories don't have to be visual. They can come from emotions.'

Rory placed his hand over hers. Elena so wanted to hug him, to kiss him, to get as close as possible, to do all she could to make him feel better. But she wouldn't let that happen. His mum's death had affected him for years. She mustn't get closer only to be torn away; it wouldn't be fair on him. In any event, the attraction was all one way.

Elena finished her drink. 'Morag may not be a villain. I was never afraid of *her* – just afraid of the promise, afraid of losing Mum.'

'We'll see.' He frowned. 'From everything Jimmy's said, she was a decent enough person and as I've said before... about mutualism... it doesn't make sense to me that she'd save your mum but take your life. Yet you are so adamant about the deal that was made.' His expression darkened.

Elena felt suddenly toasty and warm inside at how angry Rory felt on her behalf.

'On a brighter note, have you contacted Nicole yet?' she asked, in a voice breezier than the wind outside. 'You must, if only to see the look on Gary's face when you arrange to meet her.'

Rory didn't reply for a moment and then squared his shoulders. 'No. She's not the woman for me, flattering as her attention was. Okay, this is me doing me now. I'm not a model, I'm Rory

Bunker, marketing bod, who's a mediocre karaoke singer and satisfactory stir-frier; a man who gets emotionally blackmailed by stick insects, and speaks a smattering of X-rated Urdu. A man who, right at this minute, would rather be sitting here, with you, eating out of a cardboard box, than posing in a Michelin restaurant by the Seine.'

As if his words had tied her to a hot air balloon, and she was twirling like a feather, higher and higher in warm, sunny air, Elena polished off the last mouthful of her burger and went on to devour the chocolate bar, feeling as fizzy as the Coke in her cup.

35

ELENA

Using her satnav, Elena completed their journey by turning into a cul-de-sac, still wondering what Rory had meant about someone being to blame for his mum's illness. It has been a long drive. Since leaving the service station, snow had turned to mushy sleet. The reduced visibility had slowed the traffic. She hadn't been sure what to expect of Leith, having read the novel *Trainspotting*, a story of squalor in the locality. Clearly, a regeneration plan had taken place since the early nineties. She and Rory had scrolled through a gallery of photos together during their lunch stop, and before going home tomorrow, they planned to visit the vibrant centre, with cobbled streets and restaurants, the waterway and varied architecture.

Elena parked up outside a small, detached bungalow. Moss covered the grey tiled roof and a black spiked metal fence circumnavigated the tiny front garden, newly painted by the looks of it. Her chest tightened. It hit her. Elena was actually going to meet the woman who'd changed her life so irreparably, all those years ago.

'Ready?' asked Rory.

'As I'll ever be.' Legs shaky, she got out of the car, checked that she'd locked the door several times, and then met Rory by the gate. He opened it and they walked up to the front door, past Morag's garden that had an orderly wildness about it, with a beautiful array of winter leaf colours, gold to green, from shrubs and conifers, to ferns and ivy.

She flinched as the door opened. A smoky, rich, meaty, satisfying smell escaped outside. Elena gripped her handbag tightly and stared at the woman, hair grey now, and whoosh! The memories! Like those eyes as green as the ferns outside, as if Morag camped in the woods every night, and her irises had grown to reflect the surroundings. Like the long, striking nose that suited the strong jaw. The woman's aura of kindness, of warmth – Elena had forgotten that. Morag was smaller than Elena remembered – but then Elena had shot up at high school. Morag wore an impossibly woolly jumper over a thick, plaid skirt and slippers that looked like boots.

'Can I help you?' The woman's face concertinaed into friendly lines.

That accent. The lilt. Elena shivered. 'My name is Elena Swan. I... We... You see...' She gulped and took several breaths. 'Sorry... it's been a long time. We met, when I was a little girl... Your tent on the common... My mum critically ill... I know none of this makes sense, but you and I...' She gulped again.

Morag stared back. 'You'd better come in, lass. A strong cup of tea, that's what you need.'

Elena stumbled into the woman's house and followed her into a kitchen-cum-dining room on the right, at the back. It was tidy, apart from a tall ramshackle pile of cookbooks on a cabinet top. The smell of stew bubbling on the hob felt reassuring. Elena spotted no crystal balls, nor dreamcatchers, nor packs of cards or joss sticks. Pendulums weren't swinging on the shelves and no mysterious fragrance from a scented candle filled the air. No magical music welcomed them in, either. The sun was setting but it left enough light to reveal the garden, with its rows of pots with bamboo canes in, along with a henhouse and a big tree in the far corner. A bird feeder hung from one of its branches, and a lone sparrow pecked vigorously at the holes at the bottom.

'How about a wee slice of fruit cake?' asked Morag, kindly. She held out her hand to shake Rory's. 'Morag Macbay.'

'Rory Bunker,' he said in a tight voice, hands remaining by his sides.

Morag passed him plates and forks and pointed to the dining room table that was covered in a colourful, mosaic-style tablecloth. Drawn to the huge bookcases on the walls, Elena headed over. She skimmed the titles... Lots of non-fiction ones about mountain hiking and British history. Also guides to identifying toadstools, wildflowers and birds. As for the fiction, Morag's taste was as eclectic as Elena's own... Dark crime, light romance, fantasy, classics too, and several gentle reads by Japanese authors about cats and coffee shops. Under any other circumstances, she'd have quizzed Morag about her favourite reads and asked for recommendations. She gave the fortune teller a sideways glance. In Elena's experience, fellow booklovers were usually empathetic people, understanding, and open to life's differences; they looked for hope and resonance in stories; they looked for expanding their knowledge, to growing. Perhaps Rory was right and it didn't make sense that such a person would have agreed to Elena promising her life away.

'You're a fellow bookworm?' asked Morag as she brought over a tray and put it down, handing out the cups and putting the milk jug and sugar bowl on the tablecloth.

'Novels. Love them,' she said.

'Elena reads a lot on her Kindle,' said Rory in an overly polite voice.

'Ach, I like the smell of a book, me,' said Morag, 'and the feel of it between my hands. My nephews love their eReaders, but they also love skimming through my children's books.' She pointed to a bookcase at the far end of the room, underneath a painting of an old-fashioned funfair. 'I've still got my favourites from my childhood and have kept the collection up to date for them. Both of their parents work hard, so I'm spoilt with the amount of time I get to look after them. One set of grandparents lives in Portugal, the other two are divorced and don't live locally any more.' She gestured for Elena and Rory to sit down and Morag pulled out a chair for herself. 'Right. Take a mouthful of tea, lass, enjoy some cake, and then tell me – what's all of this about? I'll do anything I can to help.'

Elena didn't normally have sugar in tea, but she put in two teaspoons. The heat and sweetness ran through her veins. She could do this.

'When I was ten, my mum was in a bad accident. It didn't look as if she was going to pull through. We lived in Bridgwich, near the common.'

Morag raised an eyebrow. 'Ach, I know it well. Or used to. What a crime, it was, when property developers got their hands on that lush, green space.'

'You were part of Jimmy Fletcher's touring fair,' said Elena. The bubble of stew soothed her, as comforting as its smell. 'We visited him recently.'

'Indeed I was. How is my old pal? A decent sort was Jimmy. Made the worst coffee I've ever drunk, but his heart was in the right place – not in his pants or wallet, like so many men I met on the road.'

'He's good,' said Rory stiffly.

'It was the last night of the fair. You were camping in the woods,' continued Elena.

Morag bellowed with laughter. 'I was a one back then. Had my principles and rarely wasted money on a hotel. I grew up without heating so always coped with the cold. "Layer up," my dad used to boom. Bearing any chill became a way of life, almost like a badge of honour. Ironic that pneumonia got my dad in the end. But when you tip into your seventies, like me now, your bones start to twinge, so I've had radiators installed and wouldn't sleep outside again, not for a million pounds.' Morag took a slurp of tea and studied Elena's face. 'Your hair was a different colour back then, but you've still got those freckles.'

'You remember her?' asked Rory, with the same robotic tone.

'As a young woman I longed for freckles and painted them on, when everyone else was covering theirs up. But yes. You were lost and appeared outside my tent, a black cat by your side. I took you home. A sorry sight you were, eyes swollen from crying, and your babysitter... Pleasant woman, big necklace... Mentioned you had a temperature.'

'Do you recall the promise we made?' asked Elena, voice trembling. The world stopped for a moment and went into slow motion. Rory ran a hand through his curly hair, fiddling with his silver necklace, whereas Morag sat stock still, calm and attentive. A knack she'd probably learned from years of reading cards to customers who no doubt told her about any flawed part of their lives and expected her to unravel it. So much was hinging on what Morag said next. Outside, sleet started up again and flicked against the kitchen window, the last shafts of winter sun admitting defeat and withdrawing.

Elena's heart thumped.

'What sort of promise?' asked Morag, her brow furrowed.

Garbling, Elena spoke about the deal, a life for a life, how

Elena would die at thirty – next weekend – and how she'd pass on to 'the next stage of our world'. She talked about Mum's miracle recovery, at midnight, and mentioned the crystal ball.

'A life for a life?' Morag's teacup clattered, and she put it back on the saucer. 'Of course. It's coming back. I thought about you for days afterwards.'

Elena stiffened. A deal *had* been struck. Her biggest fear would come true. She would die in five days. She looked at Rory, sitting there, knuckles white as his fists lay on top of the table.

'You said you'd do anything to save your mum's life – suggested you swap yours for hers. Oh my days, what a selfless heart you had. I'm so glad it all worked out and she survived.'

'Worked out?' spluttered Rory. 'Maybe for her mum! But that promise has stained Elena's life, as year in, year out, she's counted down to her thirtieth birthday.'

'Rory,' said Elena, and she glared.

'Wait a minute... You believe that deal was actually made? Are you serious?' said Morag, and her eyes widened. 'Not that I read your cards that night, but even if I had, my card reading is more about reflecting on your life, making sense of it, and less about predicting the future. As for making some pact, that's not anything I would ever agree to.'

'But you said, "A life for a life, it is." You picked up your crystal ball and ran your hand over it. Then everything went blurry and before I knew it, I was home.' Elena could hardly breathe. 'You warned me about "dark forces" too, but still agreed to the deal.'

Morag frowned. 'I remember *you* saying, "A life for a life," but I ignored you, Elena. And I had no crystal ball. Cartomancy is my thing. Always has been. You did have a temperature that night, so perhaps...'

'Just a twenty-four-hour bug. This wasn't some hallucination,' she said in a clipped voice. 'Nothing else explained Mum's recovery that happened as the clock struck midnight. Even the doctors were baffled. Everyone called it a miracle. There was other stuff too. When you took me home, you told my babysitter to go to the dentist. Turned out she had the very early stages of oral cancer.'

Morag thought for a moment. 'Yes, I spotted a white patch on her lip when she was talking. My brother-in-law had the same a couple of years earlier, and ended up having chemotherapy. My warning to her was nothing to do with fortune-telling. I hope she got through it.'

'But... but my friend Lucy... You told her gran you could see money. A few days later, she won big on the lottery.'

'Sometimes I get... a sixth sense about things. Images come into my head. But I would never, ever predict something tragic, or make a deal that would hurt someone, even if it was to help another person. If I saw or sensed anything negative, I would never share it. As for agreeing to some pact, a scary one at that, with a little girl? What sort of monster do you take me for?'

The tips of Rory's ears turned red.

Morag got up and paced the room... 'But your words... "A life for a life... As the clock struck midnight"... I didn't think of it at the time, but now...'

'Those phrases have always stuck in my head.' Elena looked at Rory. 'I'm so confused.'

'What was I wearing that night?' asked Morag.

Elena shrugged. 'A purple shawl. It was really fancy. But that didn't stop you picking up muddy Bumper, to give him a hug.'

'The black cat?'

'Yes. Why?'

Morag went over to Elena and pulled her to her feet. Put her hands on Elena's elbows. 'I don't deal in gobbledy-gook, whatever people might think about card readers. The insights I give people make sense to me – and most of the time to the customer too. I give them the cards' perception of their life. It often provides a way for them to look at their problems or ambitions in a different way.' She brushed a strand of hair out of Elena's face. 'It's obvious you've had such a hard time with this, lass. But almost everything in life has a reason, has an explanation. It's simply a matter of looking at this differently. As is the case, I believe, for this episode from your past.' Morag went to the bookcase at the end of the room. Grunting, she crouched down and ran a finger over the books. Eventually, she stopped at one. She tugged the children's book out and held it up to Elena and Rory.

'A favourite classic. My nephews love it.'

Elena's mouth fell open. Memories came back of her reading that book, cover to cover, night after night. 'That used to be a favourite of mine too,' she stuttered. 'It must have been one of the tatty books that Mum threw out when I was twelve – she'd had a clear-out, thinking I'd be happy for the new shelf space. I'd completely forgotten about it.' Elena reached out a hand. Morag passed her the book and sat down again. Elena stared at the cover – a fortune teller, in a purple shawl, holding a black cat, a crystal ball at her feet.

'The book's called *As the Clock Struck Midnight*,' said Rory, in a hushed tone.

'I remember the story now,' said Elena, in a choked-up voice. 'The fortune teller had the power to let people swap lives for a day, from midnight. "A life for a life" was her catchphrase. People would choose someone who, in their opinion, led a fantastic life, full of riches or travel. But the exchange always made them realise that, actually, their own life wasn't so bad. But...' She looked up at Morag. 'My memory of us making that deal... it's so very real.'

'You had a fever. You were traumatised about your mum, lassie. Then there was a black cat there and I was wearing a purple shawl. It does add up, Elena. I can see why you, a young child at the time, might have woken up the next day, confused – especially with the coincidence of your mum recovering at midnight. If you flick through the pages, you'll see the fortune teller gets paid by potential life-swappers with a bar of her favourite dark chocolate. She makes a joke about dark forces that runs throughout the story.'

Elena's brain froze. It was too much to take in. Was this some joke? Was Morag protecting herself or getting confused?

'When I once had flu, I woke up convinced that, during the night, I'd been flying on a broomstick,' mumbled Rory.

'But this can't be true,' Elena said. Tears ran down her face. 'All these years I've worried about it. That so-called promise has stopped me doing so many things. It cast a shadow over my life for months at school, until I learned to box it up in my mind, the lid only popping open now and again. I'm so fucking stupid.'

'Don't,' said Rory sternly. 'You were ten, for goodness' sake. Children believe all sorts – that Father Christmas is real, that fairies collect teeth.'

But Elena had grown out of believing those two particular myths.

As if reading her mind, Morag asked, 'Any clue as to why you haven't shaken off this belief as an adult, lass, as you matured and would have realised, through logic, that it was ridiculous? You strike me as an otherwise sensible young woman, which is probably why this has been so distressing for you.'

Elena studied the book's cover. 'Because of a voice in my head... Whenever I dared question that night, it piped up: "Yes, but what if it's true?" That doubt held so much power, driven by the evidence of Mum's recovery, Gayle's dental appointment and Lucy's gran's lottery win.' The doubt that plagued her even now. So, Morag hadn't made the promise with her. What if the universe had? No one could deny that her mum should have died twenty years ago. Had the fortune teller been a red herring? There were no leads left to explore. Now all Elena could do was wait until the twenty-first. She lifted her head and caught Rory giving her a curious look. Fighting off more tears, she stared without blinking for a few seconds. 'One more thing, Morag. You gave me a playing card. The king of hearts. Why?'

'It represents someone who'd be important to you one day. That night, my cards were underneath my shawl, in a trouser pocket, and they fell out when I put the cat down. That card was the only one that lay face up, on the damp grass. I just got a strong feeling.'

Morag made them another cup of tea and insisted they each have a bowl of the stew. Elena's pulse slowed as she digested Morag's words, along with the food.

'What about the three near misses I've had in recent weeks?' she said, the stew restoring her logic. Elena told Morag about the firework, the swimming pool and coffee spill.

'Mere coincidences,' said Morag.

Really? All three? Mum getting better bang on midnight – was that really nothing but a coincidence as well?

Nah.

If anything was a coincidence, it was that book cover.

Since that night in the woods, Elena had held the fortune teller up as some powerful oracle. This meeting proved she was just flesh and blood, like everyone else. A lovely woman, by all appearances, a fellow booklover too. But it was clear confused Morag knew no more than Elena. The internet was loaded with quotes about there being no such thing as coincidence. Any detective knew that.

'Sorry for being a bit... offhand earlier,' said Rory to Morag as they stood in the hallway to go, a sheepish look on his face.

'Don't apologise, lad. I can tell, you're a good friend. You were looking out for Elena.' She opened the door. 'Rory Bunker. An unusual surname. Do you know the origin of it?'

'No. Should look into it, really. I used to get called Golfie at school.' He went outside, into the slushy night.

Morag put her hand on Elena's arm as she went to follow. 'I'm always here, if you want a chat. My landline's been playing up lately.' She sighed. 'My nephews have convinced me it's time to finally get a mobile phone. If you give me your number, I'll message you mine, if you want.' Morag gave a wry smile. 'I fear they've got me a smart phone for Christmas. Silly name, isn't it? As if anyone would make a phone that was stupid.' She disappeared and came back shortly with a notepad and pen. Indifferently, Elena scribbled down her number.

Yet Elena was grateful for the woman's time. 'Thanks, Morag. Sorry for just calling by unannounced.'

'Your mum is very lucky to have a daughter like you.' Morag gave her a hug. Half-heartedly, Elena patted the fortune teller's back and Morag's perfume jogged her memory, a soothing smell of heather and pine. 'I'm sorry, lass. I imagine this visit has given you a lot to take in?'

Ya think? Where to start? Morag believed that twenty years of torture simply came from a muddle over a book? No. It didn't make sense. As Gayle, as her parents, as school teachers always said, order and rationale had ruled that little girl's life. She'd never hallucinated with any other childhood bug and didn't believe that adult Elena would have continued to believe the promise, unless there was some significant reason to support it.

'That comment you remembered, about making a deal that meant you would "pass on to the next stage of our world"...' said Morag, and she nodded encouragingly. 'That's not from the book, but wherever it came from, perhaps it's food for thought. Maybe a new stage of your life is waiting for you, around the corner, and all you need is a nudge in order to move forwards to it.'

Elena stepped outside. The only direction she needed to move in was away from the bungalow and this woman who, getting on in years, quite possibly had a dodgy memory and couldn't recall exactly everything she'd said to young Elena all those years ago.

'Thanks again for seeing me.' Elena was thankful. Truly. Yet so disappointed. The explanation Morag had given didn't feel like the whole story. It was as if the last chapter was missing and wasn't to be found in Scotland. Oh, Morag had provided a denouement, explaining about the crystal ball, about the importance of the clock and midnight, the dark chocolate. However, Elena knew, in her heart, that this wasn't The End; that the story of that frightening night, still with loose ends, had a final plot twist waiting in the wings.

'One last thing. That card was important,' called Morag from her doorway. 'Don't forget that, Elena.'

Really? In *Alice in Wonderland*, the King of Hearts was weak and indecisive. As an avid reader of books, Morag should have known that.

36

RORY

Sunday 14th December

What a tedious journey back from Scotland, with a diversion and then a broken-down lorry causing tailbacks. Elena had gone straight up to bed after we visited Morag yesterday, having hardly spoken to me. She couldn't face a drink in the B&B's bar. She was still deep in thought this morning, over bacon and eggs that remained untouched on her plate. At her request, we skipped the planned trip around Leith. I mentioned her imminent birthday party, but she wasn't enthusiastic. Whatever Morag had said, Elena was still being nervous about next weekend and didn't want to talk about the children's book we'd been shown. We didn't even stop at the services, despite the terrible traffic. No sooner had we got back than the shower was running in her bathroom. I made cheese toasties and took hers up, but she had disappeared, possibly for the whole afternoon.

I wouldn't know though, as I rang up Julian and asked if I could go over. He's a good mate and he cancelled plans with his new girlfriend – a customer at the veterinary surgery who is also a primary school teacher. She'd seen a social media post about the stick insects needing new homes and wanted some for her classroom. One bramble twig led to another and they'd been out on three dates since. I felt like dating Julian myself when I arrived at his. He'd ordered Indian takeout and made one of his fruit crumbles for afterwards. He'd often left a portion of those outside my door in the past, when he couldn't polish it all off himself.

We talked about Chelsea, the teacher, and Brandy and Snap's big new tank. Julian spilled the tea about the builders working on my apartment, who sing louder than they drill and are full of banter at 7.30 a.m., when any normal person is still waking up. After 1 chicken balti, 1 pilau rice, 2 naan breads, a scoop of Saag Aloo and 1 onion bhaji, I finally got around to asking Julian about his illness and the stress that had made parts of his life a misery.

I felt disloyal for sharing Elena's childhood secret, but it was for the best, because I think I have an explanation for her promise that runs deeper than her memory simply being messed up by a children's book. Julian shared his experiences and concluded, like me, that there were things about that night, in the woods, about that death deal, that weren't explained by everything Morag had said.

I need Elena to open up more, except she's avoiding me. I understand why. Her whole persona and reputation is based upon sound judgement, on level-headedness. Those are the things that have got her to the top of her profession. She's embarrassed.

Perhaps it will do her good, having the house to herself tomorrow, as I'll be over at Tahoor's watching the footie. Dad is coming over too! When we got back from Scotland and Elena shot inside, I went over to Tahoor, who was dead-

heading a plant in his front garden. I mentioned that Dad hadn't been able to get tickets for tomorrow night, so Tahoor suggested we make a lads' night of it. He looked... happier. His manner has a purpose to it now, and he's arranged to go bowling with friends after Christmas. We batted a few football facts at each other before I left to unpack:

Football began in China over 2,000 years ago, and was called cuju.

North Korea has the biggest stadium, that can supposedly hold 150,000 people.

The average player runs 11 km during 1 game. We both felt knackered just imagining that.

Right. Time for sleep. It's a big week ahead, with the football night, staff Christmas quiz night and then Elena's birthday bash.

But most importantly, I'm hoping, with the whole of my heart, that the biggest thing will be that Julian's theory is right, and that the question he's given me, to ask Elena, will finally lead to the truth about whether she'll die at thirty.

37

ELENA

Gary linked arms with Elena as they walked towards the Three Horseshoes. He'd brought tinsel into the office and insisted everyone make scarves out of it. He'd sent out an email last week saying wearing Christmas jumpers was a must. As he did every year, he'd ribbed Elena for her tasteful, subtly sequined choice, whilst shimmying to make the knitted snowy bobbles on his shake. Caz walked behind talking to Sophie, the intern. Behind them were Rory and Derek, followed by the rest of the team.

'Ready to be thrashed?' Gary said to Elena and grinned. 'Rory may be the fun fact king, but my general knowledge is second to none – Diego's obsessed with Trivial Pursuit, as if he's living back in the eighties.'

She blew on her fingers, having left her gloves at home this morning. 'How about I go on Caz's and your team?' she said brightly. 'We'd just need to find two other people. I... I'd like to see how well I do without Rory answering every question. Just because we're housemates doesn't mean we're joined at the hip.'

Gary pulled open the door and they went into the warm, hit

by post-work banter and the aroma of hops and fried food. He gave her a sideways glance. 'You sure?' Elena nodded vigorously.

Gary started to sort out the logistics, but Rory went to sit down by Elena straightaway. 'Mate... I think our team is full,' said Gary. 'How about you sit with Derek and...'

'Oh. Right. Of course.' He and his elf jumper moved more quickly than the commuters outside heading off to do Christmas shopping, panic having set in with only one week to go.

Elena still couldn't face him. Not after the children's book revelations and the opinion he must have of her now. He'd tried to talk about everything Morag had said on the trip back down to Manchester, but she'd changed the subject. She, Gary, Caz, Sophie and marketing assistant Sanjay made up her team. Halves of lager arrived, with vodka shots to knock back before drinking, courtesy of Gary. Elena and Rory had got up extra early to catch the train to work, so they could drink tonight. Elena swigged her shot in one and gave her first genuine smile since seeing Morag.

'This is water.'

'Shhh,' said Gary. 'We need to keep hydrated if we're going to beat the others. I've looked at the categories of questions. They've got a festive twist. Caz is a great nature buff, you're on literature and I'm the biggest foodie ever. Sophie, you're a whizz when it comes to movies and celebrities, right?'

Sophie gave a thumbs up before drinking the water. She pulled a face afterwards and went up to the bar to get proper drinks for her and Sanjay, who was a self-professed expert when it came to history. Despite trying to avoid his attention, Elena laughed out loud when worldwide traveller Rory got beaten over a question on where Saint Nicholas was born. Rory confidently said Russia, having seen many statues of him there on a heli-skiing trip years ago. Sanjay duly provided the correct answer:

Turkey. Rory's strength, as well as travel and sport, was general knowledge. Yet he was no competition for Gary when it came to food – Gary knew straightaway that peacocks used to be the centrepieces in medieval festive banquets. The surprise of the evening was Derek's celebrity knowledge. Oh, the scowl on Sophie's face when she didn't know which Puerto Rican singer was born on Christmas Day – Rory's team whooped when Derek immediately wrote down the answer, later proven to be Ricky Martin. Elena's mind didn't return once to Morag – apart from that question about an old Christmas tradition in Scotland where single people would crack an egg into a cup on Christmas Eve, and the shape of the white would magically predict the profession of a potential romantic partner.

Each team had handed in their entries and tucked into bowls of French fries and chicken wings. Rory looked at Elena across the room. More relaxed, she gave a thumbs up. His face lit up and he sent one back. Gary gently elbowed Elena.

'Come up to the bar with me, will you? I'll get another round in. You can help me carry them back. We should sample those spiced clementine gin cocktails that the bar staff are making especially.'

Whilst the barman made their drinks, he nudged Elena with his elbow again. 'What are you going to do about it?'

'Pardon?'

'You and Rory. It's obvious you're mad about him.'

'*What?* Me and... I don't think so. Really, *you* are the one who's mad,' she hissed, and the barman glanced over.

'Come on, Swan, admit it, I'm right. I've always had my suspicions, but these last weeks... I've caught you staring at him, for no good reason. You become more animated, in a fun way, when he's around, as if you've binged on popping candy. It's good to see, Elena. I think you should go for it.'

'And I don't think you should drink so much.'

He opened his mouth and breathed on to her face. 'Not guilty.'

She pretended to gag and Gary laughed.

'But you've always teased about what a terrible match we'd make, and said it would be like Timothée Chalamet and Princess Anne getting together.'

'Timothée is sexy, right?'

Her eyes narrowed. 'Fancy Rory yourself, do you?'

Gary looked appalled. 'Good God, no! All those facts, the figures, the stats... Whereas a man who rides sandworms on dunes and gives out golden tickets for a chocolate factory, that's a different matter.'

'Does Diego know about this crush?' She took one of the cocktails and sipped it, keen to change the subject.

'We allow each other one celebrity crush each,' he said airily. 'Diego's is Gordon Ramsay.' He looked at Elena and they both chuckled. 'But I digress. Seriously, you should say something. I reckon he feels the same.'

He doesn't. Couldn't.

'What's stopping you, hmm?'

She took another sip and looked away. 'Rory... he's found out something embarrassing about me. For sure I've lost his respect.'

Gary paid the barman. He hesitated. 'I understand. I tried to hide it, but Diego accidentally overheard me once, on the phone to the bank, after we'd only been on a few dates. I needed to get a large sum of money back. I'd been scammed for a thousand pounds.'

Elena met his gaze. '*How* much?'

Gary sighed. 'A photographer – or so I thought – had seen my profile on socials and wanted me to, um... model. He said he'd need the money upfront and it would guarantee a great portfolio and secure a spot on an upcoming shoot that would lead to masses of paid work. He kept going on about how hot I was.' Gary turned bright red. 'Stupid, I know. People always say I've got a great personality...' He gave Elena a pointed look, and she smiled and side-hugged him. 'But they don't say so much about my looks. His offer fed into the securities I used to have that contributed to my old eating disorder problems. His compliments were fabulous, as if I were leaner and taller than any catwalk model. Guess that's why I've been teasing Rory – to try to get the shame and my vanity out of my system, and to not be afraid of talking and joking about modelling. I've only recently watched *America's Next Top Model* again.'

'Why didn't you tell me at the time?'

'I felt like an idiot. But Diego was great and made me realise it wasn't my fault. I told Rory once when I drank too much. He was really understanding. Another mate might have laughed.'

The landlord rang the bell at the bar.

Gary looked at Elena. 'Go for it, gal. Don't tell him I said so, but Rory's one of the good guys.'

They sat down and the landlord came out from behind the bar and smiled. 'It's a draw, between team Santapolitan' – Elena and Gary beamed – 'and team Mistletoehattan.' Rory and Derek high-fived. 'Sit tight, here's the tiebreaker for every team member to win one free drink a week for the whole of 2025: According to myth, why should you avoid your cat as the clock strikes midnight on Christmas Eve?'

Cat... Midnight... The fear came flooding back. Elena sat up with a jolt. No one spoke for a moment and the landlord was about to give the answer when nature expert Caz shot her hand up.

'My grandma used to tell us this,' said Caz. 'Apparently

midnight on Christmas Eve is the one time cats gain the power of speech, and anyone who hears them talk will die.'

Elena froze, drowning in a wave of painful memories around the childhood fear that Mummy was going to die. She got to her feet and almost tripped outside, escaping into the sobering air. The pub door creaked open behind her. Rory appeared with both their coats.

'Come on,' he said, 'I need to avoid Gary's jubilation. You haven't seen how the renovation work is going on my apartment. No time like the present.'

38

ELENA

Elena sat in Rory's apartment, shivering. He put on the heating and fetched a blanket. She huddled under it on the floral sofa. Like his dress sense, the apartment's décor was fluid, with a chintzy sofa and armchair holding their own amongst minimalist wooden side tables and shelves. Curtains hung at the windows instead of blinds, with multi-coloured decorations fixed to the plain magnolia walls, like the hanging alpaca blanket from Peru. However, the kitchen and bathroom renovations had both been practical, with marble fittings in grey, black and white. The apartment smelt of fresh paint and sawdust. Elena inspected his shelves, as she did on every visit. There was always a new souvenir from a sports trip to join the ones he already had, like the Matryoshka nested dolls and the Thai soap carving. He rambled on about the dust, joking that he'd need to get industrial cleaners in when the builders had finished.

She took out her phone and texted Gary, saying the cocktail had gone to her head – that she and Rory were going home. He sent back a row of winking face emojis, followed by the words *Do it*. Perhaps Gary was right. She should tell Rory how she felt. It couldn't make his opinion of her worse.

'The renovations are beautiful,' she said instead of 'doing it'. 'Real quality. You must be over the moon.'

He came over from his hot chocolate machine and handed her a steaming mug. He snuggled under the blanket with her. 'Yep. Good craftsmanship apart from a couple of small issues. Also, the crew is more or less on target, timewise.'

'About earlier and me leaving the pub,' she said. 'The cocktail made me feel a bit woozy and—'

He looked her dead in the eyes. 'I didn't know that fact about cats or midnight either.'

Dear Rory. Always so understanding. 'I've got something I want to talk to you about,' she said, heart thumping loudly in her ears.

'Me too,' he said and took a large mouthful of the creamy, sweet drink, wincing as it was still too hot.

'You go first,' she said with relief. She needed a hit of chocolate first.

'Sure?'

Quickly, she raised the mug to her lips.

Rory pulled down the bit of the blanket covering him and turned sideways to face her. 'It's more of a question really – that might shed some light on what happened years ago.'

'But... don't you, like Morag, believe that children's book provides all the answers?'

'Huh? Not all. Not in my opinion.'

Was there a chance he didn't think her ridiculous?

He put down her mug too, and took her hands. 'Let's just say, for argument's sake, that you did get confused and there really wasn't a promise made...'

'One *was*,' she said, face pinched.

'Okay. But can you recall any episode in your life where you've convinced yourself that something bad has happened – but it hadn't really?'

She pursed her lips.

'It's important, Elena,' he said gently.

She thought hard. 'Nope.'

'Nothing at all, where you've been convinced of something that would make no sense to anyone else?'

She broke eye contact. Well, there was that thing that happened at school. She was sixteen. It had felt like the end of the world. But it was nothing; she'd just been a stupid teen.

'Elena?' he pushed gently.

She sighed. 'It was just me being weird as a teenager, during a stressful time. I don't see how it's relevant.'

'Tell me about it.'

'I revised really hard for my GCSEs. The pupils I hung out with were straight-A people and I wanted to be the same. It... it happened right at the beginning of the exam period. I came home from a chemistry paper. I'd had a crisis of confidence halfway through and panicked afterwards, convinced I'd failed. It was the first exam and it really affected me. I didn't perform as well as I reckoned I should have, in the following ones. I worried about it all summer, hardly sleeping, telling myself I wouldn't be allowed to do the A levels I was interested in, telling myself I'd let my parents down. But then the results came through and I more or less got straight As. I don't know why, but the idea popped into my head that the exam board had made a mistake and muddled my results with another pupil's, especially as a couple of people in my class were devastated by their unexpectedly bad results – and one of them had a similar surname to me. That mere idea became a solid belief, fed by doubt – it grew and grew. I didn't say anything as it would have sounded stupid, but keeping quiet made me feel even more guilty, even less deserving.'

'Did you know it wasn't true at the time?'

'Deep down, yes. You remember what pupils are like – every exam we came out talking about our answers, and mine were the same as my bright friends who also got As. I could appreciate that, when the results came through, but even that logic didn't erase the doubts in my mind about being given the wrong results, not at the time. That logic couldn't overpower the 'what if' voice. Mum and Dad were so proud when I opened my results, but this obsession clung on tight. I pretended to be happy, but as soon as the fuss died down, I went up to my room and cried and cried.'

'You've come to terms with the truth now?'

'It took several years. Told you it was weird.'

Rory took her hand. 'I can't imagine how difficult that must have been. But... there's someone who could.'

Elena raised an eyebrow.

'The reason I went to see Julian on Sunday... I hope you don't mind, Elena, but I told him about the woods and the children's book, because he's been through a similar thing.'

She sat more upright. 'He met a fortune teller as a child? Did Julian make a deal? Did it come true?'

'No, nothing like that. He was doing voluntary work at an animal shelter that had a veterinary wing. A favourite patient he'd been working on, an Alsatian dog, rescued from years of abuse, died, despite him insisting on personally giving around-the-clock care. Julian was approaching exam time. He'd convinced himself he'd killed the dog in a cruel way, that he'd let it die on purpose; that the animal had looked him straight in the eye as it passed, knowing that Julian had effectively murdered it. He couldn't shake this off for a couple of years, telling himself he was a bad vet and it would only happen again. After he recovered from this, like you, Julian put it down to him being... odd, the whole episode simply being one of the quirks of his personality.'

What has this got to do with Elena's story? Exam time was stressful; they'd both simply let the pressure get to them. This had nothing to do with that night on the common.

'Then a few years ago, when he went through a difficult divorce...'

'Julian's been married?'

'He doesn't talk about it often... Things turned ugly, and what with a busy career, bad stress kicked in again. Julian went through a phase – it lasted about a year – of convincing himself he knocked pets over with his car and killed them – that he was guilty of multiple hit-and-runs and leaving the animals to die in pain and their owners bereft. Driving to and from work became increasingly upsetting as he kept having to park up and go back and check the street behind him. Eventually, he broke down in front of his boss when he was late, yet again, for his shift.'

Poor Julian. But what had this got to do with her?

'It's called False Memory OCD, Elena. False memories about the sufferer doing something wrong. The hit-and-run subcategory is, sadly, a popular one, with sufferers believing they've hit and killed passersby. For you, it's been believing you did a terrible thing: for selfish reasons, tampering with the course of nature, risking awful consequences for your mother.'

'OCD?' She rolled her eyes. 'Is that what this chat is about? Me having a mental health problem? Come on, Rory. No way. Not me. I mean... I like checking things and—'

'Exactly. The tendency has always been there. I did a little research – hope that isn't overstepping – but being bullied at school might have triggered it. That phrase you told me your gran would always say: "It costs nothing to double-check." That probably fed into it. Gayle, your parents, they were aware of how super safety-conscious you were as a child – unusually so. It's always struck me how safety aware you are too, even though I've only known you for a year. Then your routines have become heightened in recent weeks due to the stress of your approaching birthday.'

He meant to help, that much was clear, but Rory couldn't have been more wrong.

'I saw a documentary about OCD once,' she said. 'This woman had to stare at the hob for two hours, each night, to make sure it wasn't still on. Another spent the whole of her day doing housework, terrified of dust collecting. I've never been that bad! OCD hugely disables people's lives. It's insulting to them that you think that's what my problems have been about. A few bolts on the door and double-checking windows, that's nothing in comparison.' She wasn't up all night, washing her hands; wasn't paranoid about catching germs. Her food tins weren't colour-coordinated. No, rational Elena had a successful career, a beautiful house. No illness had held her back.

'Suffering for years about false guilt over exam results? Believing you'd made a reckless pact that would end your life? I'd say that's been equally as disabling and painful.'

Elena gave him a fixed stare. In Rory's opinion, she was seriously, mentally ill. But if that were the case, she'd never have coped all these years. 'Look. You're mistaken. Leave it. I appreciate the time you've taken looking into this, but I haven't got OCD. I'd know if I had.'

'Julian didn't. Not when he was in the midst of it.'

She scrambled to her feet. 'For God's sake, stop, man! I'm not listening to this rubbish.' Because accepting she had that mental illness would mean admitting that... that... she hadn't coped at all; that the stress she's suffered hadn't been about saving Mum, a belief that had made the last two decades bearable. No, it would mean that the time she'd spent these last years playing it safe and worrying was down to something truly imaginary that her brain alone had created.

What a waste that would have been. What a pointless tragedy.

Rory had misjudged this completely. Elena *had* been instrumental in saving her Mum's life, and that was a price she'd always been willing to pay. How dare Rory try to take that away from her?

'There's one more thing,' he said quietly.

Why was he doing this? Her heartbeat raced. Elena's fists curled; her face screwed up. 'I'm not interested in your amateur theories! You're going too far now. This is all highly offensive.'

'But you've mentioned the two words that plague sufferers of OCD. *What if.* What if it happened? What if I did it? The two words that eat away at any common sense and—'

'That's enough! I'm leaving! Alone!'

'Elena... I... I didn't mean to upset you,' he stuttered and rubbed his forehead. 'But surely it's good to know? Now you can get treatment and get rid of your guilt – Julian said that feeling is a massive part of it.'

Her breath hitched. Rory didn't see her as someone who'd valiantly emerged from trauma stronger, but as someone who needed fixing, instead of a person who'd saved the life of another. 'You can forget coming back to mine.' Her voice trembled. 'Your apartment's renovation is almost completed. It's time to move out of my place and... and' – her voice rose – 'take those fucking stick insects with you. I'll pack up your stuff and bring it into work tomorrow.'

Rory winced and he stood up too. 'Elena, let's talk this over. Look, I'm sorry if—'

'Why would you inflict a mental illness on me? Does it make you feel like a bigger person, thinking that I'm nuts?'

His jaw dropped.

'I am Elena Swan.' Her voice shook. 'I have a solid marketing career. I was just ten years old when I sacrificed everything to save my mum. Maybe it was selfish, maybe I risked angering some dark force, but... but I was a child, and it's... it's been so fucking hard for me. I am not ill. I am of sound mind. You ask anyone who's ever known me.' A sob escaped her lips. 'I held my family together when it mattered, when the grown-ups were panicking about Mum dying. It was *me* who saved her and this is the thanks I get for it?'

Fist in her mouth, she ran towards the door, yanked it open and slammed it shut behind her.

39

RORY

Wow. He'd messed up big time, and Rory had moved on to gin since Elena left. The door almost came off its hinges when she'd slammed it.

What an idiot. He'd gone blundering in and arrogantly announced a diagnosis instead of simply mooting the possibility of OCD and letting Elena work things out for herself. She hadn't even seen a doctor yet, for fuck's sake. Later on he could have introduced Julian. His neighbour and Elena might have spoken at the party. A few days ago she'd suggested inviting him. Julian was keenly doing the social rounds at the moment, still needing homes for the thirty remaining stick insects he was looking after.

Rory sat on the floor now, leaning back against the sofa. His knees were bent and he dropped his head onto them. What a jerk. He'd never seen her so angry. Elena was always so level, about everything. A spike of pain ran through his chest at the thought of her home alone and in a state.

One way he could start redeeming himself was to get on with arranging her party. He didn't have to be there, not if it was going to upset her. Rory reached for his phone and tapped in a journal entry that he would write up when he got his notebook back.

Tuesday 17th December

Okay. Focus. I need to firm up the party details and will email them straight to Elena. I won't be expecting an acknowledgement tonight. Maybe she'll never reply. But I hope the message will prod her to not consider cancelling Saturday.

Sigh. Our fallout is going around and around in my head. I'm sure she's got False Memory OCD. It all adds up. Speaking with Julian confirmed my view. The research pointed to it being such a devastating illness. A few facts I've stumbled across, although they vary a little from article to article:

Sometimes there is no clear cause for OCD.

It's not just handwashing or being super tidy; the sufferer often hides it.

It can run in families. Most sufferers realise their fears are not logical, yet that powerful phrase kicks in – 'but what if?'.

Prior to the 18th century, OCD was considered the work of evil spirits, and the treatment was exorcism.

The average age of onset is 19, but 50 per cent of sufferers have symptoms before then.

It affects men and women equally.

OCD affects 1 per cent of the worldwide population – that adds up to 70 million people.

That last fact takes my breath away. Elena must feel so alone at times – if only she knew she really wasn't. But I've said all I can to her. It's none of my business any more. I never want to hurt her like that again. It's her prerogative about if and when she gets help. Now may not be the right time. So I'll keep my distance and definitely keep hiding my feelings. Elena could never love such a Jurassic-sized twat as me.

Right, the party:

11 guests – Elena, her parents Don and Melanie, Gayle, Tahoor, Gary and Diego, Caz and Derek with their respective partners. I won't include me, my dad, his girlfriend Jenny and Julian – not now.

Ingredients for the Christmas punch the two of us talked about – Prosecco, vodka, cranberry juice, orange juice, limes, oranges, pomegrànates.

Festive nibbles from our favourite supermarket. Even though the celebration is for her birthday, Elena wanted to enjoy more Christmas fare – in case she never quite got to the 25th of December – so that would be those turkey stuffing crisps we tried, chestnut sausage rolls, sage and onion cheese-stuffed croquettes, cranberry and brie filo parcels, and a cheese board with black pepper crackers and olives.

Pizza takeout – we kept the main easy. I was even prepared to eat pineapple on mine again.

Dessert – Diego has insisted he'll provide that.

Party poppers, paper napkins, table glitter, balloons.

I can't face typing anything else – like the plans we had for board games, and charades once everyone got a little tipsy, perhaps even getting out her old childhood game of Twister. We were going to create a Spotify dance list together as well.

There's no more together now – not for us.

But this isn't about how sad I am. Saturday is about her. Elena is the most incredible, strong woman I've ever met, who's held her own against what may well have been a debilitating illness for years, who's always done her best for other people. I couldn't respect and admire her more.

Despite what I've learnt from Julian, and the internet, despite the solid evidence, I'm worried about the weekend. That's what I should have said to Elena tonight. Sometimes the facts, the logic, they aren't enough for anyone.

My worry about her turning thirty is nothing to do with an obsession or compulsion; it's nothing as extreme as what Elena's been through. But even if it was, it wouldn't mean I was nuts or loony, or that I'd got a screw loose, or that I was a basket-case or a psycho. None of those offensive, old-fashioned insults that used to be bandied about apply just because someone believes in something that can't be explained, or has suffered any other mental illness. So often the people who come out the other side are the most resilient amongst us... like Julian with his own OCD, and Dad who brought me up with such care, despite his depression after losing Mum; like Gary, who's suffered an eating disorder and told me once about a terrible time after he was scammed about his looks – yet you'd never guess, with all the banter; like my childhood neighbour who suffered from agoraphobia after being mugged, yet always had a smile when she saw me through her window; like Caz, who's told me about the social anxiety she suffered at uni, even though she now enjoys the office outings as much as anyone. Then there's her husband, suffering from stress with his family in Ukraine. Like Pete at work, too, having panic attacks because of his increased mortgage payments, and Sanjay hardly sleeping thanks to his son's online bullies. Like Tahoor, whose grief made things slip after Isha died, but who has found the strength, recently, to turn things around.

Like Elena, for a long list of reasons.

Being led astray by unhelpful thoughts is simply called being human – even if they are completely false and have no solid grounds whatsoever.

With one caveat – not if you're a flat earth believer like Carl.

(Elena would laugh at that last line.)

40

ELENA

Elena pulled up on her drive. Friday. She exhaled, impatient to get inside and spend the evening escaping into fiction. Last night she'd finished *The Light We Lost*, the story of a couple continually brought together, then torn apart. Elena rested her forehead on the steering wheel for a moment. She'd taken Rory's belongings to work in bin liners on Wednesday, the day after their argument, and gave them to him, from the boot of her car, at lunch. Neither she nor Rory had mentioned their fallout. Thankfully everyone in the office was too hungover to notice the lack of banter between them, and the rest of the week, with Christmas imminent, and all the preparation that entailed, took the others' attention. She'd batted away Gary's questions, saying she was still thinking about what he said.

Rory had come over to her desk after she'd handed his stuff to him in the car park. She was reading. 'Elena...'

She'd not replied.

'I won't come to the party. I'll take Dad, Jenny and Julian out for a meal instead.'

She'd not looked up from her book when she replied, 'Mum and Dad will ask questions. Tahoor too, Gayle maybe, and everyone from the office, especially Gary. It's probably best that the four of you just come.' Despite everything, she'd love to meet his father and the girlfriend.

'You're sure? Okay. Whatever's easiest. Shall I come early and help arrange—'

'I don't need any help, thank you.' This was true. She'd cracked on with organising it the last couple of days, and, begrudgingly, admitted Rory's email had helped. Elena Swan would see her twenties out with a bang.

Yesterday Rory had approached her once more and asked about Brandy and Snap. Again it was lunch time and she was reading. Books had always been her safe place when the real world got too scary. She'd dived into a new story today, a light-hearted romance by a favourite author, who focused on the journey, not the destination, of the story, understanding that her readership liked a predictable ending, because life is so often not like that. Knowing what was going to happen, at least in fiction, offered security at a hazardous time.

Elena suggested Rory take Brandy and Snap home after the party. Truth is, she was hoping he'd somehow forget. She'd apologised to them as soon as she got home after the quiz night for asking Rory to take them away, and for swearing. She'd never normally refer to them with the f-word. They were beautiful and clever, merging in with their leafy background, and she admired the contented life they led, a life humans might consider boring. Snap looked especially clever lately, hanging upside down.

The sharp December air brought Elena back to the present as she opened the car door. Tahoor came out and hurried over as sporadic snowflakes tumbled down.

'Now, I certainly have not been curtain-twitching and waiting for you to return...' he said, a guilty look on his face.

She couldn't help smiling.

'But I was hoping you'd come in for a cup of tea and try a samosa. I made a batch for the party tomorrow. Young Sharnaz encouraged me. Isha always did the cooking. I didn't want to come empty-handed. She wouldn't have approved of that.'

No thanks. I just want to go into my house and lose myself in a novel.

'How lovely! Sounds great, Tahoor. I didn't have time for lunch, so a samosa will hit the spot.' Didn't have an appetite, more like.

She followed him inside, telling herself to cheer up for her neighbour's sake, and sat in the lounge that looked more like it used to when Isha was around. Half-heartedly, she scrolled through her phone until Tahoor came in, looking proud of himself, carrying a tray with a teapot on it, with two cups, milk and sugar.

'I feel like a queen,' she said to Tahoor, and beaming he went back into the kitchen. Elena thought of the card Morag had given her, the king of hearts.

He came back with a bowl of samosas, handed her a plate and she helped herself to one. He sat down in the armchair.

'They are vegetarian,' he said. 'Just in case. You never know what anyone is these days. Sharnaz has one school friend who is gluten-free, another is vegan. I can't keep up. In my day, you ate what was on your plate or you got nothing. This is one of Isha's recipes. I hope I've done her justice.'

Elena took a bite. Wow. Those flavours. Subtle but zingy.

Tahoor held his breath.

'It's delicious! Any chance of another?' Elena asked, realising how hungry she was.

Tahoor's chest plumped out and he beamed again. 'No Rory with you tonight? Has he gone off on some sports expedition? Take a couple back for him. I never realised how relaxing cooking was.'

She choked on the flaky pastry and had a coughing fit.

Tahoor put down his plate. 'You okay, lass? What's up? You look as if I've made those pastries sour, not savoury.'

'Oh... it went down the wrong way.'

He tilted his head. 'That's all?'

'I'm tired, to be honest – drank a bit too much earlier in the week, what with the Christmas staff night out.' She told him about the pub quiz questions, but eventually he put up his hand.

'Elena. What's up? I may be a silly old man, but I can tell when someone's sad. I've seen that look enough in the mirror these last months. You might try to hide it, but I can also see through the bluster. Have you and young Rory argued?'

'What makes you say that?'

'Because you've been so happy these last few weeks, since he moved in.'

Like popping candy, Gary had said. Her shoulders bobbed up and down. Tahoor folded his arms.

'Our friendship's probably over,' she mumbled.

'Oh, Elena. I'm sorry, lass.'

'Don't start up about me running out of time to get married, Tahoor,' she said playfully.

He cleared his throat with embarrassment. 'I wouldn't. I've done a lot of talking in the past few days with my daughter. You see, since, well... that red card you gave me.' He pointed to it on the mantelpiece.

'You kept it!' she said.

'It's helped me realise that maybe I *have* held all my grief in. I was telling young Rory that... that recently, crying has helped.'

She leaned forward. 'I'm so very glad.'

'It's brought me and Yalina closer. We've shared tears like never before and talked a lot on the phone lately. Every day, and not just checking in; we've talked about "things that matter", as she puts it. My... my attitude to women and marriage came up.'

Elena put down her drink.

'It's as if my daughter can say more to me, now that we're... sharing feelings. So I explained. You see...' He wiped his mouth with a napkin; a small touch, but it showed how much better he was. 'My mother had big ambitions for me – and for herself, back in Pakistan. Despite not having the chances in education that I did, she'd forged a career in the customer service side of banking. Dad always supported her. She was most unusual compared to the women in our street and compared to our relatives. Some of them agreed to look after me when she continued to work after I was born – only part-time, but it was enough for the community, for some of our family, to frown. She was called names, and was sneered at once by a disgruntled customer at the bank who said women belonged in the home, doing housework, not in an office, sticking their nose into his finances – he refused to be served by her.'

'Tahoor, that's awful,' she murmured, forgetting her own problems for a moment.

'I was proud of her, like Dad. She was one reason I went into banking – but I used to think her life would be so much easier if she'd stayed at home. The other children used to make nasty comments, said I didn't have a proper mummy. I hated seeing her upset. She cried after that episode with the rude man. She worked so very hard, too, getting up early to make dinner before going to work. Dad backed up her career, but it went without saying that she still did the housework and cooking. I don't blame him. It's the way it was, at the time.'

'But this isn't Pakistan back then. This is England, now, and us women still have big battles but there are laws in place to protect us and—'

'I know, and Pakistan has been slowly moving forwards. I'm working on changing, too.' He put a hand on his chest. 'It's a gut instinct, I've got to care. You've been a good neighbour and it's hard to ignore that voice in my head hoping a man will come along and look after you. It's not because I think you're less capable.' He gave her a sheepish look.

Elena wanted to hug him.

Though it didn't mean she'd be getting rid of the card system.

He talked about how proud he was of his Yalina, how she'd worked so hard to become an IT consultant. 'My Isha had always wanted to be a homemaker. She got on well with my mother, who said life was about respecting each other's choices. Nothing gave Isha more pleasure than watching us enjoy her cooking, than keeping things neat and tidy, than organising Yalina's school life, and she was a whizz with budgeting. She instilled in Yalina that she could achieve anything she wanted; that she should follow her heart. Isha would give me a pointed look if I ever went on about grandchildren and Yalina giving up the IT work.' He picked up his drink again. 'The old me would be very sad that you and Rory had argued because that would mean a potential husband, to provide for you, was maybe out of your life.'

Elena got up and went to the mantelpiece. She waved the red card at him and they both smiled as she sat down again, clutching it.

Tahoor gently tapped the card. 'You're allowed to share too. Cry even. What happened with Rory? It might help to talk about it.'

Caught unawares, a tear did trickle down her cheek. She'd

been so blindsided by the situation with Rory that she'd hardly thought about the prospect of her death day tomorrow. Tahoor delved into his pocket and pulled out a clean, cloth handkerchief, ironed into a square. 'Keep it,' he said.

'You're very kind.' Elena dabbed her eyes. 'He... he reckons I'm a weak idiot. Not that people with... with what he talked about are somehow less, they're not... but me, my common sense, my... my solidity... it's how I've always defined myself. Take that away and what's left? Something bad happened years ago, you see, and he's come up with an explanation that questions everything I ever believed about who I am.' Her body shuddered. 'I thought he and I were friends, good friends, that he understood me, had respect. But in his opinion, I made this whole traumatic thing up when I was ten and...' She gave a wry look. 'Sorry. I'm probably not making much sense.'

'The opposite, my dear – this shows how very much you care for the lad. I can't imagine him – or anyone – ever believing you're an idiot.' He patted her arm. 'You and Rory work together on the same team. You must disagree every now and then on a professional level. Goodness knows I did with my colleagues at the bank, over differences from how best to pitch a new product to food going missing in the staff fridge. So how would you handle a disagreement at work?'

Elena stuffed the handkerchief up her sleeve and sniffed. 'Research his point of view for myself.'

Tahoor shrugged. 'There you go.'

Elena stayed for another cup of tea, finding, to her surprise, she didn't want to leave. She suggested a game of cards and tried to give him a very stern look when she worked out he'd let her win, but instead blew him a kiss. Back at hers, Elena settled in the lounge after spraying Brandy and Snap's bramble leaves.

Tahoor was right. The only way to convince Rory he was wrong would be to come at it from a position of knowledge.

Coat still on until the heating warmed up, she ignored the light-hearted romance she wanted to dive back into, opened her laptop and typed 'OCD' into the search engine.

41

RORY

Friday 20th December

My 3rd night staying over at Julian's. As soon as I bumped into him on Wednesday, and told him about the fallout, he insisted I sleep there until the renovations on my apartment are completely finished.

I'm in bed after our 3rd takeout meal since I moved in. Yes, that's 1 every night. Julian's veterinary surgery is pre-holiday busy, owners fearful their pets' minor complaints might worsen during the closed festive days. Whereas I have no zest for cooking, no zest for anything much. I've insisted on paying. Japanese night one, curry yesterday and full-blown fish 'n' chips tonight, with buttered baps, mushy peas, tartare sauce and pickled eggs.

4 chocolate baubles from Julian's tree lifted my mood even further, but only for as long as it took to swallow them.

I miss the 2 insectile ladeez in my life. The natural world has always inspired humans' creations; it's called biomimicry. Scientists considered the way desert spiders moved when inventing space rovers, and beavers have been looked at closely in terms of creating fur-like wetsuits for surfers. These 2 stick insects inspire me to stay humble. Sounds pretentious? Maybe it is. But they don't ask for much, just the basics. They blend into their environment, and Brandy and Snap are self-sufficient in terms of reproduction. Yet, like all insects, they're important, clearing vegetation and fertilising the soil with their waste. Us humans make our lives so complicated, attracting stress instead of repelling it.

Most of all, I miss Elena, a zillion times a day (it would take a boring amount of zeros to write that as a number) every time a silly fun fact, or an idea for work, comes to mind, or I've watched a great thriller like the film Julian and I put on last night. I miss the look on her face when takeout arrives, how those blue eyes light up and she gets bossy with the plates, insisting we must eat before the food gets cold. I even miss her jazz music, it's grown on me like a weed that turns out to be beneficial, like clover that fixes nitrogen in soil. Those tunes are comforting, gentle, like Elena's presence when it's just the two of us in her lounge after a gruelling day in the office. We don't need to talk, and we automatically sense if the other needs a drink or snack. It's easy. Reassuring. It's homely.

Or used to be. 4 chocolate baubles go down a lot easier with 4 whiskies, don't you know? Julian didn't say anything but ran me 1 large glass of water to take to bed, and here I am humming 'Ocean Eyes'.

What if something fateful does happen to Elena tomorrow? I can't block out that concern, because I care so very much for her, like she cared for her mum, like Julian cared for that Alsatian dog. When emotions run high, people can fall into the trap of believing internal lies to be external truths.

Will Elena disappear for good in the next 24 hours?

42

ELENA

After heading to the supermarket last night, after work, to pick up the party provisions, Elena had spent most of the evening and this morning on the computer, researching, researching. Since lunch, she'd sat in the lounge, letting what she'd discovered about OCD sink in, and how it would effectively end any chance of romance with Rory, due to his theory about her promise twenty years ago.

But now it was time to party! Her guests would arrive in two hours. The light snowflakes that had fallen this week were coming down stronger, heavy, with purpose. She got up and headed into the kitchen, yawning, to fetch plates and cutlery to set up in the dining room. She'd hardly slept this last week. Elena took through the robin-print paper napkins and carefully shook out red and green table glitter. Mum and Dad had wanted to come round early to help once she'd let slip that Rory was 'out'. But she didn't want to risk an intense session of questions about her housemate. Elena set out nibble bowls on the break-fast bar in the kitchen, along with glasses, and went to get changed before making the Christmas punch. Yet she had to charge down again, having forgotten to light the pine candles to set the mood.

In just a few hours, it would be midnight.

None of the research had changed her mind about what would happen on her thirtieth birthday.

No matter. She was going to enjoy tonight. Now 21 December 2024 had finally arrived it was almost a... relief. Her fate was out of her hands. The moment of reckoning was here; no point fretting about avoiding it.

Elena luxuriated in the hot shower, the steamy water as soothing as a warm embrace. Maybe it was a goodbye hug. She shrugged. Half an hour later, she stood in the fancy red gown she'd worn for the early Christmas dinner with Tahoor, her blonde bob stylishly blown, make-up on. She looked skywards. Fuck destiny. She was going to go out in style, having one hell of a time.

The doorbell rang and she hurried downstairs. Elena pulled open the door and the appearance of Rory took her breath away. Coat open at the front, he wore a cranberry-coloured velvet suit, no shirt underneath, nothing but a silver necklace, sexy and naturally confident. He still had a key, could have still let himself in. But here he was, acting like a stranger. He came in, followed by Julian and a grey-haired man who had the same shaped nose as Rory, along with a middle-aged woman with a friendly face.

'Happy Birthday, Elena – you've met Julian, and this is my dad, Mike, and his girlfriend Jenny.'

She shook their hands, exchanged pleasantries, good-naturedly telling them off for buying her presents. Rory shook everyone's coats outside, due to the snow, before hanging them up. Elena suggested the three of them make themselves comfortable in the lounge. She'd bring in Christmas punch. Rory went after her.

'How are you?' he asked tentatively.

'Still alive, as you can see,' she said. Then she caught his eye and smiled. 'I'm great. Looking forward to tonight. The pizza should arrive in an hour. Tahoor and I discussed which games would be best to play and—'

'I miss you,' he blurted out. 'I was a twat. I'm sorry.'

The doorbell rang again and she held up her hand. 'I can't do this, Rory. Not now. Let's speak later. There's something I want to say to you, anyway.'

Eight o'clock.

Rory busied himself pouring out punch. Mum and Dad arrived and shot her worried looks, but they slowly disappeared as Elena sang along to music and laughed at her dad's jokes. She told them about the broken biscuit campaign and how excited she was for its launch in 2025. After catching up, they handed her an envelope, her Christmas present. A long weekend trip for two to...

'Berlin?' Elena looked up at her parents.

'Now that you've started travelling, love, you've a fair bit of mileage to catch up on,' said Dad.

'You could take Rory, seeing as you both went to France... Or I'd love to come, for a gals' trip,' said her mum. 'I've always wanted to see a burlesque show.'

'This is too much! I don't know what to say,' said Elena with a stutter, imagining, for a second, a future, with no promise hanging over her.

'Well, it is a big birthday,' said her dad. 'Can't believe I've got a thirty-year-old daughter.'

Gayle and Tahoor arrived next, at the same time, and it wasn't long before they were comfortably chatting about the snow and whether Manchester would have a white Christmas.

Half past eight.

Gary and Diego turned up late, a while after Caz and Derek and their respective partners. Diego, ever the perfectionist, had been finishing a selection of Spanish Christmas desserts – a walnut cream pudding, marzipan sweets, cinnamon festive cookies, churros and mini nougat bars, and a colourfully decorated brioche-like cake, sliced in half and filled with cream. Gary held a huge helium balloon with '30' written on the side, and he handed Elena a Birthday Girl badge.

The pizza arrived on time, and over a large slice, Elena chatted to her guests, complimenting the wine Gary had brought, and pointing out to Tahoor that all of his samosas had gone.

Five to nine.

She listened to Caz and Derek's Christmas plans and laughed with everyone else when Julian attempted to persuade them that stick insects made the perfect present – as long as they were cared for responsibly. Cue a chat about everyone's pets over the years. Tahoor had apparently had a pet turtle as a child in Pakistan!

Ten fifteen.

This could be her last night. She should have been terrified at the prospect, curled up in a ball under the bed. But after all the upset, all the stress, she hadn't got any tears left and she wouldn't lose her last precious hours to pointless panicking. She got Mum and Dad talking about the eighties. She loved their stories about making mix tapes, JR from *Dallas*, and leg warmers.

Ten fifty-five.

Gary turned up the music and she danced with him, before swirling around the lounge with Tahoor to Frank Sinatra, and then gently she pulled Gayle to her feet once he'd collapsed on to the sofa, breathless. Holding hands, Gayle and Elena danced, like they used to when she was a little girl.

'How's everything going?' asked Gayle over the music. 'I got your text about Scotland. You said everything had been sorted.'

Elena gave her a thumbs up, but Gayle led her into the hallway.

'We may have lost touch over the years, but I can still tell when you're worried. Your voice gets a tad too bright and your shoulders droop when you think no one's looking. Do you want to tell me about the fortune teller?' asked Gayle.

Elena squeezed her hand back. 'No. Not tonight. I really, really, just want to enjoy myself.'

Gayle paused. 'Of course you do, love. But I'm always here if you need a chat. Or a slice of cake. Or even someone to read you a story.'

'I'm sorry for backing off all these years.' Elena's voice sounded full.

Gayle placed her other hand over Elena's. 'Now, we've put that to rest, love. You and I are back in touch and I don't intend on kicking the bucket for a few years yet.'

Eleven thirty.

Elena's mum appeared and frowned. 'Everything okay?'

Gayle looked from her to Elena. 'Fine, Melanie. We were talking books.'

'No change there, then,' said Melanie, and her features softened. 'Have you seen the snow? It's falling even more heavily.'

They went into the dining room and looked out onto the back lawn. Elena loved how excited her mum got every winter, sounding like a small, rapt child if the white stuff settled. It was a couple of inches thick now. The three women returned to the hallway and Tahoor came out of the lounge, a twinkle in his eye.

'A person could die of thirst in this place,' he said. 'How about a coffee?'

'I'm sure Elena can show you how to use the machine,' said Gayle smoothly, eyes twinkling back.

Elena had overheard the two pensioners talking earlier, both sharing how difficult it was to get over a spouse's passing.

Tahoor lowered his voice. 'Truth is, my energy is lagging. Diego wants to show me some Flamenco moves, and Julian and Derek have been playing a party guessing game. I'll need a large shot of caffeine if I'm going to join in.'

'Tahoor!' said Rory's dad, Mike, striding into the hallway. He shook the old man's hand. 'We've hardly had a chance to chat. I'm still baffled by that missed goal that...'

Elena acted as if her eyes were glazing over, and her mum grinned. Elena looked into the distance and saw Rory talking to Caz and Derek, pointing out Brandy and Snap in the tank.

Gary boogied up to her. 'There's me thinking the best parties take place in the kitchen.' He rubbed his hands. 'Who's up for a game of strip charades?'

Tahoor looked horrified and everyone laughed.

Elena consulted her watch.

Twenty minutes to midnight? Already?

She hadn't even had time to talk privately to Rory. It was too late now.

'I'm just going upstairs to freshen up,' she murmured to her mum. 'Do you mind starting up the coffee machine?'

She put her arms around Mel, not wanting to let go, thanking her again for the incredible present. Searched out Dad and spotted him in the lounge still, teaching Diego how to moon-walk. A lump formed in her throat as she waved at him. That's exactly how she would want to remember her dad – if the worst happened in the next fifteen minutes. She wanted to go around the room and hug everyone tight. But she didn't want to draw attention to herself. She began climbing the staircase; however, there was no chance of slinking off quietly with Gary around.

'Elena Swan. Don't disappear. We haven't got long left to sing you Happy Birthday yet.'

'No time like the present then,' said her mum, and everyone stared up. Guests in the lounge piled into the hallway. Mike and Tahoor sang loudly, as if they were chanting at a football match. Gary swivelled his hips, giving the tune his best karaoke moves. Rory stared up at her, hardly mouthing the words. She stared back for a fleeting second.

I love you, Rory Bunker.

Raucous applause followed the last words of the song, and Derek insisted they give her three cheers. Elena gave a little bow and then headed into her bedroom, her heart full of gratitude for her kind, fun, wonderful family, friends and colleagues. She sat on the edge of her bed and stared out of the window, at the moon and stars, at the chunky snowflakes spinning down to the ground, counting off the minutes. Shouts drew her attention and she stood up. Below, to the left, where the cul-de-sac stretched, two teenage boys appeared, having bombarded the sentry boxes with snowballs. One skidded and fell over. They both doubled up with laughter. A tear trickled down Elena's cheek and ended at her smiling mouth. *Don't ever lose that carefree spirit, lads. Don't ever lose the ability to see humour in adversity. And if that voice in your head tells you you're a bad person, a failure, ignore it. It's not your friend.* She sniffed, wiped her eyes and then, orderly as ever, in her head she went through the paperwork... She'd checked over her will a couple of weeks ago and paid all her bills in advance and...

It was ten to twelve. Elena shivered. She dropped to the bed and lay down. If anything was going to happen, it couldn't be in front of her guests.

Be brave, Elena. Like you were twenty years ago. You've had a great life. Enjoyed more than so many people. Sure, you've had your challenges, but no one's life is flawless.

Now that the deciding moment had come, Elena's breathing slowed, her brow relaxed, satisfaction and thanks for the life she'd led running through her veins. Whatever would be, would be. She closed her eyes as the sound of 'Last Christmas' drifted upstairs.

43

RORY

Why had Elena gone upstairs? Rory stood at the bottom of the hallway. Everyone else had gone back into the lounge to drink coffee and polish off Diego's desserts.

Nothing was going to happen. Crystal balls, fortune tellers, black cats... Thanks to Julian, a logical explanation for Elena's promise had emerged.

Still, Elena should be warned that a minute longer and there wouldn't be so much as a cinnamon cookie crumb left downstairs. Taking the steps two at a time, he headed towards her bedroom. Rory consulted his watch.

It was a minute past midnight!

It wasn't Elena's thirtieth birthday any more! Any apparent, possible danger was definitely, inarguably, over! He could have swung from the light fitting above, or sat on the balcony and helter-skeltered down. Instead, he knocked on her door. No reply. Excitedly, he pushed it open.

Rory stopped.

Blinked.

The colour drained from his face.

His mouth felt as if he'd eaten nothing but dry crisps for four hours straight.

Elena lay in the foetal position, at a strange angle on the duvet, mouth open, arms hanging over the side of the bed, an open book by her body.

No. No, this hadn't happened. Yet... he narrowed his eyes.

She wasn't breathing.

Rory stood rigid. Elena had lost her life with so much of it ahead to enjoy – more travel, career promotions, chats with Brandy and Snap... And he'd lost Elena before even declaring his love for her. Numb, unable to release the tears building up, he stumbled over to the bed. 'I love you,' he whispered. 'I love you, Elena Swan, with every tick tock of every second, with every thump, thump of every heartbeat.' Only because he'd seen it in movies, a procedure he felt he had to follow, Rory pressed his trembling palm against her eyes to make sure they were fully closed before putting his finger on the side of her neck.

44

ELENA?

Elena let out an ear-piercing scream and grabbed Rory's arm. She sat bolt upright, almost falling off the bed in the process. 'What the hell?' she yelled.

'Whoa!' yelled Rory back, both of them with eyes wild, her heart pumping.

'I thought someone was strangling me,' she hissed and let go of him, catching her breath as the song 'All I Want For Christmas Is You' pumped out from the lounge below.

'My God. You're alive. You're really *alive!*' He gulped, stared for a moment then preceded to do some sort of Good Times Dance on his own. 'I was only checking your pulse. What with today's date and...' His face split into a grin and he lunged forwards to give her the tightest hug.

'Jesus, can't a girl get a bit of kip on her own bed?' she said, loosening herself from his embrace, secretly wishing it would last forever. 'I was knackered. Must have nodded off. Can't remember the last time I slept through the night.' She wiped dribble from the side of her mouth.

'You missed a bit,' he said and brushed his hand across her skin and then looked at his wet fingers.

'That's disgusting,' she said and their eyes locked, her mouth upturned, along with his. Laughter rang around her bedroom and tears of mirth poured down their cheeks, until they turned into something different. Her tone was scratchy as she spoke. 'It's gone midnight, hasn't it? I... I'm safe.'

He jumped up, grabbed her hands and insisted they do the Good Times Dance properly, together. She'd never performed it with more gusto, swinging his arms, throwing out her hips. Eventually, they fell on the bed and both lay on their backs. She looked sideways at him and croaked, 'It's over, isn't it? All my fears.'

Rory took her hand.

'You were right,' she said, 'about the False Memory OCD. But I still believed the worse – right till the end. Couldn't get rid of that voice in my head saying I'd made some fateful pact. I... I know that means that I am – I am ill, if I still believed it, despite having an alternative evidence-based explanation.' Elena squeezed his hand. 'I've been unwell all this time, not under the spell of a promise.' She shook her head. 'But if that night was a false memory, what else has been?'

He ran his thumb over her palm. 'False Memory OCD is about the person thinking they've done something wrong – about guilt and shame. It's not about other memories, like other people upsetting them or about trips, events, feelings, relationships, the world at large.'

She sat up. 'I've done my own research, last night and this morning. I've read dissertations on it, visited medical websites, and the patient cases given all resonated. I've also gone into chat rooms, and the despair felt tangible. People like me, so confused about what is happening, angry they can't ignore the voice in their head doubting them – part of them knows it's telling lies. Being locked in a prison where you hold the key is soul-destroying.' She stared at the duvet. 'I'm so stupid. For most of my life I've feared that I'd die at thirty, and even worse, that Mum would go to some terrible place in the afterlife, as a punishment. The guilt over that has overwhelmed me at times.'

Rory sat up too and put an arm around her shoulder. 'Julian's given me the number for his therapist. He said go to your GP in the first instance, but the waiting list for treatment might be long. If you can afford it, Julian's counsellor transformed his life. He also used to think that OCD was just about people washing their hands too often, but it's much more complicated and there are multiple subtypes – as you've probably found out from your own investigations.'

Elena's body shook. Tears rolled down her cheeks with relief.

'I googled what you said, about a common form being people believing they've run someone over. Poor Julian. Yet seeing him tonight, you'd never guess.' She exhaled. 'Like so many mental illnesses, it's invisible. How arrogant of me, thinking I was any different, any less susceptible to suffering.'

'Not arrogant,' he said in a soft voice. 'That ten-year-old girl felt she had to be the strong one, I'm guessing?'

She met his gaze.

'Maybe your OCD became a coping mechanism.'

'I came across something else, as well – Magical Thinking OCD. You kid yourself that if you do something specific, you can magically prevent certain things happening. Like if I turned my pillow over exactly five times before going to sleep, it would mean nothing bad would happen to Mum or Dad during the night. I went through a phase of rituals like that as a child, and different ones have appeared as I've grown up. Stupid really, believing I have some sort of power.'

'You've not been stupid, Elena – you've been stressed.'

They sat listening to the music coming up from the lounge. Her whole life didn't flash but steadily replayed before her, the parts where she'd checked the oven, the windows, bolted the door, and so much more, often a particular number of times. She'd told herself that everyone was like this, that there was nothing wrong with being careful. But she was beginning to see what drove that checking... The 'what if' voice, taking control, ravaging her good sense.

But what if you leave the window open and a burglar breaks in?

What if he's got a knife?

What if he kills you? It would be your own fault.

And when she was a child, there was that huge sense of responsibility for her parents, especially after Mum's accident.

What if they left the cooker on?

What if I don't check it? And then don't go back to check it exactly five more times? Then I'll be to blame if they burn to their deaths.

Elena thought back to primary school and the bullying – how little control she'd felt she had when the children ganged up and circled her, imitating her lisp. The OCD had given her back a sense of being in control. Protecting herself. Then protecting Mum.

'Nobody is going to die. At least not now,' she mumbled.

'Don't get carried away. I for one will combust if I have to listen to any more of Gary's singing.'

They smiled at each other.

Plans. For the first time in years, she dared to look forward to the future. She could travel the world, live dangerously, act impulsively. Her eyes filled. Yes. All of that. But really, the dreams that mattered were much simpler – to be happy; to spend more years with Mum and Dad; to be adventurous. Morag's words came back to her – over the phrase about passing on to the next stage of our world, and what that might really mean. Even if those words had simply come from young Elena's imagination, they *had* given Elena food for thought.

Perhaps the next stage of her life was about facing her problems, trying new things and... and giving love a go.

Forcing herself to ignore Rory's bare chest, solid and firm, visible down the front of his cranberry-coloured jacket, she lay her head on his shoulder. The velvet felt comforting against her cheek. He'd be too polite to ever let slip how he must think her a joke. Her research had proved him right – and because of that, she wouldn't blame him for keeping her at a distance. The idea of a romantic relationship with him was, now, even more implausible than ever.

'There's something I need to tell you,' he said. 'I... I've been holding it back since Paris.'

Oh God. What a meltdown she'd had on the aeroplane on the way there. What a relief it must have been for him to move out of her house and away from the drama. Yet he'd been there for Gary and Tahoor, a good listener during difficult times. Rory wasn't a man to dismiss other people's problems. And he'd shared the struggles he'd had over his mum. However, perhaps he was taking a much-needed, well-earned break from her problems, by changing jobs or taking a year out to do extreme sports. Or maybe he'd met someone. She didn't want to hear that, not right at this moment, not when the future now looked so fucking amazing!

'Me first,' she said. 'I've got something to show you. No one else has seen it before.'

He suggestively raised an eyebrow and she burst out laughing again. Elena stood up and took his hand, pulled him off the bed and headed onto the landing, glad to be holding on to something due to feeling so light as if she might blow away. Tahoor was in the hallway.

'Wit woo, as my granddaughter Sharnaz would say,' he called up. 'We wondered what the hostess was up to.'

'Tahoor!' said Elena, trying to look as cross as possible, failing miserably, and blushing. 'It's nothing like that. You can tell everyone we'll be down in a minute.'

'No worries. Gary and Diego have roped me into a dance-off. God help my back tomorrow.' Tahoor grinned and headed back into the lounge, carrying a bowl of crisps.

Elena walked past the spare room, where Rory used to sleep, and led him into her home office, with the tidy pen pots and stationery stacks, the minimalist décor and desk facing the wall. She stood staring at the oil painting of the cottage made from books on the wall that was several feet forwards, to the right of the window.

'You've been puzzled about where I disappear to sometimes,' she said and turned to face him.

'Oh. Yes. But it's private, you don't have to share.' He shrugged. 'I've checked in here at those times and the room's been empty.'

Elena paused and then turned back to the painting. She held the right-hand side and pulled it outwards. The painting swung out like a shutter, to reveal a handle. Rory's jaw dropped as she pulled on it and the wall halved, down a line that matched the edge of a strip of wallpaper. A door opened out. Elena didn't stop until it was wide open and she jerked her head, indicating for Rory to follow her in. Once inside, she switched on the light and closed the door.

Rory looked around and gave a low whistle.

45

ELENA

And relax... Elena was in her special place – with Rory, who speechlessly gazed around. She was a huge fan of reading on Kindle, but paperbacks were an equal love. Three walls were lined with shelves, packed with every genre of novel and autobiographies. The narrowest wall housed her childhood collection of books, including replacements of the ones she'd remembered Mum throwing out. On one wall the books were sorted according to colour, another alphabetically. The fourth wall had a shelf on it for teabags, coffee and biscuits. There was a mini fridge underneath. To the right of the door was a beanbag with a lava lamp next to it. In the middle of the room were a tiny table and a chair. The ceiling was sky blue and had white clouds painted on it.

'Elena. This is so cool. Your very own library. So you do collect paperbacks after all.'

'You don't think it's strange to be hidden like this? Especially as I live alone anyway.'

'Not at all. It takes me back to being a kid... If you've had a shit day at school or argued with a parent, your room is a safe haven, not on show. Like when you're a teen and have posters of your crushes on the walls. You don't want everyone to see them.'

Rory got it. Of course he did.

'These authors are my crushes. They've lifted me on so many occasions, as if they are therapists, or made me laugh, as if they're comedians – or cry, as if they were the very best moving actor.'

Rory ran his finger along a row of book spines. 'Damn. This room means you aren't really an alien who's been flying to visit the mothership every time you disappeared. What a let-down.'

'Sorry to disappoint. I'm just a reader.'

Rory reached up to the coffee pot, having spotted something behind it. He pulled it out and twisted it in the air. A playing card.

'The king of hearts?' he said. The back was ornate, with a colourful pattern, and it was creased, with a tear on one corner. 'It's Morag's? The one she gave you? That night, in the woods, she said the pack fell onto the grass and that was the only one that lay face up. You've kept it all this time?'

Elena took it from him and sat down in the small chair. Rory pulled up the beanbag and settled opposite her.

'Yes. And when we visited her, she said it represented someone who would be important to me one day. I've been thinking about that since. I had a boss whose surname was King once, but he turned out to be a real creep. A friend in the sixth form had the surname Hart, but she moved away and we lost touch. I've hoped to find an answer and that the card would point to someone who might help me make sense of the way my life has been.' She stared at the card for inspiration.

How odd it was, to have a guest in her private, precious den. Odd in a good way, because it was Rory. He sat, legs apart, jacket undone, completely unaware of how beguiling he was. Rory, who'd been there these last weeks, through all the ups and downs.

Elena hesitated and then took out her phone. She tapped away whilst they chatted about Paris and her parents' gift of the trip to Berlin. He began telling her a fun fact about Berlin being nine times bigger than Paris when her typing hand dropped. Elena's eyes remained fixed on the screen.

'Holy shit!' she muttered.

'What?'

Elena looked at him, then looked back at her phone.

Rory leant forwards. 'You okay?'

'Talking about names reminded me how Morag asked if you'd ever looked into the origins of yours. I felt a sudden compulsion to google it. You've really never done that?'

'Nah. A name's a name, right? Why? With this talk of travel, do you reckon Bunker is German? It does sound like it. Perhaps my ancestors were Berliners.'

'It's actually rather lovely. Bunker comes from the Old French *bon couer*, meaning good heart.'

'Cool.' Rory shuffled and made himself more comfortable in the bean bag. He beat a hand on his chest and smiled. 'Glad to know I'm truly a good'un.'

'*Rory* comes from the French *roi*, meaning...'

'King! One of the few words I remember from a French-subtitled historical Netflix series I loved. I've never connected my name with it before but, of course, it makes complete sense,' he said and grinned, giving a regal wave.

'But don't you see? *Good hearted King*. That's what your name means. The king of hearts.' She picked up the card. 'This card has got to represent you, Rory.' There was someone – it was *him* – who'd helped her sort of the mess she felt her life was. Unlike the King of Hearts in *Alice in Wonderland*, Rory was bold, and strong in the sense that he supported people who needed it; he wasn't afraid of recognising when he needed help too, such as moving on from trying to live his mother's life for her.

Of course, along the way, he'd stolen Elena's heart, even though he must never find out.

Rory stared at the card. He reached out and took her hand. 'Wow. Okay. Because actually, the word heart... it makes sense. That's... it's... amazing! You see...' He covered his eyes for a moment. 'Gah! I just need to go for it. Okay. Elena Swan, I know you don't feel the same, but Paris helped me see the obvious – that I'm wholly, irrevocably' – his voice broke a little – 'in love with you.'

He was *what*?

Her heart pounded.

She'd do anything to believe those words, anything to be able to act upon such a declaration. But she must have misunderstood.

She slid her hand out of his. 'Look... I... I don't know if this is some joke or... you think those words will make me feel good... but how could you be? I've been convinced about an imaginary promise for twenty years. How could anyone trust what I say now? Or hang around until I sort myself out? You deserve someone who's got their shit together. I'm going to need time, lots of it, to... to reassess so much of my life.'

Rory's cheeks matched his festively coloured jacket and trousers. 'You truly believe I'm that shallow? That I'm only interested in the good times I make you dance about?'

'No,' she said quietly. 'It's one reason I... like you so much. But I don't even know who I am any more, so how can you? You *are* my king of hearts, Rory – Morag *was* right, you've been more important than anyone ever has. You're up there with Gayle and Mum and Dad. But I'd never go out with anyone who must have changed their opinion of me – Elena, the supposed go-getting, successful marketeer who works with numbers and statistics, with concrete facts, yet who was convinced that uttering a few words twenty years ago put her life in jeopardy.'

'My opinion hasn't changed.'

'Rory, stop.' This was too painful, rejecting what she'd longed for so very much.

He straightened up. 'Wait... I'll prove it.' He got out his phone. 'I wrote this journal entry, Tuesday night, when I stayed at mine and didn't have my notebook. It's a private note. Why would I lie to myself?' Rory showed her the screen.

Elena is the most incredible, strong woman I've ever met, who's held her own against what might well have been a debilitating illness for years, who's always done her best for other people. I couldn't respect and admire her more.

Oh.

'As for the OCD stuff... I understand... to a degree. You see, I've convinced myself of something for years, about my mum – and talking things through with you, about why exactly I've done extreme sports, has made me come to terms with it; has helped with the guilt.' He took a deep breath. 'Mum had ovarian cancer. She found out when she was pregnant with me and refused to terminate the pregnancy to have treatment. They cut out a tumour as soon as I was born, but the cancer came back the next year. For so long I've believed her death was all my fault.' His voice hitched.

'Oh, Rory. I'm so very sorry. But... it was your mum's decision and utterly out of your control. And didn't she tell that teacher of yours who knew her at baby group that you'd made her life complete and she wouldn't change a thing, given her time again?'

His eyes glistened. 'Yes. I've realised lately how much of my life has been spent living for her, because of that guilt – so I understand the guilt you've felt over your mum. We've both suffered. I can see now Mum *would* want me to live my life for me, like she did during the years she was alive.'

They sat in silence for a few moments, holding each other's hands, understanding flowing between their fingers.

Rory cleared his throat. 'I know I'm not your type,' he said briskly, 'but I had to get my feelings out there. I, Rory Bunker, think you're fucking amazing. Jacques – the hotelier in Paris – helped me work it out that night we went back to the hotel, after you told me about the fortune teller at the Sacré Coeur. Jacques said that the person you are in love with is like home... like an escape from the world. You're my hidden library, Elena. My feelings for you have created the high that's made me realise lately I don't need to do extreme sports to feel alive. You're an incredible person, not only in spite of your challenges, but *because* of them.'

'Why didn't you tell me before?' she asked faintly.

'You needed a good friend. I didn't want to ruin the solid relationship we've got.' He sighed. 'Did that anyway though, barging in, telling you you'd got OCD instead of gently suggesting it.'

'Nicole was so stylish, so chic, so... together...'

His brow furrowed. 'Elena. Everyone's got broken bits inside. You know that, right, from that night in the pub with our colleagues, them telling us how they felt like broken biscuits? It's the basis of our whole product campaign. Anyway, I've exchanged the occasional text with Nicole and she's leaving her job. The pressure to look good, to find new models, she's been finding it too much.'

'She has?'

'I was only pretending to be interested in her, at the cemetery, embarrassed that I'd almost kissed you, thinking you'd be horrified at the thought of you and me together.'

Elena's eyes widened. 'That's the very reason *I* encouraged you to go for it with her.'

'Huh?'

'I almost kissed you then!' Her voice sounded full. She'd never said these words to anyone before. *Here goes.* 'I love you too, Rory Bunker.'

He frowned. 'Now who's joking? Or had too much Christmas punch? Come on, Elena. Don't take the piss.'

Elena got up and crouched down by the bean bag. She slid her arms around his neck. 'I'm not. I swear on Brandy's and Snap's lives. I worked it out in Paris too.'

Neither of them moved. Neither of them blinked.

'In Paris? You too?' he said eventually. 'Wow, what a clichéd pair of saps we are.' His pupils dilated as he moved closer. He ran a hand through her hair, letting his fingers fall to the side of her cheek, holding her face tenderly. Her skin sparked with his touch. 'I've wanted to do that for such a very long time. Tell me I'm not dreaming.'

'You're not,' she said, oh so tenderly.

'Your beauty struck me the very first day we met, Elena. Not just because of your cute nose that twitches before you laugh, or those ocean eyes that ripple with every emotion... It's the way you were with people in the office. Fair. Faithful. Firm. Funny. I watched you spar with Gary and take a difficult meeting with Derek. You're all the f words, Elena.'

'All of them?' she asked, and her nose twitched.

He tucked a blonde lock of hair behind her ear.

'My attraction to you is much more trivial, I'm afraid,' she whispered. 'You had me at wearing my silk dressing gown.' She nudged closer, their lips almost touching. 'But most important of all... Jacques was right. You are like home to me, as well. I can utterly be myself when you're around. I'm able to take off the mask.' Her breathing quickened and her lips touched his, gently at first. But when his mouth responded with a passion that also blazed inside her chest, Elena became part of a story even more exciting than the ones on the shelves in her little oasis.

46

ELENA

Eventually, they surfaced. It was almost one o'clock in the morning. Their guests might have left! Elena straightened her dress. Rory did up his jacket. They beamed and she took his hand.

'Let's hurry. I'm the worst hostess in the world.'

'Not sure I'd agree. You've been most accommodating,' he said.

Suppressing a laugh, she led him downstairs. They were welcomed by the lingering smell of pizza. The music was off. They went into the lounge and everyone looked up. The guests were spread across the sofa, two armchairs, the floor, and chairs brought in from the dining room.

'Well, well, well,' said Gary, looking at Tahoor. The two men nodded at each other smugly.

'I was just showing Rory my... book collection,' Elena said.

'Is that the same as Gary's collection of etchings?' asked Diego.

Everyone in the room chuckled.

'I hope you don't come to work with your jacket buttons done up in the wrong order, like that,' said Derek.

Rory looked down and blushed.

'Guys, guys, my parents and Rory's dad are here,' said Elena, blushing.

'I think it's rather lovely,' said Gayle.

'Perhaps this is our cue to leave,' said Melanie, and she grinned, got up and gave Elena a big hug. 'Playing charades has worn me out.'

'How about a caffeine hit and another round?' suggested Elena.

But Gayle and Tahoor both looked tired, and Diego was up early for work tomorrow. Caz thanked them for a lovely evening and whispered to Elena that she wanted all the details about the 'book collection' on Monday. Mike slapped Rory on the back and said to Elena he looked forward to seeing the pair of them for dinner at his, with Jenny who nodded enthusiastically. Mike also suggested to Tahoor that they arrange a trip to the pub, to watch the next match. Tahoor nodded enthusiastically and then took Gayle's number, the two of them saying it would be nice to go out for coffee, the more companions at their age the better. In fact, she should come to his for cake in a couple of weeks, Tahoor added. He'd need help choosing the perfect names for the two stick insects he'd agreed to take from Julian.

Before he left, Derek showed Elena and Rory his phone. 'The chair of the board sent this today. Her granddaughter made it. She loves the sound of our new campaign.' It was a photo of a biscuit, with red and green icing on it in the shape of a Christmas tree, broken in half.

Elena and Rory both grinned. She went to open the front door.

'Look at the snow!' she exclaimed, and held out her hand to catch a flake. 'Loads has settled! You can't see the lawn.'

Don walked onto the drive and moonwalked across it, almost falling over. Melanie kissed Elena again, and Rory then took Gayle's arm and walked her to the car. Rory's dad's taxi arrived and Caz's husband got out his keys and insisted on giving Derek and his wife a lift.

Promising to drive carefully on his motorbike, Julian went to leave.

Elena caught his arm. 'In the New Year... if you're free for a drink one day I'd really appreciate... You see, Rory told me...'

Julian put his hand on her shoulder. 'That would be great. You've got a lot to get your head around, but you'll be fine, with the right help. I felt as if I was going crazy at one point and never dared hope I'd shake that off. But I did and you will too.'

Elena couldn't speak, simply giving him a heartfelt hug as they said goodbye. She went to the window in the lounge. Rory came back from walking Tahoor home, having insisted in case the elderly neighbour slipped. He draped an arm around her shoulders.

'Everywhere looks so beautiful,' she said as thick, clumsy flakes continued to swirl to the ground.

'Not as beautiful as my view,' he said, and she turned to face him looking at her. He took her hand. 'Right, Swan, snowman-building time.'

'At this time of night?'

'I'll grab our coats. You open the kitchen back door.'

She hesitated but not for long, and by the time he'd come outside she'd rolled her weapon and hit him square on the chest. He threw her coat over through the darkness, their grins lit up by the kitchen light. A competitive spirit kicked in and half an hour later two snowmen stood on the lawn, Rory's wearing

Elena's plum beanie hat. She'd scooted into the kitchen and came out holding a gherkin pickle. She pushed it into her snowman's face so it stuck out, like a nose.

'Guess who?' she asked.

'Looks like we've both built each other.'

The pickle slipped out and slid down the snowman, getting stuck in the lower part of its body.

'I feel obliged to point out, that is in no way a life-sized representation,' he said, with an indignant tone.

'It is very cold out here, but are you sure?' she replied, and shrieked as Rory chased her around the garden. Hair dripping, cheeks tingling as snow fell heavily, once more, the two of them trudged indoors, hung up their coats and left their sodden shoes standing on old newspaper. Whilst the kettle boiled, they went into the lounge and warmed themselves by the radiator.

Shyly, Elena took his hand, lifted it to her lips and kissed his fingers. The insect tank caught her eye and she picked up the water spray bottle. She'd not paid much attention to Brandy and Snap the last couple of days, what with the party to arrange, and then the OCD research. Elena bent down to look for them and she gasped. Where Snap had been hanging upside down, now hung an old skin, white, dry and brittle. A few twigs away Snap lay on a leaf, still missing a leg, but now, at least, it should grow back. The insect's skin was fresh, olive green, soft.

'Looks great, doesn't she?' said Rory. 'Julian and I spotted her earlier.'

'How amazing it must feel to shed your skin,' Elena said and put down the spray bottle. She and Rory sat down on the sofa.

'I guess you'll find out, because that's what you're about to do in the coming months, right?'

Her eyes pricked. Yes. An exciting future lay before her, bright and shiny, like the most eye-catching bauble. There'd be travel – Berlin first – and a commitment to... to giving romance a real shot. Snap would be growing a new limb. Elena would be growing a resistance to the phrase *What if?* And like Snap's, over time, Elena's new skin would thicken and become more resilient.

'Of course, the best thing about all of this?' he said. 'We're 100 per cent justified in using those cute housemate nicknames now that we're together. In fact...' He moved close, oh so close, his breath stroking her neck, causing her pulse to race, her skin to flush. Sensations stirred, deep within, that she'd never allowed before. 'It's the prerequisite for kissing me, Houdini.'

She cupped his face in her hands and ran a forefinger over his lips. Cute nicknames? That wasn't Elena Swan's way. Nope. Nuh uh. Was never gonna happen.

Well, not in her old story, anyway.

'Whatever it takes, Pickle,' she replied, and they smiled at each other before she pressed her mouth against his and lost herself in the first of many new adventures.

AUTHOR'S NOTE

Dear Reader,

Thank you, thank you, thank you for choosing my books out of such a colossal selection, and for your feedback that gives me confidence in the stories I tell. My biggest wish, as an author, is to use my words to make a reader feel they aren't alone with their feelings, in what's a challenging world – and by feeding back to me, how a story resonates, you make me feel less alone too.

I hope you enjoyed Elena and Rory's story as much as I loved writing it. Even more thanks, in advance, if you decide to write an online review – without revealing OCD has been at the root of Elena's difficulties. Your time and discretion would be hugely appreciated.

Take care, and don't forget – it doesn't always pay to listen to the voice in your head.

Sam x

ACKNOWLEDGEMENTS

It's only as I've reached my fifties that I've gained the opportunity and ability to look back on my life and understand certain tough patches. I wish I'd known earlier what I know now. I'd encourage any of you with difficulties, to reach out for help, to talk to someone, to open your mind. Don't delay.

My first thanks have to go to my husband Martin, and children Immy and Jay, for their support and love. My fortune in having them in my life is too great to ever be measured.

Professionally, I'm grateful for the support of my multi-talented and very lovely agent Clare Wallace, and everyone else who works so hard at Darley Anderson Agency & Associates, including the finance, foreign rights and film rights teams.

Huge thanks to my wonderful editor Isobel Akenhead, whose sense of humour and enthusiasm I value as much as her clear editorial acumen. I'm equally grateful for the dynamic Boldwood team including Nia Beynon, Jenna Houston, Isabelle Flynn, Claire Fenby, Ben Wilson and Candida Bradford, to mention a few.

I'm thankful to my fellow Boldies from the Boldwood Author Facebook group. Your good-humoured chat and knowledge about publishing are both is reassuring and appreciated. Thanks as well to the amazing Friendly Book Community on Facebook. The reads, reviews and laughs mean a lot.

Much research goes into writing a story and I'm extremely grateful to wonderful author Jessica Redland, who worked as a recruitment manager for a number of years and also gained the Chartered Institute of Marketing Diploma. She gave me real insight into the inside workings of a company, and thanks to her also for her invaluable sharing of a bungee jump experience – she's a braver woman than I! I'm also grateful to my lovely friend, Jo, for the great football referee cards idea! Gotcha, Tahoor!

The blogging community is made up of some of the most generous, bookishly passionate people I know, and their support for my books over the last eleven years has been brilliant. Thanks to all of you – old friends and new.

Sam x

DISCLAIMER

Whilst the issues I write about in this story are close to my heart, and I've also done research, I'm not a medical practitioner.

If you're worried about yourself, or a loved one, talk to a GP. OCD can exist on its own, or alongside other disorders. It can also be similar to other conditions. To get the correct diagnosis and help, seek professional advice.

ABOUT THE AUTHOR

Samantha Tonge is the bestselling and award-winning author of over fifteen romantic fiction titles. Her books for Boldwood mark a broadening of her writing into multi-generational woman's fiction. She lives in Manchester with her family.

Sign up to Samantha Tonge's mailing list for news, competitions and updates on future books.

Visit Samantha's website: www.samanthatonge.co.uk

Follow Samantha on social media here:

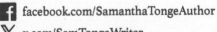

facebook.com/SamanthaTongeAuthor

x.com/SamTongeWriter

instagram.com/samanthatongeauthor

ALSO BY SAMANTHA TONGE

Boldwood

Boldwood Books is an award-winning fiction publishing company seeking out the best stories from around the world.

Find out more at www.boldwoodbooks.com

Join our reader community for brilliant books, competitions and offers!

Follow us
@BoldwoodBooks
@TheBoldBookClub

Sign up to our weekly deals newsletter

https://bit.ly/BoldwoodBNewsletter

Milton Keynes UK
Ingram Content Group UK Ltd.
UKHW021520240924
1811UKWH00007B/78